KALADON

A Novel

by

Richard W. Steeley

ISBN 1-56315-252-5

Paperback Fiction
© Copyright 2000 Richard W. Steeley
All rights reserved
First Printing—2000
Library of Congress #99-65310

Request for information should be addressed to:

SterlingHouse Publisher Inc.
The Sterling Building
440 Friday Road
Pittsburgh, PA 15209
www.sterlinghousepublisher.com

Cover design: Michelle S. Vennare – SterlingHouse Publisher
Typesetting: Kathleen M. Gall

Dedication

With love,

this book is dedicated to my children,

Bonnie, Diane and Richard.

Acknowledgments

To my good friend Chris Swindell,

his encouragement, expertise, and professionalism

helped make this novel possible.

To my sister Gladys,

my pals Leslie L. and Bill W., thanks.

Your support was greatly appreciated along the way.

CHAPTER 1

THE BEGINNING

It was a warm night in the Nevada desert with scattered clouds allowing the moon to occasionally peek through. There was just enough of a breeze to make it a beautiful evening. There were 20 to 25 buildings scattered throughout the base. Most were single story, except for the larger buildings and the control towers near the runways. There were a few hangars and even those were no more than three to four stories.

There was a 12 foot heavy-duty cyclone fence around the perimeter with razor wire and an electronic security system attached. Security had been beefed up due to an incident that occurred at the Mojave Air Force Base in southern California two months ago. They had added a third person in the rear of the vehicle to operate the rigidly mounted M-60 automatic weapon.

Lieut. Powers, Corporal Race, and Private Baldwin were on patrol to ensure no abnormalities existed, a procedure that was required every half hour. The base was sufficiently covered with electronic monitoring, but old military tradition dictated that personnel maintain the exterior perimeter. Three patrols alternated every half hour, which dictated that two would be out at all times. Lieut. Powers randomly decided to accompany Corporal Race and Private Baldwin on patrol. It was also a requirement that an officer make various patrols throughout the shift.

While approaching a security station at 2210 hours they noticed it was unmanned. The two men in front exited the vehicle and Private Baldwin stayed behind to man the automatic weapon. No movement was observed in the immediate vicinity. Lieut. Powers reported the discrepancy to the security office and automatically initiated a priority-three security violation. This was standard procedure upon observance of any abnormal condition, no matter how minor the infraction.

"See anything, Corporal?"

"No sir," a wide-eyed and frightened corporal replied. "Don't see nothin, sir." Catching sight of a different configuration forced a change in his answer. "Wait! Yes sir, there," he whispered, pointing to the fence as they approached. "Damn!," he said, looking at the ditch under the fence. The lieutenant was cautiously checking the area by the fence while the other played the eyes in the back of his head. "This doesn't make any sense, sir. Why would anyone want to make a ditch through the blacktop after they cut the bottom of the fence?"

"Perhaps they wanted to stay below the trip wires. That would certainly keep the alarm system quiet."

"But how'd they make it so smooth, sir? I mean that's asphalt, not playdough."

Within minutes of the initial report, two vehicles and six more men arrived at the scene. Sergeant Waller and the lieut. were studying the area by the fence. "Sergeant, are you thinking the same thing I am?"

"Yes sir, the melted asphalt appears to have been heated from the outside. The wires are bent inward and you can see by the dirt that whoever did this is probably still inside."

"It certainly does appear that way." Both men started looking more carefully at the shadows next to the buildings nearby.

The lieutenant keyed his mic. "Security, this is Lieutenant Powers. We have a priority-one security violation with intruder alert. Notify command headquarters at once."

He never heard the reply as a fireball streaked through the air and exploded on impact near the fence. It destroyed about 20 feet of barrier, flipped a vehicle and formed a two foot crater about 10 feet in diameter. Five men were thrown into the air and when they hit the ground their charred bodies were lying motionless.

A split-second later, a second blast from the same direction destroyed one of the smaller buildings nearby. A moment later, a third shot from a different direction turned yet another building into an inferno. All the buildings and vehicles damaged by the intruders were on fire, and bodies were scattered on the ground.

Sergeant Waller observed weapons fire from Corporal Race across the front of his vehicle. Just as he observed what Race was shooting at, another dark figure was taking aim. "Jump," he yelled. The men just cleared the vehicle as it exploded, lifting it six feet into the air, and falling on its former occupants. The sergeant and his team were killed instantly. Another shot hit the corner of building 124 and the end results were the same.

It appeared Race's team was the only viable fighting force remaining. While maneuvering to get a better shot he hit the edge of a large hole next to a damaged vehicle. His shots went wild and the hole was deep enough to tip him over, throwing them out a few seconds before it was hit by yet another blast. It lifted his vehicle into the air with incredible force. He had fallen into the hole and Private Baldwin fell in on top of him. Race was not seriously injured, but the private above him was not as fortunate.

The next two blasts hit a four-story building and another standing next to it. Both were on fire, which would finish the destruction the blasts hadn't already completed. The last blast was a direct hit on the security office. The occupants inside never had a chance. The whole incident occurred so quickly it was difficult to tell exactly what took place.

The pilot of Major Coleman's helicopter was just setting down near the security office when the building exploded. The shock wave almost tipped them over. En route he contacted Nellis Air Force Base. They scrambled two fighter groups to assist, but he was sure they'd be too late.

About 20 miles closer, two marine Sky Fox 7 helicopter gun ships were utilizing the gunnery range when the alert came in. They were the latest design for this type of encounter. Within minutes they were flying over the area surveying the damage.

"Christ! What a mess," said the pilot. "Jack Rabbit, Jack Rabbit, this is Sky Fox 1, over."

"Sky Fox 1, this is Major Coleman. A few minutes ago some intruders in a small low-flying vehicle headed in a southeasterly direction. It's certain they're the perpetrators of all this. Be very careful and approach with caution."

"I roger that, Major." They turned and left the area. In a short time they picked up a silhouette on radar moving rapidly across the desert. "Captain, looks like our objective up ahead, sir," said the technical operator.

"Jack Rabbit, Jack Rabbit, Sky Fox 1, we have located the intruders, request permission to engage, over."

"Engage immediately, Sky Fox 1," yelled Major Coleman, very excited.

The helicopter pilots never acted on those orders.

Off in the distance, the personnel on the ground observed two reddish-white streaks moving rapidly skyward, followed by two explosions. The men at the base saw fiery debris falling from the sky, and then, nothing.

★   ★   ★

Judy and Frank were out in the Nevada desert one Sunday evening, on one of those clear nights when it seemed that all the stars in the universe were bringing forth their splendor. The light from the moon cast their shadows on the ground. They had just been enjoying a super weekend camping together. They had been dating during the three weeks he'd been there, and she had been very helpful in getting him acquainted with the area.

He had just finished another assignment for the Air Force and was transferred to this part of the arid west. They were a few miles north of highway 95, near the military's gunnery range, just north of Indian Springs, about 45 miles northwest of Las Vegas, Nevada.

They were talking, laughing, and having a good time. She was riding him about his age, he being 30 and his hair with gray tint. "You know, you must be getting old," she said with a grin, her eyes gleaming in the moonlight. "I mean, you've been complaining about how tired you are from that short walk in the desert. Sounds like an age problem to me."

"Hey, now wait a minute, I never said I was tired. All I said was that I'm not used to walking on the soft sand. It isn't my fault I couldn't get my Jeep down into that canyon you wanted to explore. And by the way, that was no short walk either." He shifted his tone and said, "You know, it really was worthwhile or we never would've found those rocks and odd metal fragments."

"They sure look different from anything I've ever seen before. Hey, I know what," she said, with that bright-idea look on her face. "Take the samples into Vegas to that professor friend you told me about. I mean, if anybody could help out, I'd think it'd be her."

"You're right," he said happily, gesturing with his hands. "And even if she can't, I'm sure she'd know of someone who could." Pausing a moment, he thought, *This has been a very satisfying weekend.*

He called Professor Sheila Boundry the next morning. He hoped the items they found were as important as they looked. The thing that interested him was the metal fragments. Their coloring and weight were very unusual. He knew she was a busy woman, so he suggested lunch as a way to have their little conversation. He must have convinced her when he told her that no matter how busy she was, she still had to eat, and besides, it was on him. They served a very good crab tortellini soup at this restaurant he knew about, remembering how fond of seafood she was.

A few days later, Judy had off and they were on their way to Las Vegas. As they came down off the mountain, with their hair blowing in the breeze, they could see the smog lingered over the city. When they arrived at the restaurant, Carter introduced them.

After a pleasant lunch they walked to his vehicle, where he pulled a small cloth bag from the locker in the rear of his Jeep. He dumped the contents gently onto the lid. They rolled a short distance and came to a stop, still a little dusty.

Looking at Sheila he began, "We were out in the desert this past weekend and found these items. If you can't identify them, perhaps you might know of someone who could."

"Let's take a look." Sheila reached out while displaying her usual pretty smile. She rooted through the objects and picked up the rocks, as these were her specialty. "I can take these to the lab and analyze them, but as far as the metal objects are concerned, I can't help you there. I think perhaps Professor Johnson could, and I'm sure he'll call you if he can."

Frank thanked her, got a friendly hug, and they left. She was wearing his favorite perfume that day. He remembered the scent and the good times they had together back East. Perhaps it was intentional, but he wasn't sure.

They stayed around Vegas for a while and decided to take in a movie. It was a lovely drive back to Pahrump. There was a cool breeze, the air was fresh and there was no smog. He dropped Judy off and went home. It wasn't much of a place, an efficiency, but it was home to him and his dog, Nikki.

Going in, he went straight to the back door to let Nikki out. Walking by the phone he noticed the message machine was blinking. He went over to the answering machine to check his messages, in case it was important. *Huh, that's a laugh,* he thought. *I've been told that nothing important ever happens around here.*

Carter was quite surprised to have a message from Professor Johnson, who wanted him to call as soon as he got in, no matter what time. Carter looked at his watch and noticed it was almost midnight. The phone didn't ring more than twice before he heard, "Hello, this is Professor Johnson. May I help you?"

"Professor Johnson, Frank Carter here, returning your call. Sorry about the late hour. I just got home."

"Mr. Carter, please, no apology necessary. I'm just glad you called," he said in an anxious tone of voice. "I'm interested in the items you dropped off at the university with Professor Boundry this morning. Tell me, where did you get them?"

Carter detected enthusiasm in his voice. "As a matter of fact, I found them in the desert the other day, a few miles north of Indian Springs, up off highway 95."

"Mr. Carter, could you relocate the place where you picked up the metallic-looking objects?"

"Please, Professor, call me Frank. And in answer to your question, yes, I'm sure I can find that place again."

"Good, I was hoping you'd say that. I'd like to accompany you the next time you go out there, if it's all right with you?"

"Sounds good to me Professor, as a matter of fact, I was planning on going there this weekend."

"Let's see, today's Wednesday, hmm, I don't suppose you could make it any sooner, could you?" The anxiety was evident in his voice.

"Since I'm in the middle of changing jobs, I'm not pressed for time. I suppose I could make it just about any time. If it's that important, how about tomorrow?"

"Splendid," he said, really excited now. "That's just fine."

"I guess what you're trying to tell me is that this is a very important issue."

"Well, I'm not absolutely sure of what you found yet. But for now, let's just say it appears important enough to get me out there for a closer look."

"Okay, you're on for tomorrow."

"If you'll give me some directions, I could meet you saaay, around 10:30 in the morning?"

"10:30 it is." After giving the professor directions he hung up and started thinking. *Could it be possible that this is what we've been looking for all this time? I'm sure the General will be interested in Professor Johnson's report and so will I. Wonder why the satellites haven't picked anything up in this area yet. There's certainly enough of them up there, and still nothing. Hmm! Sure seems strange*, he thought.

He let the dog in and went to bed. He figured he'd call Judy in the morning. He knew she'd be in bed by now because she had to work the next day.

The alarm went off at 7:30. He rolled over in bed and got his face licked. Perhaps Nikki was trying to tell him something. He got up, let her out, stood in the open doorway and took in a deep breath. "Whew," he stopped short. The air would smell much better if it weren't for the neighbor's horses. If they cleaned their stables more frequently it wouldn't smell so bad. He went back in, showered and started getting his things ready. He was ready to go by 8:30 since his vehicle was still packed from the past weekend. He picked up the phone and called Judy.

"Well, hello. This is a nice surprise. I mean, calling me so early, and at work even. I thought you'd still be in bed. So, what's up?" she asked, a hint of excitement in her voice.

How can she be so pleasant this early in the morning? Hell, I'm just barely awake, he thought. "Just wanted to let you know what was happening. You know the metal samples we took to the university? Well Professor Johnson called and left a message on my machine."

"He did? Wow!" She said excitedly.

"So anyway, I called him back and we're going to meet in a few hours. He wants to see where we found those samples."

"Say, that was pretty quick. Maybe it really is something."

"Yeah, how about that?" he said.

"Wonder what it means?" A little calmer now. "You be sure to call me later, okay?"

"Yeah, sure, hey listen, I have to get going." He hung up, fed the dog and headed for the door. "See ya, Nikki." She gave him a droopy look as he left. Nikki wasn't fond of being left alone, so his cute neighbor always stopped by to keep her company while he was gone.

He arrived at the casino in Indian Springs by 9:45. He was early, so he thought he'd eat something while he waited. At 10:30 the professor pulled into the parking lot. He got up and went out. "Hello, Professor." After the introductions Carter offered, "Cup of coffee maybe, or breakfast before we get started?"

"No thank you, I'd like to get started as soon as possible." He didn't even get out of his vehicle.

Carter went to his own vehicle to get his pistol. After he locked it, he returned and climbed in next to the professor. *Glad I ate earlier*, he thought.

It was about 20 miles or so up over the mountain to Indian Springs. The professor was in a talkative mood and Carter was glad, because he hated riding with someone he just met who didn't talk. He asked Frank what type of job he left and what he was going to do at his new place of employment. Carter told him it was at an Air Force base and he was going to be an instructor at one of their schools. He also told him he felt like he was still in the military, what with being transferred from base to base even though he was just teaching. The professor didn't ask any more questions about his employment and he was glad about that.

It was close to 11:45 when they stopped at the place Carter had parked his Jeep the last time. He told the professor they had about a thirty-minute walk before they got to the exact location. The professor indicated he didn't mind the walking, but he didn't want to be that far from his equipment. He looked pretty fit for his age. Perhaps his work kept him that way. Carter tried to stay in shape too. Keeping a six-foot frame in the 210-pound range wasn't easy.

After about 20 or more minutes of driving the professor found a little slope going down into the canyon. Carter must have missed it the last time he'd been here. It continued down into another area of the same canyon Carter told him about. Coming to a stop they ended up about 30 yards from their destination.

Then the professor turned all business, as if Carter wasn't even there. Walking around quietly, he scratched the soil a time or two and kicked over a few rocks. Carter didn't say anything, he just observed. They went around a small outcrop, then the canyon narrowed and came to a dead end. Next, Carter followed him back to his vehicle, where he took out a metal detector. A few minutes later he pulled a small rake from his vehicle. At one place he found more of the metallic objects like the specimens Carter had left with him at the university. After an extensive search on the soil around the small canyon near the dead end, it looked as though he would finally say something.

"Frank, is this as far as you were able to explore in this canyon when you were here the last time?" He asked, pointing his finger.

"As a matter of fact, yesterday when we were here this area was wide open, way down into the canyon. This dead end wasn't here," he showed some concern in his voice. "I had planned on coming out here today even before you called."

"Interesting," he replied, standing there deep in thought. "Frank, because of the delicate issue involved here, I would appreciate your not discussing this with anyone."

"I have no objections with that request."

"Obviously, Frank, the closure at this end of the canyon is not nature's work. It appears someone is trying to conceal something from us and they're not doing a very good job of it. These items I picked up, I'm sure you see, are exactly the same as the pieces you brought to the university. They're non-ferrous. In fact, they're not metal at all. I have no idea what they are.

"Some things have happened here in Nevada and a few months ago in Southern California that are very puzzling. I'm sure the Air Force will be very interested in my report. They're covering this area pretty well, and it's possible something is going on right under their watchful eye, but I sort of doubt it. I can tell you this, Frank, I'll be doing some extensive research on these items and I'll try to let you know what I find out. You know," as the professor stood and looked around, "I'm surprised we haven't been approached by the Air Force or Clark County deputies yet."

"Don't concern yourself, Professor. They know we're here."

"Well, thanks for the information and if I uncover anything new, I'll surely contact you as soon as I can."

"Sounds good to me, you know where to reach me."

They climbed into the professor's vehicle and headed back. It was a quiet ride back. Neither one of them had too much to say, but they were both doing a lot of thinking. Carter asked the professor to have a late lunch with him, but he was in a hurry to get back to the university.

On the way home Carter pondered the events that had taken place and what Professor Johnson had said. He wondered if the professor knew General Harrison.

When he got home he thought about giving the General a call, but there wasn't much proof of anything at this time. He wasn't sure what he should tell Judy about all this. He knew he shouldn't say anything, seeing as how it was all classified information. Still, it would be hard keeping anything from her, because she was already involved. When he got home he thanked his neighbor for watching Nikki and called Judy.

"Hi Frank, what's up?"

"Well, not much. When the professor completes his report I'll know more. How about we discuss this over dinner at seven?"

After a long discussion at dinner, she convinced him to let her go along with him the next day. He figured she was already involved. He could understand her way of thinking, but if he thought there was any real danger she wouldn't be going no matter what she said. Besides, the Air Force didn't indicate to him there was any danger at this point of the investigation.

It was about 10:30 Friday morning when Judy arrived at Franks' place. She had to finish a few things at work before getting the rest of the day off.

"Well, guess we have everything," he said.

"I packed a lunch for us so we wouldn't have to stop along the way," she said, acting like she was happy just to be going along. "I see you brought your shotgun," she said, glancing down between the seats, "and your pistol. I hope that doesn't mean what I think it does."

His shotgun rarely accompanied him anywhere. But for some reason, he needed sort of an insurance policy. "No, hon, it's just in case, I guess. Don't know what's out there and the professor didn't seem too concerned, but it makes me feel better. Call it a security blanket, if you will."

Just as they started to drive away he heard the phone ring. "Aren't you going back to answer that?"

"Nah, don't think I'll bother. You know what they say, `Nothing important ever happens round here', anyway I'll get the message when we get back." He gunned the engine and they drove away.

It was a little cloudy, but there wasn't any rain in the forecast. "I'm kind of glad it's cloudy today. Makes for a cooler drive," he said.

"You got that right. I prefer clouds any day to sunshine while driving in the desert. This is a hellish place to be in August with the sun beating down on you," she said.

They were both quiet for a while and very tense. It was difficult for them to relax, almost as if they knew something was going to happen. Arriving at the turnoff on 95 they started into the desert. They must have traveled about a half hour or more and they were both deep in thought.

"Look out," she screamed, with fear in her voice. Frank slammed on the brakes, sliding sideways as they came to a stop, almost hitting a boulder as out of nowhere came a herd of wild horses. Thick dust churned everywhere, as they crossed the road in front of them. What a racket they made! They were both coughing from the dust and grabbing for some water. She almost jumped out of her skin, and he had to admit it scared him too. They had been tense all day and then this had to happen.

A short while later, they arrived at the place where they had camped before. The incident with the wild horses combined with wondering what might be out here had them both on edge. "Well, what's for lunch? I'm hungry," he said, trying to calm the situation.

"You're always hungry," she said, a gleam in her eye. After lunch they prepared for a long hike, calmer now and much more relaxed since they'd eaten.

"I'd like to go around the rim of the canyon first and see if we can spot anything from there," he said.

"Sounds good to me," she said. "Lead on."

They walked around slowly for about a mile, zig-zagging and using the binoculars often. "Huh, nothing out of the ordinary here," he said, "Sure is peaceful."

"Yep, sure is," she said, looking off in the distance with the binoculars. "That's one of the things I love most about the desert." It was getting toward the middle of the afternoon and they decided to head back to his Jeep.

"It seems a little cooler this year for the end of August, compared to the last few years. Don't you think?" she said.

"Wouldn't know, I ..." he stopped short, in mid-sentence, turned around quickly, brought up his shotgun, and flipped the safety off.

"What's wrong?" she asked, a little fear in her voice.

"Thought I heard a noise behind us." Standing still, he looked around for a while. *Huh! Nothing I can see*, he thought. He had his shotgun ready, anyway. It really was a security blanket for him. He felt better in the middle of nowhere carrying it. "I think perhaps we should leave."

"Why do you say that?" Almost immediately, she changed her tone. Answering her own question mentally, "I think you're right. I don't know what it is, but something's not right here." She was looking past him to her left, and then yelled, "Frank!" She pointed at a brown hairy creature wearing a black vest and pants. He was holding a weapon of some kind.

"What's the matter?" he said, standing a few feet from her.

She felt the hair bristling on the back of her neck. "Over there by that boulder," she yelled, pointing frantically. "Over there," she yelled again, "some kind of—." The creature raised its weapon as she panicked, spun around, and ran toward the vehicle.

The ground started vibrating as the hidden spacecraft was preparing for take-off. Cold fear hit his thoughts like a runaway train. "Let's get the hell out of here!" he yelled, as he spun around, shotgun ready. Then he saw what she was looking at. It was aiming a weapon toward his vehicle, in the same direction Judy was running. The alien didn't see Carter until he came from behind a boulder. The alien fired and a split-second later his blast hit the Jeep. As he turned, Carter fired and hit him right in the chest. He saw two more of them and fired three shots in their direction. Trying to change position, he slipped, and was hit on the head. He fell, then everything was fuzzy. He faintly remembered seeing two people, looking down at him and holding a weapon of some kind. Things were still fuzzy, it was hard to focus. He couldn't clear his head, couldn't think, and then it was dark.

As he lay there barely conscious, he regretted his decision to bring Judy. Perhaps if he had been more cautious, he'd know if she were still alive. It was one of those times when he wished the Air Force wasn't so damn secretive. Had he been aware of the danger, he never would've allowed her to accompany him that day. Come to think of it, he might know where the hell he was, too.

CHAPTER 2

THE JOURNEY

"God, my head hurts," he murmured. Moving a little, he muttered, "Uh that hurts too! Can't remember much, all I know for sure is that someone took a shot at us. Least I guess that's what you'd call it, if shots lift Jeeps in the air and come on a trail of fire. No hunting rifle, that thing. Remember shooting back, least four times. Don't know how many there were, how accurate I was. Saw someone, tried to change positions, stumbled. Something hard hit my head, a club, maybe? Lying on my back now ... I ... I can't seem to remember much else. Where am I? Lying on some kind of bed, tired, very weak.

"Wonder how long I was out," he murmured some more. "Didn't like the looks of them two standing over me, pointing that thing my way. Better than my shotgun, no doubt. Head clearing a little, keep mouth shut, don't let on. Easy, Frank, assess surroundings, think, observe. Faint voices, language unfamiliar, a sort of growling accent. Dizzy, probably wouldn't understand, no matter what language it was. Recall hearing faint laughter, being picked up, carried somewhere. Ohhh! Wish my head'd stop throbbing.

"In deep, Carter, ya blame fool, poking yer nose in things ya didn't understand, totally unprepared. Nearly got yourself killed, and Judy. Situation not good, surroundings not very familiar. In a small room, possibly some sort of detention cell. Feels like I'm going somewhere. Right! Real funny. Still on my back, slight odor, sort of an animal smell. Lying on some type of small bed. Chair close by, no windows, doorway with horizontal bars. Bars, geez! I am in jail! Best just lie here and rest my throbbing head. Maybe when I'm fully awake this'll all be gone. Yeah, right! I'm not that far out of it."

He slept pretty soundly; it must've been hours. Sitting up, he checked all his body parts and everything seemed to be working. "Guess I was lucky." He murmured again. "A few scratches here and there, plus a large lump under the bandage. Bandage! Where'd that come from? Got to get up, maybe walk a bit. No cuffs at least."

He was standing, looking around the room, but couldn't tell what he was looking at. *Maybe later. Whew! Got to lie down, very dizzy,* he thought. *Wish the room would stop.*

"I wonder how long I was out this time," he murmured again. "My head seems clearer now. Hmm, another familiar smell, sterile, like a medical facility. I also detect a faint noise and a slight vibration. It's like being on an airplane, only more faint. If I took a wild guess, I'd say I was in a vehicle of some kind. Flying maybe. Nah! That can't be."

Out through the doorway, Carter saw a long table near the center of the room. Someone was lying on the table on his back. He was wearing shorts, no shirt. A hairy one this was, with high pointed ears. "Heh, bet he got teased something fierce at school about his ears," he said softly, so he wouldn't be heard.

Then reality set in. He turned around with his back to the doorway wanting to scream. "This guy's an alien! Geez, this isn't a dream at all," he said softly. "Where the hell am I? Sit down, Frank, get a grip. This is crazy." He'd always known they were out there somewhere, but he never thought he'd see one, you know, up close like this. "Damn, Frank, get hold of yourself. This is no time for panic—. Like hell it isn't!"

He started to calm down and gather his thoughts. His knuckles weren't white anymore, but he thought his heart would jump out of his chest and he was perspiring. *What is real?* He thought. *This isn't. The situation I'm in right now can't be possible.* He went back to the bunk to lie down and try to sort this out. He really had some thinking to do. His head was starting to clear, but he was still weak. It was obvious to him he had a severe concussion. He drifted off again.

Waking to noises in the other room, he got up slowly and went to the doorway. Two more aliens were standing by the table looking down at the body. One of them appears to be a medical person. *Yep, the odor rings true,* he thought. *It's a medical facility and he's working on the guy using various instruments.*

Carter must have made a little noise, because one of the aliens standing at the table looked over at him, then back down to what he was doing. It seemed the person on the table was wounded in the right shoulder. *Christ, blue blood and all,* he thought. *Looks like they're about through, because the whole shoulder's being wrapped. There's also a bandage on its left leg. That shoulder wound must be giving him some trouble, because he's on some sort of life support system. With all those tubes that are sticking in him, it looks pretty bad.*

As Carter looked around the outer room, he saw what looked like a medicine cabinet against the wall. Next to the cabinet was a chair and on the floor by the chair were his clothes. All he had on was a three-quarter length robe. His watch and ring were gone, but he didn't think he was going to need either of them. Above the table in the center of the room was a long light that was similar to the one in his cell. In fact, all the lights were the same.

He knew there was more to this room, but from his position he couldn't see past the doorway. He didn't see an exit door, so he assumed it was also on the other wall. The place wasn't built for tall people. The ceiling was no more than six and a half feet, seven max. He had to be careful not to bump his head if he had to move fast. Lord knows the last thing he needed was another lump on his head. He still tired easily from his ordeal. Even thinking wearied him, so he went over to lie down and rest. In no time at all he was fast asleep.

He awoke fully rested, with no idea how long he was out. *It's odd without a watch,* he thought.

Voices in the other room might have awakened him. He slowly got up and walked over to the door for another look. Before he got there he noticed a tray of food on the table in the corner by the door. He was sure it wasn't there before. Carter hadn't even thought about eating, but now that he saw the food, he realized how hungry he was. There was a slight vapor coming from the food so he knew it was hot. It didn't smell bad, either. Right next to the tray was a small box.

When he got to the door he saw the same three aliens looking at the body on the table. It still had some life left in it because he saw it move. He didn't know what kind of life it was because he'd never seen anything like it before. They all looked similar, but with some noticeable differences. One of them turned and looked over at him again, but their conversation continued as if he wasn't here. They weren't ugly, but almost—familiar. He probably didn't look too good to them either.

Picking up the tray, he went back to the bunk and sat down. *I'd better try to eat this stuff,* he thought. *Hope it tastes good. It appears to be some type of vegetable and it isn't bad. I guess when you're this hungry, almost anything will taste good.*

"What do they call you?"

Being startled, he almost dropped the tray. Never in his wildest dreams had he ever expected to hear a familiar sound. One of the aliens was looking at him through the bars. It sounded like English, so he answered. The sound was coming from a square box hanging on the wall next to the door. "My name is Carter."

"If TanKor dies, you die," he said in a threatening voice, with an accent that ended with a slight but ominous growl.

I really needed to hear that, he thought. Carter assumed he was talking about the alien on the table. Apparently his injuries derived from the attacks at the Air Force Bases. *Good, at least our guys got some licks in and these things didn't get away scot-free,* he thought. As he stood in the doorway he observed a small bandage on this one's left arm and right leg, above the knee. *Good, heh, heh, furry bastard, somebody got you, too,* he thought.

"How is it you understand English, and what do they call you?" he asked as pleasantly as possible.

"I don't know this English you refer to, and my name is MarKor. We have a translator device on the wall." He pointed to the small speaker box to the left of the doorway. "In that small box on the table are a pair of translators. Use them. It will save you from a severe beating when you don't obey me. This is going to be a long voyage." He turned and left.

Carter certainly wasn't impressed by what the alien had to say. Opening the box he found two small earpieces, which he put in his ears. They seemed to fit okay. *I'm not real sure I want to hear what this alien has to say. Anyway, I don't think I'll have much choice. I must be careful and go along with everything until I learn just what kind of a mess I'm really in,* he thought.

Suddenly, one of the aliens gave out a loud growling cry. Looking at the doorway he saw the bars slide open and this MarKor guy, eyes on fire, a snarl on his face, coming toward him. *Boy, I'm in for it now,* he thought. The alien was coming at him with clenched fists. Carter was more fearful than he realized, because all he could think of was how weak he was. Even though he'd do the best he could, he just hoped it was good enough. MarKor was a good six inches shorter, but that didn't seem to bother him.

As he came toward Carter he had an angry look on his face that nobody could mistake, no matter what planet they were from. He swung with his left, but Carter ducked and turned it into a glancing blow. *Damn, I'm glad that wasn't a direct hit. This guy has real power in his punches,* he thought. But Carter had the advantage of more speed, even in his weakened condition.

He got by him quickly and ran out of the room, realizing then where the animal smell was coming from. Another alien tripped him just outside the door. He fell and slid crashing into the chair next to his pile of clothes. Then another alien came into the room and yelled, "MarKor, stop!" Ignoring the command, he continued and got to within five feet of his prey. The guy who told him to stop grabbed him from behind and repeated the command in his ear. MarKor spun around and connected with a wicked right that knocked him to the floor.

MarKor pulled a dagger from his belt and was going to stab the guy. His expression was far from angry; he seemed almost jubilant. He had a wide grin on his face as he approached. *How can I stop this from happening? If MarKor kills this guy, I'm next. Plus, I kind of owe him,* he thought.

While leaning against the wall Carter felt something hard pressing against his side. Probing with his hand, he found the familiar and welcomed shape of his semi-automatic pistol, wrapped up in his clothes. Without thinking he picked it up, pulled the slide, chambered a round and squeezed the trigger. The noise was deafening to everyone in the small room. He hit MarKor in the left shoulder and it spun him around. As accurate as Carter was with a pistol, he figured the shot would be fatal. Instead, he turned, and displayed a shocked look of disbelief on his face. This look turned to blind rage as MarKor came at Carter again. It didn't even seem to slow him down, so Carter pumped three more shots in him, right across his chest. The other aliens were holding their hands over their ears with pain written all over their faces. The impact threw him backwards: he was dead before he hit the floor.

Two aliens stood, almost frozen in place. They looked at Carter with their hands still covering their ears. He waved his gun at them as they slowly lowered their hands. The same disbelieving look MarKor had was on their faces, too, but they were in no mood to join him. They were as shocked as Carter was about the gun. They certainly never expected him to get hold of it, much less use it. He wasn't going to be allowed out of the cell in the first place, so nobody was concerned about it. Until now.

The third alien got up off the floor and looked at Carter, saying, "I want to thank you for saving my life, I think." This noise started as a multi-toned growl, then the translators tuned to the home speech Carter learned as a child, good old English.

"What do you mean, you think?" Carter said.

"I suppose it depends on what you're going to do next." He was staring at the business end of Carters' 9mm.

"I guess—I'm, ah, I'm not sure."

"I'm Captain RomMen and I command this vessel, at least I do until you decide whether or not you're going to use that weapon again," he grinned as he pointed a claw at my gun. "I could go deaf or you could kill me. Neither option seems very pleasant."

"My name is Carter. And I think I like an alien with a sense of humor. Continue, Captain, you have my undivided attention." As RomMen started to speak, Carter, noticed he never took his eyes off the gun or its holder.

"First order of business, put the weapon on the table."

"And if I do, what happens to me? Surely you can understand my delicate position, Captain?" he said, with eyebrows raised.

"If you do as I say, you may go back to your cellroom and no harm will come to you while you're aboard this vessel."

"How do I know you'll keep your word? I mean, we hardly know each other and I know nothing of your honor." The gun gave Carter a false sense of courage. Then it was the captain's turn to break the tension.

"I have no intention of having you killed. The only threat to you on board this vessel is now dead." He glanced down at the body and the pool of blue running beside his shoe.

Carter wasn't sure that MarKor was the only threat, thinking about the guy that tripped him. He figured there really wasn't much choice except to do what the captain said. He didn't have enough bullets for all of them, and even if he did, who'd fly this damn thing?

He wondered how much they knew about his gun. "You don't mind, do you?" He said, gesturing toward his clothes, while trying to keep his robe closed. The captain nodded his approval. He picked up his clothes and as he walked toward the table, the captain bent over to pick up the dagger. Neither of them saw Carter pop the clip about an inch and eject the chambered bullet into his hand. He slid the clip back in and laid the gun on the table. He turned and started back to his cellroom. *Geez, I feel like a kid. Go to your room!* he thought.

Of course it happened, it was a sure thing. The alien that tripped Carter picked up the gun from the table, pointed it at Carter's back, and squeezed the trigger. Naturally it didn't go off because the hammer fell on the empty chamber, but what happened next Carter never expected. At that instant the captain swung his arm around and plunged the dagger into the right side of the guy's chest. *Huh! So much for loyalty,* he thought.

"I can't have anyone on board this vessel who doesn't obey orders." Carter hadn't noticed before, but there were two more aliens in the room behind the captain holding some sort of small weapons in their hands.

With a slight grin, Carter knew he made the right decision. He didn't even hear them come in. The bars closed behind him and he went over to his bunk to lie down. *Boy, am I beat.* he thought. He was asleep in no time.

He awoke, sat up, and decided to get dressed. He was glad he had his clothes again. His pockets were empty, but he still had the bullet. *You know, except for my situation, I'm really starting to feel pretty good,* he thought. He got up and walked over to the doorway to look out into the other room. It was empty except for the table in the middle of the room and the rest of the fixtures, no more bodies or blood on the floor, either.

He looked around the room and thought he'd check it out this time, figuring he'd probably be here a while. The walls were smooth and had a strange light greenish color. The floors were a blue-green and felt spongy, sort of like an indoor-outdoor carpet. The lighting in the ceiling resembled fluorescent, but no outlining tubes were visible. He felt heat emitting from them so perhaps they had a dual purpose. *That'll work,* he thought.

"How are you feeling?"

He was startled, but the voice was familiar. He looked over at the doorway and saw the captain. "Pretty good, sir."

"Well, you can just relax and enjoy where you are as best you can. It's a long journey and I'll be stopping by now and then to see how you're doing."

"Say, captain, what are the chances of getting out of here for a little walk now and then?" he asked, trying to be friendly.

"Not a chance. I don't want you producing any more weapons. That was a pretty slick move you made before and you're quick. Perhaps you've had some military training? Nothing personal, but I feel much better with you in there. You're a very foxy guy, and this is definitely not a hen house." Turning, he walked away.

"How the hell does he know the story of the fox and the hen house?" Carter said out loud. *He seems like a nice guy. I'm not even sure he's the enemy. I'd better sit down and think this one over. There's a lot going on in my head right now,* he thought.

The last time the captain visited he told Carter they're of a race called Tygerians. And like any other race, there were good and bad elements. *Fair enough,* he thought. Gathering from our conversations during the trip, he appeared to be a very good and efficient captain. He was loyal to his beliefs and supportive of his crew. *Too bad he's on the opposite side of things. I could probably use a friend like him,* he thought.

Tygerians seemed very strong for their size and they didn't look too bad. It was hard to put them in a category! They looked almost like cats, but they didn't have whiskers. Their nails were pointed which give them the appearance of claws, but they didn't have a tail. Their teeth were somewhat flat and they had small fangs. They didn't have real thick hair, but what they had varied in color. One thing he did know for sure: they'd mastered interstellar flight and killed with little or no concern. *Easy, Frank, don't plunge off the deep end again. You've been there and it sucks,* he thought. *But hey, things must be looking up, even my head stopped hurting.*

Captain RomMen had explained some basics about space travel the last time they talked. When traveling in hyperspace the vessel moved so fast one had to decelerate to light speed first and then slow to normal speed before coming to a stop. Early space travelers learned a hard lesson about speed reduction versus vessel stress because their spacecraft blew apart. It required as much power output from the main engines to decelerate as it did to accelerate when transiting to and from hyperspace. This also affected the sensors and enhanced the ability of detection by an unfriendly foe. It was on this weakness that Gorgins, or space pirates, had regularly preyed. The captain knew better then to get caught in a trap coming out of hyperspace, so he always had a response plan.

Carter was listening to all the various noises that were emanating from the vessel. He wanted to familiarize himself with every sound he heard.

During their last conversation the captain was in a jovial mood. "Captain, I've been thinking," Carter said, with a slight frown. "For a conscientious person, which at least your crew seems to think you are, why the incidents and killings on Earth?"

"We stopped on Earth to conduct minor repairs to our spacecraft and do some research. We needed special materials, but what we were looking for was hard to find. The closest solution was at your experimental military installations, and we had to be careful about detection." He paused a moment. "I'm sure if we had gone to your base commanders and requested the materials we would need, the destruction would've been enormous. And that would have really increased the casualties. MarKor wasn't as concerned as I was about being detected, because he would rather fight and kill than do anything else. That's why there was more destruction than I had anticipated. He also knew that when this spacecraft was airborne and over 1,000 meter's in altitude, there weren't any weapons on Earth that could have caused us any damage."

"He killed a lot of people for those materials you needed."

"I know," the captain said, almost too softly for the translator. "It wasn't supposed to happen that way and I wish it would have been different." He spoke with more resolve than he had before. "I had no control over MarKor when he wasn't on board this vessel. We spent the equivalent of about three of your months on Earth to conduct research and complete our repairs. Perhaps MarKor was a little overzealous. I wanted to leave peacefully, but as you know, that didn't happen. We never take captives from another planet, but I had no control there, either. However, on occasion we do transport prisoners to Calverone if it's en route. MarKor was very angry when you wounded his brother."

"Oh, I thought he was wounded during one of the raids on the military bases."

"No," the captain said, a little surprised. "You wounded TanKor, and killed another in the desert before we took off. Three other members of MarKor's warriors were wounded during the raids on your military bases and have since died. This whole situation infuriated MarKor, and that's why you're here. He lost five warriors in the raids and then you killed his brother. I guess he just lost control.

"By the time I found out you were a prisoner on this vessel, we had already gone too far to turn back. As you can see, there's nothing that can be done to correct your situation. I'm very sorry for that, Carter. You don't seem so bad, for an alien."

Who's calling who an alien here? he thought. Carter wanted more information from him about Calverone and the Na'Reen people, but that went nowhere. The captain didn't want to discuss those subjects at all.

Time sure goes by slowly when that's all you have on your hands. It seems as though we've been traveling forever. I wonder what's happening back on Earth. I don't suppose I'll ever see that place again, he thought.

He was starting to feel a slight movement in the spacecraft. He figured they would be landing somewhere soon. *I have a feeling I'm going to regret this. Huh! Big choice in the matter. This is definitely not going to be my day,* he thought.

Now he knew there were more aliens in some of the other rooms, prisoners just like he was. But he had no idea who or what they were. He heard noises and movement on the blind side of the room. The bars slid open and in came three Tygerians with shackles and chains. *Boy, what a feeling of panic that gives you after months of confinement,* he thought.

They walked down a corridor and around a few corners. The farther they walked the weaker his legs felt. He thought he was going to fall any second. They went down a ramp onto what looked like a helicopter pad, only much, much larger.

He couldn't believe how wobbly he was, almost falling. So this is what the spacecraft looked like on the outside. There were two more right here next to it. `Where is here? He thought. *And now who's the alien? Perhaps it really is me.*

Suddenly, down he went. He was sprawled on the concrete-like substance. The chains rattled and made a lot of noise. Everyone laughed at him. For Frank Carter it was one hell of an entrance and he couldn't have been more embarrassed. As he struggled to get to his feet two dwarf-like aliens began pushing and poking at him with clubs. "What the—? Where did they come from?" he said, still struggling to get up. He didn't understand this at all, but once he got to his feet the short ones backed off. He had a little trouble breathing. *Perhaps the air was thinner here than on Earth*, he thought. He glanced around and saw the two that were hitting him a few moments ago. They were short squat aliens with facial hair, mustaches and beards. They wore rust colored outfits and had pointed ears. He didn't hear them say anything, so he was wondering if they were able to speak. *I think I'll call them dwarfs,* he thought.

CHAPTER 3

THE ARENA

They were huddled together in a group. The others seemed no more aware than Carter as to what would happen next. One of them became disorderly, protesting perhaps. The handlers converged, began yanking on his chains, and hitting him with clubs. *Guess he won't try that again*, he thought. The protester had a greenish-brown complexion with rough, lumpy skin, and had pointed bone-like teeth, little ears, and a rough voice. He appeared to be part reptilian from the looks of him. He was saying something about unfair justice and not belonging here. Carter didn't catch the rest. *Man, is he ugly*, he thought.

There were 12 of them in all, most of a sort that reminded him of a circus freak show. Aliens, like him, who were no longer in charge of their own lives. They shoved five aliens together and moved them to one side. The rest of us were herded into small individual cages and put onto what appeared to be their version of a flat-bed truck.

Three of them had exoskeletons with small spines that tapered from the middle of their forearms, getting larger and longer all the way to their elbows. Three thin spikes resembled fingers on their hands and two stubs on their heads compared to antennae. They were slender and had compound eyes. Another one resembled the guard, having very light green-tinted skin, and yet another appeared to be human, much like a Polynesian.

They traveled from the landing area onto a small road toward a city of some kind. Carter turned to study the area they had just left. Immediately he focused on the three spacecraft sitting on an oversized cement slab. One looked identical to the vessel that brought him. There were no markings on either, but the third one bore an insignia on the side. Along the roadside he noticed a peculiar variety of vegetation. *Could this be their version of grass?* he thought. It was more of the leafy variety than blades. The air seemed clean and fresh, but a resort it wasn't.

Turning, he concentrated more on their present direction. They skirted the edge of the city he had seen off in the distance. It looked different than any city he'd seen on Earth. The taller buildings stood near the perimeter and had odd shaped windows. Linking them together were low flat-roofed two-story structures. The windows in these structures were about two feet high and a foot wide, sort of resembling gun ports! He wondered about that. The road appeared to be cobblestone, but didn't produce the clackety clack noise as they traveled upon it.

As they went by people started badgering them; some even threw rocks. *Maybe this cage isn't so bad after all,* he thought.

After about ten more minutes of traveling, they came to what could only be described as a large stone structure. The walls were about 20 to 25 feet high on all sides. In the front there was a moat and a drawbridge, with towers at every corner. "Hey, I'm for the medieval look, but where did you guys learn this castle stuff?" he asked an unpleasant-looking guard, who didn't respond. He thought he could see weapons protruding from every tower. There was an entrance in the front and across the corner on the far side there appeared to be a parking lot. They turned right and onto a small road alongside the castle.

When they came around the rear of the castle he noticed a second entrance with yet another drawbridge, which raised as soon as they crossed it. Then a large door with square holes fell to the ground behind them with an ominous thud.

They went into a courtyard, about 20 feet past the entrance, where the vehicle came to a stop. "I guess this is where the fun begins," he said to his new friend, the guard. Still no answer. An alien that looked like a dwarf came to each of them and unlocked their cages. He motioned for them to line up in front of a small platform.

Two other aliens came out of a small building that was off to the right of them. One was a dwarf, and the other resembled the guard who accompanied them. The taller alien got up on the small platform in front of them and said, "If you can understand what I'm saying, take two steps backwards." The translators were doing their job because Carter understood him perfectly. The other two aliens from Captain RomMens' craft also followed suit.

While the rest of the group was given translators Carter checked out his surroundings. There were two guards on each side of the entrance at the drawbridge and three more up on the walls. He noticed the drawbridge didn't have any chains or rigging to support the weight and the large door with square holes didn't either. As he scanned the interior the aliens crossed his line of sight. *Boy, some of these clowns are ugly,* he thought. One thing did catch his eye, however. The guards on the ground level were armed only with clubs, but the guards on the walls had what resembled rifles. *Now that's security-conscious. A rebellion in the pit wouldn't yield good weapons and the rebels would get slaughtered in the process. Hmm, that would be ugly. Okay, so they're not stupid,* he thought.

At the far end, around past the drawbridge entrance, was a row of small rooms. They looked like jail cells, but he wasn't sure. Over to the left was a small archway over a closed door. On around to the drawbridge there was nothing but empty space, giving him the impression they didn't want anyone to escape.

As Carter pondered what might be next on the agenda, his hosts accommodated by marching them into the small building one at a time. It looked as though he'd be last, and that was fine by him, since he didn't think he'd like what they said anyway. The first two guys taken were locked in the small rooms at the other end of the courtyard. Next came the being who had given the dwarfs a hard time. They took him through the door under the archway and into the castle. The next three prisoners were also locked in the small cells. Carter had bad vibes about those three. Since the cells were full, he had to wonder where he would spend his evening, for it appeared they had plans for him, too.

When he got into the small building there was an alien sitting behind a small desk. He wasn't a dwarf either, he was too tall. He looked up at Carter and said. "According to the papers we have on you from Captain RomMen, you killed a Tygerian on board his spacecraft. Is that correct?"

"Yes, it is," he replied as nicely as he could.

"You are here against your will and no criminal charges have been filed against you thus far. Is that also correct?"

"As far as I know, yes, it is," he replied again. *Well this is going smoothly,* he thought. "Ahhhh! Ugh." A hit in the stomach from the club of a dwarf sent him to his knees.

The alien asking the questions said firmly, while pointing a finger, "That's twice you forgot to say, `sir'. I can forgive your ignorance once, but not twice."

"I'm sorry, sir. I won't forget again, sir," he said loudly, coughing, bending over, and trying to catch his breath. *That was real stupid, Frank, you should've known better,* he thought.

"That's much better," the alien replied. "Captain RomMen stated in his report that you saved his life by killing the Tygerian who threatened him. He also spoke well of you. However, that will not get you released. There will be an investigation, but in the meantime you will be our guest. I must warn you that any infraction, including disobedience, violence of any kind or escape attempts, will make your stay here permanent. In case you didn't hear me when I used the words escape attempts, I shall explain. No one has ever escaped from Calverone. Do I make myself clear?"

"Yes, sir, perfectly," he answered in a loud voice.

"Take him away," he said firmly, making a sweeping motion with his hand. A dwarf led him through the door under the archway and down some steps on the other side of the courtyard. They walked through a narrow corridor that had two thick wooden doors about 20 feet apart. Each had a small barred window. The window offered a clear view of the corridor behind it. At the end of the corridor they turned right and went up some steps. He figured they must be on ground level again. But he was more concerned about his gut, as he rubbed it, trying to ease the pain.

They passed through an archway and he was led to the left, through another corridor out into bright daylight. Momentarily blinded, they stopped. He couldn't believe his now-adjusted eyes. This looked like it belonged back in ancient Rome. It was an arena, an actual gladiator ring just like in the movies. He saw aliens at the other end practicing with swords.

Then his silent tour guide motioned for him to turn around and they went back through the same corridor. They turned left and crossed under what he thought to be the underside of the seating area.

When they got to the other side they went through another archway and down some steps. At the bottom on the left was a closed door with symbols on it he had never seen before. He had no idea what they meant.

On the right was an open doorway that led into a large room. On the left behind a counter were two aliens who appeared to be the same species as the guy in the small building. The dwarf gave one of them some papers and left. *Here we go, check-in-time,* he thought.

After one of them silently read the papers he looked up at Carter, grinned, and said, "Welcome to the pit; here you may die. My name is Phi'Lik and this is Bor'Tzz." He pointed to the alien next to him. "We are here to look after you. If you have any difficulties, get hurt, or need anything, just ask. We'll help you as long as they let us." He handed him a list of symbols, one of which was circled. "Go down through the middle of the large room behind you," he said, pointing with his out-stretched arm. "Go up the stairs at the far end and you'll locate station number 58 on the level above us," he pointed to the paper of symbols. "There you'll find everything you need. Get out of line and they'll make it very painful for you, understand?"

"Yes, sir," he replied, with emphasis on "sir."

"Carter, we are the only one's around here you don't have to address as `sir'," said Phi'Lik.

Carter turned around and walked down the middle of the large room. He noticed more doors with weird-looking symbols on them and at the far end was the staircase. To his surprise he found no doors on the second floor. It was a large room filled with bunks and lockers, dormitory style. As he walked down the middle he was searching for the designated symbol that was his.

On the left side, about halfway down he found what he was looking for. On the bunk he saw his gear and all his fears were confirmed. There was a medium-sized broad sword, a small shield, and a locker full of clothing, that also looked early Roman. *Shuuu!, smells early Roman too,* he thought, recognizing a strong leathery odor. *Looks like one size fits all.* He changed clothes, then walked down to the two aliens he had just talked to and said, "Who are you? Where am I? And what am I supposed to do?"

"Well, Carter, that's a lot of questions at one time. First, we are of a race called Na'Reens and are native to this planet. We are criminals and this," he motioned around the room with his arm, "is what we received as punishment.

"Second, you're on the planet Na'Reen and the city you went through upon your arrival is called Calverone.

"As for what you're supposed to do, well, that's easy. You go to the arena." Pointing, he said, "You go up the stairs, turn right, go all the way to the end, turn left, then left again and into the arena. Oh, by the way, Carter, one more thing, never uncover your sword in this building except for sharpening. And you can only sharpen your sword right there." He pointed again. "At the tables where you eat. If they catch you with your sword drawn anywhere else they'll punish you severely."

"Thanks for the advice," he replied and left for the arena. He passed some jail cells on the right and in a room at the corner on the right, he saw someone banging away on an anvil with a large hammer. Huh! looks like a forge of some kind, probably making weapons. *Good, nice to keep a fresh supply*, he thought.

In the arena was a big brute hollering some instructions to a few of the other aliens. He wasn't the same color as the rest of the Na'Reens. He had a ruddy complexion and was very muscular. You could almost compare him in size to the Tygerians, but with no hair. When he saw Carter, he came over and delivered the usual greeting. "Welcome to the pit, Carter. I've been expecting you. This is where you may die."

"That's exactly what Phi'Lik told me, sir. Guess I'd better get used to the idea pretty soon, huh, sir?" Suddenly Dor'Get burst out laughing, big loud laughs. He apparently thought it was funny. *It wasn't that funny*, Carter thought. *Oh well, maybe someone around here has a sense of humor.*

"I'm called Dor'Get, sir," he said, stopping his laughter as quickly as it started. "From this time on and until you or I cease to exist. "You got that, Carter?" He grinned; his stare was really starting to annoy Carter. I have a hunch you'll be the first to go. Heh, heh," he laughed again, but not as loud. Carter had finally realized what was annoying him—the guy had no eyelids and he never blinked.

"Yes, sir, Dor'Get, sir," he answered loudly, unable to hide his nervousness.

"Saaay, you catch on pretty fast, don't you? Good, now let me give you the rules. Follow them or die, makes no difference to me. Rule number one: never draw your sword unless you're in the arena. Rule number two: never kill anybody, unless you have my permission. Rule number three: you'll obey me or I'll kill you myself. No questions asked. I don't need anybody's permission to kill anyone. Those are the rules, Carter. And one more thing: do you know how to use that?" He pointed to Carter's sword. Carter was speechless. "Carter," he yelled again, but louder. He must have jumped a foot. "Do you know how to use that sword?"

"No sir, Dor'Get, sir. I've never used a sword in my life."

"Then take it back to your station," he replied, expressing foul words the translator couldn't change to English, "and leave it there until you are told otherwise. Now get moving and get back here fast." He raised his sword as Carter took off running.

When he returned, Dor'Get handed him a wooden sword and paired him with a veteran. By the end of the first two weeks of his training he was positive there wasn't a place on his body that wasn't sore from being hit by this guy. All he was trying to do was stop the blows. The guy never said a word. He just kept swinging and hitting him, swinging and hitting him. It was getting old and he was very frustrated. He had many lumps and welts. You name it, he had it, all over his body. And to make matters worse, he was being pushed around, harassed, tripped and kicked by the veteran warriors even when he wasn't in the arena.

That night while lying in his bunk thinking to himself, trying to rest, his mind drifted back to the three years he'd been in the Orient. *Damn, if I would've taken up swordsmanship, along with martial arts, I'd be doing so much better than I am. But how could I have known for one minute that I'd be in this situation*, he thought.

Sleep eluded him. He got up, weary and confused. He walked to the far end and went into the small room. *Even smells like a sweat box*, he thought. The windows were about six feet off the floor. Moonlight streamed in so he could see he was alone. "What the hell am I doing here? Lord, what did I do to deserve this? Ahhh!" He screamed, "I can't handle this anymore. Ahhh!" He screamed again. "I can't—." No more words would come.

Leaning against the wall, his legs gave out, and he slid to the floor. He just sat there, trying to relax. "Hell, I can't even cry. Can't do nothin' right. Dad, where were you when I needed you?" Yelling again. "I never got any help, no direction, no nothin—. I feel terrible. And now, I could easily die in this horrible place and who would know, or even care for that matter. What am I going to do?" His voice softened, slipping off. "What am I going to do?" he said again, only softer this time. His chin rested on his chest and his words were replaced by thoughts. *Never felt so lost in all my life. Almost wish I could die. Can't think clearly. Must get this monkey off my back, get myself straightened out, but how? Damn, RomMen, why'd you bring me to this wretched place. If hell is real, it's got to be here!*

He must've passed out or fallen asleep, he wasn't sure which, but when he awoke it was getting light out. Struggling to his feet, he thought, I *must get hold of myself. Take charge, Frank, This is not you, get a grip, it's time to pull yourself together. You'll never make it if you don't.* Shaking his head from side to side it came to him. "The arts, that's it," He said out loud. "I gotta start practicing again. I've neglected my training far too long. And it's the best way I know of to pull myself through this. So that's it then, I must learn the art of killing in order to survive."

Struggling to the next practice, he took the bull by the horns, literally confronting the bull who was daily beating him almost senseless. Being angry, he became more aggressive, and for the first time his opponent didn't get in as many hits, because he was dodging a few himself. *About time, damn it,* he thought. *It's take-charge day, Frank. I've been a screw-up most of my life. So let's go,* he thought. *Meet the new and improved Franklin Jonathan Carter.*

About two weeks later he started using a real sword. During his so-called three-month training period he wasn't allowed to speak to anyone except Dor'Get. And at the end of that period he was supposed to be pitted against other prisoners at the same skill level.

One of the aliens who came here about the same time Carter did spoke to someone earlier in the day. *Man, they beat the hell out of him. It's no wonder he didn't make it to practice the next day. I'm surprised he's still alive,* he thought.

The fighting had become easier since his near breakdown. And it didn't hurt to see his handlers adjust the attitudes of others to know what he'd have been in for if he hadn't changed.

He could have beaten his instructor a time or two, but he decided against it. He figured he wasn't here to win a few fights; he was here to learn how to handle himself and fight the way he had been taught. The other things he knew could only help him later when it really counted. *Stay alert, Carter*, he thought. *The only important thing now is survival. Still, I wonder how the Cleveland Browns are doing? And I miss the good steaks at the Outback.* He shook his head, knowing those thoughts were getting him nowhere. It was just making things worse.

Some of the aliens thought he was a little crazy, the way he was practicing his routine every day at the far end of the second floor. Before the end of his three-month probation, he'd be back in shape again. He had also learned that the best warriors, which they were called when they finished their training, got the first floor private rooms, supposedly an honor. All it really meant was that you were a better killer than most.

The warriors were still a real pain in the ass, but he could put up with them until probation was over. He wouldn't have to deal with them much longer. Turning off his translator wouldn't help either, because that would be worse than listening. They use verbal and minor physical abuse and he still had to take it. He certainly didn't want to give them a reason to really get tough. He was told that before he arrived, some of the trainees resisted and they got hurt really bad. Dor'Get didn't seem to care as long as nobody was killed. Every day was the same: eat, train, eat, and sleep. Some days passed almost unnoticed.

During the last two weeks they paired him with others of the same experience. During the matches he held his own, but it just didn't feel right. Something was still missing. His timing was off and it was like he was all thumbs. He wasn't really ready for a genuine fight. *I must work harder*, he thought. *Perhaps more room would help, like the arena. Hmm! That's an idea.*

At last, the three-month training period ended and he could finally speak. He wondered if he'd have to ask permission first. He wasn't in any hurry and thought perhaps he'd wait and see. He hadn't spoken this long, what was a few more days. Sure enough, the guy who arrived when he did, Mr. Protestor himself, started talking and shooting his mouth off. Dor'Get hit him with a club and he was lying in the dirt, out cold. Carter walked over to where Dor'Get was standing and looked him firmly in the eye. This got his attention. Glaring back he said, "You got something to say?"

"Permission to speak, Dor'Get, sir?" Carter asked, and hard ass softened immediately.

"Of course, you may speak. Now that you have asked properly, I have no objections."

"Thank you, Dor'Get, sir. A request."

"What is it?" he said with a glare.

"Dor'Get, sir, request permission to practice by myself, in the arena at night with my sword. Perhaps two hours every night while the arena's not in use, sir."

"That's an unusual request." He eyed Carter suspiciously. "Everyone else is tired and wants out as soon possible. And you want to go back?" He paused a moment. "Perhaps it would be good for you," he said in a fatherly sort of way. "I have noticed you're having difficulty in the arena. Perhaps the extra practice will improve your ability." Pondering a moment, he blurted out, "Yes, Carter, you have my permission," he said, almost smiling.

"Thank you, Dor'Get, sir."

★   ★   ★

There was a lull in the arena, a season break, so to speak. Nothing was going on for at least three months, maybe longer. It was perfect for Carter, to try what he had in mind. He wondered if anybody was watching during his nightly sessions. He hadn't seen anyone, but one never knew around here. He was confident this extra time to himself was exactly what he needed. With martial arts skills and the sword training, he was now improved and less Earth-sick. If he combined his skills, maybe he'd even be able to survive in this death camp. They said it wasn't for keeps, but he knew that all someone had to do was demand a grudge match and the fight was to the death. "Six warriors were killed in the last two weeks, not for keeps, huh? Damn bloodthirsty wackos," he said.

After two weeks at night, he wouldn't set the planet on fire, but he figured he'd be able to hold his own. Deep in thought, he barely heard the footfall of the alien approaching him. He turned sharply because the noise grew louder. Sure enough, in the dim light he could see someone approaching. He started whipping his sword around, such as a student of the arts might do when showing his prowess with the tools of his trade. It was a little something he put together, not that he was expecting any trouble, but it was supposed to be impressive, like a warmup for combat. He recognized the alien who approached him, but he didn't know him by name. He'd seen him fight and knew he was very good.

"Heard you were spending some time here at night practicing. I wondered how someone could practice alone and still get anything accomplished." KorRak had doubt in his voice. "I've been observing your training and you're definitely showing signs of improvement. For a while you weren't progressing well at all. My name is KorRak. I'm a Tygerian. And you're Carter, aren't you?"

"Yes," he replied, pausing. "I knew you were a Tygerian the moment I saw you." Turning slightly he returned to his routine.

KorRak looked at him a moment, then politely said, "Don't make the mistake of judging all of us from your experience with a few, just as I'm sure all Earthlings are not the same. As a matter of fact, I thought all Earthlings were brown," he said, glancing at his hands and face.

KorRak probably detected his annoyance, but it didn't seem to bother him. Carter was wondering why he thought all Earthlings were brown. "Well, now that we're through with the preliminary garbage, what can I do for you?" said Carter, not too politely.

"I have taken an interest in your practice here at night. Frankly, I'm quite surprised. Dor'Get usually lets no one in the arena at night for any reason. Perhaps you have impressed him in some way. Or maybe he thinks you'll improve and become a great warrior. That would make them all happy. Actually, since you're so far from Earth, I thought perhaps you could use a friend."

"I suppose a man can always use a friend," he said, quickly softening. That last statement removed any annoyance toward KorRak that he might have had. Since he was hundreds of light years from home and someone had offered genuine friendship, it's something that's hard to turn down. "It's true, I am a long way from home and I'll probably never see Earth again. I'm just trying to adjust and do the best I can to stay alive." *Still, I don't know him or his motives, so I'll keep the old guard up,* he thought.

"You attitude's good. I think you and I will get along just fine," said KorRak, seemingly satisfied about his trip to see this Earthling.

"I'd better get going, because my two hours in the arena are almost up. I don't want to anger Dor'Get."

As they started back toward their stations KorRak said, "Your station number is 58. That leaves 57 unaccounted for. A lot of them are dead, but right now most of them are at other arenas. They cycle around for about three months during the season break, but they will be back soon. In time you'll have developed your skills enough to be a warrior, but for now take it slow, my friend. Try to avoid the other Tygerians when they return."

"I'm sure that's good advice and I thank you," he said, remembering how hard just a glancing blow felt from MarKor. KorRak didn't ask him how he got here or about Captain RomMen, so he didn't mention it either. Because their conversation drifted he also forgot to ask him why he thought all Earthlings were brown.

One thing that KorRak said concerned him. It was about their better warriors being in another arena. According to KorRak there were three such arenas on Na'Reen. That would explain where the aliens were that came here when he did. Since he'd been here he'd only seen one.

After he'd showered, with cold water again, he crawled into his bunk. He'd been really tired these last two weeks, but it was well worth the extra work.

The next day in the arena Dor'Get called him over. "Carter, Skish here says you're a no-good ass-kisser and he wants to carve you into little pieces." He looked at the guy he was referring to, and saw it was Mr. Protester himself. He didn't even know his name because he was too busy practicing and keeping to himself. This guy Skish came at him, with sword drawn and a menacing look. With no time to think, Carter drew his sword, and not a moment too soon. His came slashing down at him. He ducked from underneath and came around with a slice for his midsection. Skish blocked it and they parried back and forth for a few minutes. Truth be known, Carter was only fighting defensively. He didn't want to hurt him in this world where killing was expected.

He got in a slice on Carter's leg. It stung more than it hurt and it wasn't bleeding too badly. He swung at him again and nicked Carter on the arm.

That did it. He was getting tired and had about enough. Carter parried a little more aggressively, then moved in. He blocked one of Skish's thrusts and sliced open his arm. Skish moved to the opposite side, then a karate move knocked him off his feet and onto his back. With Carter's sword at his throat, he decided to quit. *Wise, very wise,* Carter thought.

Two dwarfs came out hurriedly with a stretcher, but it wasn't needed. Skish walked out mumbling to himself and went to the sickroom on his own. "Well, Carter," said Dor'Get, "I didn't know for sure if you'd even fight like a warrior. But I guess you'll do for now. But, if you expect to survive here you'd better improve, and quickly I might add." Carter didn't say anything as he left the arena. He also went to see the doctor to get his wounds taken care of.

"Hello, Carter, I'm Doctor Zark. I was wondering when we'd meet. My good friend KorRak told me about you. Come on over and sit up here," he said, patting the place for him to sit. "Let me see what your opponent's done. Huh! Looks like your friend Skish got it worse than you."

He didn't tell him who fought Skish. "Thank you, Dr. Zark. I appreciate it, although I don't think they're very serious."

"Carter, all wounds are serious if not attended properly, so let's get started. You're going to have to answer a few questions before I work on you. Alien physiology's my specialty, but I don't get many Earthlings. By the way, your flesh tone's awfully light, isn't it? Anyway, I'll need your blood type, normal blood pressure, and a few more vital statistics."

Carter never expected the third degree, but the doctor sure was thorough about his anatomy. He thought doctors were supposed to know these things until he began to realize the monumental task it must be to keep track of the numerous races within the arena. After Dr. Zark finished, he thanked him and left.

He had 10 fights during the next month. He seemed to be holding his own, but something was still missing. He had less then desirable results in half his matches. Some of his opponents went down, but got right back up. He thought he'd win them all.

A few days later all the warriors were returning from their tour. He heard they received a real hero's welcome when they came through the city. Some of them really looked strange, in ways he didn't have words to describe. He saw the six Tygerians come in and for some reason they singled him out for some nasty looks. All six of them. *Don't know what that's all about, but I'm sure I'll find out soon enough*, he thought.

The next day KorRak looked him up. He was on the second level of the warriors' quarters, so they moved down to the end near the room. "Carter, do you know Captain RomMen?"

"I, uh, yes I do," stammering somewhat. This caught him off guard. "Why do you ask?"

"The captain of the small craft that brought the warriors back from Ratoon had an interesting story to tell," KorRak said quietly. "It seems an Earthling being transported here on Captain RomMen's war cruiser killed two Tygerians by the name of MarKor and TanKor. Did it pretty handily, too, I'm told." Then he looked at Carter. "Do you know anything about that incident?"

"Damn, word travels fast. I suppose that would explain why the Tygerians looked at me in an angry way yesterday when they arrived," he said, understanding full well what it meant to anger them.

"So it was you, wasn't it?"

"Uh huh." He nodded his head. "It was me."

"Heh, heh, I thought it might be you," KorRak chuckled. "Listen, my friend, I know you're not aware of this, but MarKor's cousin is also a prisoner here. He's considered an outcast and I'm sure he's thinking he'll get back in good graces if he kills the one who got MarKor. I wouldn't even be surprised to see a small Tygerian fleet swing by here to settle the score. You see, MarKor was the favorite nephew of Lord GorDon. He's a War Lord in the Tygerian Empire. But I'll save the history lesson for later."

Hmm, I guess I really stirred up a hornet's nest didn't I?" He stared at him until his translator found an appropriate phrase and then they both laughed.

"They also said Captain RomMen was being detained for questioning and possible action against him."

"I wonder if Captain RomMen will get in trouble for what I did?" He displayed a sober expression. "But I will say that I have some ill feelings toward him."

"I'll help you all I can, Carter. I think even Dor'Get is on your side, although I'm not exactly sure why. You'll have to try to avoid DanKor as much as possible."

"DanKor. So that's his name."

"Yes it is, and he's a bad one. There's something else you should know." He had a very serious expression on his face. "RomMen and I are very good friends. We grew up together on our home planet. He probably thinks I'm dead. But I'm worse than dead, I'm here. I've been in this place for over three years and I sure would like to get out some day—alive, I mean. And I might add that your situation with Captain RomMen is between him and you."

"I've thought about escaping many times myself, but at the present time I have neither the means nor the plan to do so."

"Perhaps we can work on that when this business with DanKor is over," said KorRak, smiling as he got up to leave.

The hide-and-seek tactic with the Tygerians was in its third day. It wasn't a big place and avoiding them wasn't easy. As KorRak said, Dor'Get could be helping to keep them separated. Perhaps that's why he assigned him to the weapons forge. It was tough work, but it helped build his muscle tone.

Ordak was the master of the weapons forge as far as swords were concerned. He didn't know if Ordak had any other skills, but he made all the weapons used in the arena and was good at it.

"Carter, come over here. I want to show you something," said Ordak, smiling through the beads of sweat rolling down his brow. He followed him as they went behind some cabinets to a small table. Ordak unrolled something that was wrapped in a clean thin piece of leather lying on the table. Whatever it was, he could see Ordak was very excited about it.

"It's going to be a beauty when it's finished," Ordak said while holding it up. "It's going to be the best sword I ever made. I fused three different metals to make this. I couldn't tell you how many times I folded it. One of the metals is from the arelian sun. The whole universe is loaded with ferrous metals, plenty of titanium and seanthrite for spacecraft. But arelium, ah," he gazed down at his masterpiece. "Only the arelian cold sun has this stuff. That's what's going to be the difference in this sword. It'll have a new kind of power and much more strength." He looked up. "Only you and I know about this."

"Your secret's safe with me," he said. "I have to get going, or I'll miss the evening meal they're holding for me." *Ordak, you need to get out more,* he thought.

The next morning he got up earlier than the rest because he wanted to get to the forge before anyone saw him. This time it didn't work. Nearing the forge, movement caught his eye. It was DanKor, stepping out from behind a pillar in the hallway, waiting for him. Carter looked around quickly and saw that the other Tygerians had closed off his escape. "Good morning, Carter," said DanKor with a grin Carter knew he was going to loathe. "Slept well, did you?" He put his hand on his sword and looked directly at DanKor."Ah, ah, ah, Carter, you know the rules. No drawn swords anywhere except in the arena. Let's just go there and wait for everyone else. Then we can have some fun."

When Dor'Get got to the arena he saw the Tygerians standing around Carter. "What's going on, DanKor?"

"Nothing much, Dor'Get, sir." He smirked.

Dor'Get gave an unseen signal to the guards on the wall. In a few minutes all the warriors had assembled in the arena. "Okay, DanKor," resuming his authority. "What now?"

"I declare a grudge match with Carter, the Earthling." He drew his sword slowly and pointed it at him.

Carter drew his sword, pointed it at DanKor, and answered as strongly as he could. "I accept the challenge, DanKor." There was a low hush from the warriors. All had known this was coming. The match was scheduled to occur in three days. News had spread fast and the Na'Reens were making wagers through a credit system Carter didn't understand. After all, gambling was what this place was all about.

★   ★   ★

It was late afternoon and the arena was filled to capacity. Carter knew that DanKor was heavily favored. He couldn't blame them. Since they had only seen him in a few preliminary matches, they had no reason to bet otherwise. For Dor'Get it was a sign that the Earthling was not yet the drawing card he expected.

DanKor and Carter approached Dor'Get and drew their swords. He nodded his approval, which started the event. As Carter turned to face DanKor he stepped back a few feet to size him up. They paced each other, getting closer all the time. DanKor looked like he was really going to enjoy this. Either that or it was a strategy to throw Carter off. Probably both.

Damn it, play games back, he thought. So he started smiling, too. Suddenly DanKor lunged, swinging his sword from side to side in hopes of scaring Carter right off. *Not today furball!* He thought. Carter parried, shifted his weight, used a karate move and knocked DanKor to the ground. Just as quickly Carter came around and thrust at DanKor's shoulder. He cut him on the left arm and it started to bleed. "Blue furball!" He corrected, yelling again. Translators were never turned on during combat.

It appeared lady luck was smiling on DanKor, because he just had time to avoid Carters thrust. The smile left his face immediately as he suddenly realized how he'd underestimated his opponent. The two of them jabbed, parried, and banged on each other a few more minutes. Carter realized they were pretty evenly matched, but he still wanted an edge. He knew he'd get it if he didn't let his anger cloud his judgment.

As if by some signal, three of the Tygerians moved toward Dor'Get and crowded him over to the side. *Damn*, he thought. *DanKor didn't need a translator to understand my concern. So much for the edge.* Dor'Get was out of the way in case he would try to interfere with their plans. KorRak and the sixth Tygerian were about 15 feet from the rest. KorRak didn't indicate he knew anything was going on either.

Still, it was the kind of fight the spectators wanted. They cheered and waved their arms, encouraging their favorite warrior. They stepped back for a little breather and he could tell DanKor was starting to weaken because his movements were slower and his thrusts were not as strong. *Now I have the advantage*, he thought. *And he knows it.*

Suddenly the Tygerian nearest to KorRak moved in and tripped Carter. Seeing this, DanKor quickly bashed Carter alongside the head with his shield. The blow almost knocked him out. He was flat on his back, dazed and somewhat disorientated. DanKor stood over him and quickly plunged his sword into the right side of Carter's chest. He remembered letting out a

low cry before he passed out. The tip of DanKor's sword coming out of
his back.

★   ★   ★

Carter was told about what happened later. KorRak turned around and
killed the Tygerian that tripped him. The three Tygerians who had Dor'Get
surrounded continued with the plan. Before he could raise an alarm, one of
them whispered, "Dor'Get, you're far too soft for this job and you picked
the wrong side." The closest Tygerian plunged a handmade dagger into his
chest. The guards fired immediately at the Tygerians and killed all three. The
crowd was giving the warriors a standing ovation. So much death, so much
entertainment. They were all elated and had a great day at the arena.
Everyone except Carter and the dead warriors.

The warriors immediately dropped their weapons and spread their arms
above their heads. They knew anyone who didn't would be shot on the
spot. It was standard procedure when a disturbance occurred. Three dwarfs
came out quickly with their stretcher, picked up Dor'Get, and hurriedly
carried him to the sickroom. Two more came out and picked up Carter.
Everyone thought for sure he was dead. "It seemed a shame," many had
said. "He was a likable alien. Too bad he had to die at the hands of a
cheating, low-life Tygerian."

After the fight DanKor had picked up Carter's sword and left the arena.
"It was a very high price to pay for Carter's death," BriCon had said,
troubled at the loss of their four comrades. DanKor, flushed with victory and
fatigue, had said nothing. He had only thought about what Carter's death
would do for him with his uncle.

★   ★   ★

Dor'Get had been the first patient, but he died a few minutes after they
got him to the sickroom.

Doctor Zark had to perform a temporary procedure to stop the
bleeding in Carter's shoulder, knowing full well he'd have to be transferred
to the city hospital immediately to operate on his right lung. He had put

Carter asleep for the ordeal, all the while knowing he would have a full recovery. Zark had decided to keep Carter's condition to himself for a while, as well as the secret he learned from a dying Dor'Get.

*   *   *

There had been minor chaos in the warrior quarters because Dor'Get was dead and they had no direction. Of course, the warriors didn't want to get too unruly because they knew what would happen.

Res'Itz held an immediate council meeting and sent for Warrior Master Jackson, ordering him to come to Calverone and take control. Res'Itz thought about training Carter for the job. He guessed it was a little late now that Carter was dead.

The next day Jackson arrived and took over. Most of the warriors knew who he was and they respected him. He restored order as soon as he arrived. Jackson was a very different Earthling than Carter.

*   *   *

"Well, doctor, how'm I doing? Could you fill me in on what happened?" said Carter.

"You're doing fine. Your friend Dor'Get's dead. It was the Tygerians, of course. Only two of them survived. The guards killed three and KorRak got the other one. The good news is that you're being transferred to Harzzton. I also might add you were very lucky yesterday," Zark said, almost congratulatory.

"I guess I was tripped by one of the Tygerians. Geez, that's the second time that happened. I fared much better the first time, doctor," he said, thinking back to the confrontation on Captain RomMen's spacecraft.

"That's not what I'm talking about," Zark shot back. He paused, then said, "I guess you should hear the whole story. Dor'Get and Res'Itz were withholding information from you about your imprisonment here. I convinced Res'Itz to transfer you to another arena to keep the Tygerians from knowing you were still alive. I told him that as long as they knew you survived he risked a retaliatory invasion from Lord GorDon. There are no

Tygerians at Harzzton. But the irony of it all is that you should not be here at all. Your release approval came to Res'Itz. The ruling council set you free, but the final approval still rested with Res'Itz, because he's the senior magistrate. And he decided not to let you go. His reasoning was that you had nowhere to go and what would you do? He had some thoughts on the possibility of training you to be a warrior master."

"So that's why Dor'Get helped me," he said, the pieces now falling into place. "That explains a lot." Then the anger came, the kind he usually saved for his sword. "Doctor, could you leave me alone for awhile?"

"Of course, I'll be back later." He left the room.

The next morning Zark stopped by. "How's my best patient doing today?"

"Better, I guess." He moved his shoulder a little. "Yep, still hurts." He was no Earthly physician, but his bedside manner was comforting.

"It's not the wounds I'm—."

"I know what you meant," he cut in, displaying a little sarcasm. "I've done a lot of thinking during the night and I suppose Res'Itz could be right on one point, but wrong on another. I feel like I'm lost in a time warp and I'm definitely out of place here. I know I can't go out into this world and start life over. I also know I don't want to spend the rest of my life in these damn arenas, either." Fists still clenched and angry, he continued. "If I trust my instincts and wait till the time comes, I'm sure I'll take the right course of action."

"That sounds reasonable to me," Zark said.

"By the way, doctor, last night you said I was very lucky. There aren't any vital organs in the right side of my chest area except the lung," he said, wondering.

"That's exactly the point. DanKor thought your heart was in the right side of your chest. He has no idea about human anatomy. In his mind, you're dead. He thought for sure he killed you with that thrust, but he was wrong. The only other race that's like yours are the Kaladonians."

At first Carter just sat there, not fully grasping DanKor's mistake. Then it hit him like a brick. "Doctor, you just made my day." Now he was smiling again. "You've just given me the last piece of information I've been looking for all along. It's like getting the last piece of the jigsaw puzzle." Zark's translator couldn't deliver on the last two words. "Doctor, will you help me acquire a base knowledge of the anatomy of these aliens I fight?"

"I don't understand about the jigsaw puzzle, but I'll help you all I can with the anatomy." Grinning, he turned and left.

I can see it clearly now. That's why I hadn't been doing as well as I should have in the arena. I didn't know my opponents' insides or what made them tick, he thought. "Strange, how the final piece of information needed for success in the arena comes not from experience, but Dr. Zark and his medical books. Yes," he said out loud, clenching his fists. He was almost looking forward to Harzzton.

CHAPTER 4

A NEW GOVERNMENT

The decor was appropriate for a person of his stature. A small table was in the corner on his left and a large credenza sat behind his desk beneath a medium-sized window. An adjoining room contained a large table and chairs. The walls were plain except for three-inch-square touch pads on both sides of the door. It was a comfortable environment for him to spend his time planning for the future of Kaladon. He was the leader of the High Council and felt this was his responsibility.

Gart Zordek was a slender person of just under six feet and weighed about 170 pounds. When the new government was officially installed he had visions of being named emperor. There had been much turmoil and lack of trust within the government and it was time for change. Just this morning a member of the council staff had been found guilty of conspiring to commit treason. The worst problem was the Tygerians. They never seemed to be far away when there was trouble. The need for a strong and stable government had never been greater. And he thought perhaps he was the one who could make it happen. Zordek was no fool and with the help of his good friend, Tak Byrokk, who excelled at details, allowed him to concentrate on other more important matters. Byrokk also accomplished an enormous amount of public relations work for their cause.

Zordek was sitting at his desk, shuffling through some of the papers he needed for the meeting that evening. He was deep in thought, when a loud, "Hi, Daddy," broke the silence. The always jovial Dovina came bursting into his office. "How's my favorite person today?"

"Huh, what? Oh, ah, fine my dear, just fine," replied a very startled father at her abrupt entrance. He had to admire his daughter's spunk and charm, but he wished she'd slow down. As pretty as she was, he didn't understand why there was no male in her life. Ever since she was a child she had been interested in the military. Her and Shanza, that tomboy friend of hers, seemed more interested in military tactics and various types of military weaponry than anything else.

"What can I do for you, my dear?" displaying happiness.

"Oh, not much, Daddy." She looked around the room, much as her father had done moments before. "Why the dismal look, is anything wrong?" She hugged him from behind and rubbed the back of his neck.

"Nooo," he said slowly, giving out a sigh as he felt the tension ebbing from his body. "You know the situation here right now. Until we conclude the negotiations with our allies and get this new government installed, it's going to give me medical problems for sure," displaying a slight frown.

"Now, Daddy, only you can get this accomplished," smiling now, "just remember what you always tell me. Think things out carefully, don't overreact, and everything will be just fine."

"Thank you for that, my dear. It's not just Kaladon I'm concerned about. There's our moon Mylaar to consider. And what about Krynta and her moon Pendari? You know this government and Pendari nearly broke off diplomatic relations, more than once! I wouldn't exactly call us friendly." He was slowly shaking his head from side to side. "A lot to consider. Krynta's trade market might be affected, so we have to be very careful there. They've been our closest ally, for longer than I can remember.

"By the way, my dear, are you going to the conference on Krynta with me next week?"

"Yes, of course," displaying an even bigger smile, knowing full well that Krynta had the best trade markets in their solar system. They were right in line with the trade routes to the Darien Way and beyond. "I wouldn't miss it for anything. Do you mind if Shanza accompanies us?"

"No, of course not, my dear. You know she's always welcome."

"I have to go now, Daddy, see you at dinner." She left in a flash, only the fragrance of her perfume remaining.

He sat for a moment, thinking about Shanza a few years back. She had been extremely distressed by her father's accidental death. It had been an emotional time for everyone. Drey Mytlaq was his closest friend and was slated to play a big part in his political career. After Drey's death he sort of looked after Shanza and took her in, treating her like a daughter.

The meeting in Ozlonz, the capital city of Kaladon, came to order and all were present. The attendance told him that all were interested in accomplishing their objective. The topics for debate were critical and by evening's end he had won some and lost others, as expected. The meeting concluded very late and most everyone seemed happy with the results. Upon conclusion, all knew it would be good for Kaladon. "I'm sure the Krynians will be pleased too, because these new revisions will only help their economy," he said to his aide as they left. "Wealth was always their main concern."

His driver dropped him off and then left to take his aide home. He went in and Dovina met him in the foyer with a hug.

"What's wrong, my dear? You're trembling," he said.

"I'm not sure," she said, "I can't seem to associate the feeling with anything right now. But I think we should be very careful on our trip to Krynta." He gave her a reassuring hug and she started to calm down.

In the morning, four days later, they boarded a travel cruiser for Krynta. Since the trip was considered top secret the date, time, and departure place had been kept secret.

A fighter group escorted them until they went to hyperspace. At that time, however, the fighters had to turn back because of their inability to travel in hyperspace. About halfway they were met by two Krynian war cruisers. All knew these security measures were a necessity. There were too many sightings of Tygerian war cruisers near Krynta. "If anybody could wreck their travel plans, it'd be them," said the captain.

"They can wreck much more than travel plans," replied Gart.

It was hard to believe, but amongst all the treachery and fighting, there was still a city that lived in peace. It had good laws which were strictly enforced. Anybody visiting Korinze, the capital city, came in peace or was confined. Civil disturbances were never permitted. Dovina and Shanza were excited about the trip for different reasons. Like a lot of females, the market was the number one priority on their list.

Departing the spacecraft, Gart and his party boarded the transport for their quarters. En route they passed over miles of roads with hundreds of shops on both sides. Some buildings were multilevel with large cultural centers and others were single story. All were well-appointed and well-stocked.

A number of years ago a major technological break-through in communications had been established with the development of language translators. This enabled all races to broker their own financial transactions in this market where hundreds of alien races made their livelihood and interpreters were no longer needed.

Gart was anxious to get the meetings underway and complete his business here. He also wanted to relax and spend a few days in Korinze. After eight days of meetings, all parties were basically content with the plans outlined for the new alliance. Much to Gart's surprise, even Pendari gave its full support.

His mission accomplished, Gart was now ready to relax. He sent a coded message to the high council in OzLonz that all had gone as planned. He'd return in about a week to help implement the new government. Then the hard work would really begin. *Yes,* he thought. *And it would be done.* His anxiety was very high.

On the day they were scheduled to leave for Kaladon, low clouds threatened rain from the east. The low chatter from the crowd of about 35 people waited to give them the proper send off. But their travel cruiser was nowhere in sight.

The Krynian military commander was visibly disturbed by this situation and thought it very odd. He turned to his assistant and ordered, "learn the reason for this delay."

"Yes sir," he clicked his heels and hurriedly left.

They heard a low roar coming from the far side of the wide open padport. Beyond the field, past the padport, they saw three spacecraft traveling in a semicircle toward them. "They're not our vessels," the commander yelled to the unsuspecting travelers. "Scatter! They're Tygerian war cruisers!"

Many screamed as they ran in all directions. The only cover were canopies. The padport was a wide open area.

When the commander's assistant opened the door to the control building, he was immediately shot. The Tygerians hiding inside came rushing out. They started firing toward the crowd, with emphasis on the governing party. The small detachment of Krynian military forces on hand returned fire. But they were out- gunned and soon yielded ground.

When one of the Krynian defenders fell dead next to Dovina, she picked up his weapon and started firing at the Tygerians. On impulse Shanza grabbed a stray weapon and did the same. The fight only lasted a short time because everyone was out in the open. The best marksmen killed the most, which was why Dovina and her tomboy friend did well.

One of the Tygerians, surprised at this much resistance, fired a blaster into the crowd. All the action from the defenders had halted immediately. Both Dovina and Shanza had been knocked unconscious. Dovina, being closer to the blast, had more severe wounds. It looked as if Gart was one of the first killed. He wasn't moving and neither were most of the others.

"Speed," shouted the Tygerian in charge, while waving his arm. It appeared there were only six survivors and these were being taken prisoner. All the others were checked to confirm their condition, because they wanted no witnesses.

When the Tygerian commander heard the first rescue vehicle approaching, he gave the order to withdraw. His orders were very specific, in and out, no second encounters. It meant they had to leave as soon as possible. It also meant an important figure would be left behind. Had they but known, they would have stayed. They fired their blasters at the approaching vehicles as they turned and began boarding their craft. They picked up their casualties, the prisoners and left.

"Shoot," yelled the new military commander rolling up to the scene. His troops fired and did the best they could, but their weapons were not adequate to take on a war cruiser. The fleeing enemy was fast and too determined. The only things visible were departing spacecrafts.

When the rescue vehicles arrived, the medical personnel hit the ground running. They ran toward the crowd to render help to anyone still alive, but it appeared hopeless. "Another senseless attack on unarmed, but not unimportant people," said a paramedic, as she checked for a pulse that wasn't there.

Then a dazed and painful call sounded. "Help, please help me," said a person, falling backwards almost passing out. Too weak to sit up, he was placed on a gurney, put into a small rescue vehicle and rushed to the nearest hospital.

Five days later, a bandaged Gart Zordek opened his eyes, and saw his friend Tak standing by his bed. "Where am I?"

"Try to relax, my friend. You were wounded during the fight at the padport."

"What the hell happened? Where's Dovina? What's going on?" He looked around, eyes searching for nothing in particular. "Tell me." He was almost delirious.

"Take it easy, relax, and I'll tell you."

"How long have I been here, Tak?"

"It's hard to say anything if you keep asking questions."

"Okay, go ahead. Talk, no more questions." He leaned back on his bed, but before Tak could say anything, he passed out.

"Doctor," Tak yelled without taking his eyes off Gart. He yelled again, then a doctor came into the room and rushed to the patient. He checked his vitals and observed the visual display.

"He just passed out from exhaustion," said the doctor. "He'll come around again soon. Try not to let him get so excited next time. If he doesn't stay calm, call for assistance. Someone will be nearby." Two assistants also responding to the call met the doctor in the doorway, bumping into each other.

It was in the middle of the afternoon on the following day before Gart stirred again, waking more quietly this time. "Well, my friend, shall we try again?" Tak asked.

"What happened? Where am I?" He was much more sedate.

"That's what you asked me yesterday, but you tuned out before I could answer."

"Yesterday? I don't remember talking to you yesterday," he said, almost in a whisper. "I'll just lie here and let you do the talking, I'm very tired."

"First, I must tell you, nobody knows where your daughter is." The sorrow appeared on his face.

"And Shanza?"

"Her too. You're the only survivor of a Tygerian attack at the padport. Everyone was killed or captured but you. I could have been killed too, but I was running late. You've been in this medical facility for five days.

"I notified the council on Kaladon of the events. They all wish you well and consider your being spared as a major failure for the Tygerians." Tak spoke this way to try and help his friend balance the needs of government with his personal losses. "I am sorry about Dovina and Shanza. For awhile no one must know you survived but the doctors and council members. If the Tygerians think you're dead, they'll be less likely to return and create more turmoil on Kaladon during its transition." He could see the tears forming in Gart's eyes.

"Please, leave me," he pleaded, trying hard to swallow his emotion. "Come back tomorrow. I need to be alone." Tak nodded his head, got up, squeezed Gart's arm, and left.

The Krynian government expressed their condolences over his daughter and wished him well.

They would be landing at Ozlonz in a little while and Gart would be happy to be home. He was eager to delve into the arduous task before him so as not to dwell on his missing daughter and Shanza.

A meeting was set up with the government to begin the transition of power. This long and slow process would take some time to complete. Much to his satisfaction, everything was progressing much better than he had anticipated. The present government was giving their full cooperation. In fact, all looked to Gart as some kind of hero, some even taking his survival as an omen.

The meeting came to order in the Senate Building, one of the city's newest structures. Because of the good representation of the people they all agreed to appoint the council members as the new senators. Tak Byrokk was voted in as secretary of this new senate. General Wydorf was appointed Brigadier General in charge of the military and he appointed his fellow comrade and trusted friend General Sizdroz as chief of security. Gart Zordek was elected Emperor of Kaladon for life and his heirs to follow. Menk Froks, the previous emperor, was appointed first assistant to the emperor and it took a few months to draft the "Articles of Law" to govern by.

They decided to build an academy for their officers and set up training facilities for the enlisted ranks. They would also have to build a space fleet because they only had ten spacecraft for all of Kaladon, which included only one small war cruiser. They would contact Mylaar, Kaladon's moon, Pendari, Krynta's moon and Ra'Tor, moon of Na'Reen in the Ta'Rae solar system for their construction and purchase. These were the builders of the best spacecraft. The companies on Kaladon built excellent fighters, various transports and small military hardware.

The emperor sent messages to summon the senate secretary, his two generals and the first assistant to a meeting in his study. An hour later the meeting began and they went over a number of items; the most important was the need for large military weaponry. Nobody wanted a war with the Tygerians, but they knew peace would only come by bargaining through strength.

They agreed to send an emissary to Ra'Tor to negotiate for the purchase of war cruisers. Their order and number being the last items for discussion, the meeting adjourned. As general Wydorf was turning to leave, the emperor said, "Wait, General, one more thing. I neglected to mention Mylaar and Pendari when we ordered spacecraft. They build quality spacecraft, don't they?"

"Yes, they do, your highness. I will take care of this personally." Secrets were best kept in small circles, the existence of which would not be so accessible to the spies who were probably already informing the Tygerians.

"Yes, that will be fine."

Two days later the emissary left for Ra'Tor. The following day, the other emissaries left for Mylaar and Pendari.

★   ★   ★

On the moon's surface of a remote planet in the Nacid solar system, deep valleys between mountain ranges served to hide the work underway. On the floor of these valleys various structures were being constructed. Mingled within was an occasional larger structure. These were the entrance areas to very large caverns beneath the moon's surface. Part of the caverns were natural formations and the remainder were handiwork of the Tygerian engineers. Of course, they used slave labor for the manual part, but took credit just the same.

Within the caverns were various structures consisting of office buildings, stores, living quarters, and a military complex. Some structures were 90 stories high. They were all interconnected by clear transportation tubes. Openings near the surface housed an elaborate air curtain system connected to sophisticated electronic holoshields.

In other areas were industrial complexes powered by large generating stations churning out lifelines for the machinery of war. It was a large cavernous environment going on for hundreds of miles beneath the surface of the moon. In short, it was a secret world, inhabited by a large part of the Tygerian Empire.

The moon, called MarQ, was as large as some planets in the Nacid solar system. The friendly atmosphere, augmented by oxygen generators, and the natural resources beneath the moon's surface amply supplied all the requirements for sustaining life. As far as anyone else was concerned, the moon wasn't inhabited.

The moon was also occupied by a race called Bendoatiis. Aliens with very little hair on their bodies, light gray complexions, thick dark brown hair on their heads, green eyes, and an average height of six feet. They had drooping earlobes, as if they wore heavy earrings, and various markings on their faces. They had occupied the inhabitable moon for years before the coming of the Tygerians.

Below the surface on this uncharted moon, Lord GorDon, the war lord of the Tygerian Empire, held council. He was a person of stature with an infinite craving for quality and perfection. His command headquarters was a cluster of rooms in which he had a private office, a study, a war room (conference room), and small living quarters. He was in his war room meeting with Regent BryQat, his second in command.

"What do you mean he's still alive? Explain," he shouted.

"My lord, that's the report we received from Krynta."

"How can this be? How could they have possibly failed? I sent three war cruisers to carry out this assignment and you're telling me they failed. Are you sure the information from our agent is correct?"

"Yes, my lord, all the information we received about this mission is correct," replied the regent, somewhat nervous.

"Who was the Commander in charge of this mission?"

"It was Captain MyrAak, my lord." Still a little uneasy, "the officer at the scene was "Captain SenKez."

"Hmm," said Lord GorDon. "Those are very capable officers," He was calmer now. "There must have been some unforeseen problem during the mission. Where is Captain MyrAak now?"

"He's en route to Calverone, to drop off some prisoners from Korinze. While he's there he will also check on the status of the Earthling, Carter." The tension between them was subsiding.

"Did they have a personnel transfer en route to Calverone?"

"If you're asking about Captain RomMen, yes, my lord, he was transferred to Captain MyrAak's vessel two days ago. They will arrive at Calverone tomorrow," He frowned slightly, hoping Lord GorDon wouldn't see.

"Good, at least something is going right today." He noticed the frown on BryQats' face. "I see you don't approve of Captain RomMen being sent to Calverone, do you, my friend?"

"My lord, I do have reservations about losing such a capable and well-qualified captain over this matter. I may not agree with your decision, but I do understand how you feel."

"You are second in command of this sector and one of my most trusted officers. Careful what you say, it could be dangerous."

"I'm well aware of that, my lord. But you can't execute all your good officers and trusted friends just because they disagree with you from time to time." He felt more at ease as time went on. Lord GorDon just looked at his friend with a stone face, which broke into a slight grin.

BryQat decided to continue. "According to the rest of the message, your nephew DanKor will kill Carter in the arena. Perhaps we should wait for the final report from Captain MyrAak and see if he succeeds."

"Excellent idea," he stated, immediately changing his grin to a full smile. "Maybe we'll have another plan successfully completed soon." In an elevated tone, he continued. "Send a message to our contingent on Kaladon. We must make it as difficult as possible for this new emperor. Have them create as much turmoil and unrest as possible with the locals. Get a revolt going in the border area of the Esterk Province and the Central Government. Then let's see what other discontent we can cause for this new emperor." Yelling now, "that cursed Zordek." He raved, banging his fist on the table. "I curse him to die in fire." Almost instantly Lord GorDon's mood changed again, mellowing, he said, "And by the way, they're sending an emissary to Ra'Tor for the purpose of acquiring spacecraft to enlarge their space fleet. Immediately after Captain MyrAak completes his mission at

Calverone, have him intercept this emissary."

"Yes, my lord."

"After completion of these new orders, have him return to the Ta'Rae solar system near Na'Reen and out of sensor range; we'll contact him in a few days. Also have Admiral ZynTak deploy his fleet. Inform him he is now the fleet commander of the Tarn solar system. He is to go there and await further orders."

"Very good, sir," said Regent BryQat. While walking down the hall toward the communications room, he wondered how Lord GorDon could have possibly found out about the new spacecraft being ordered by Kaladon before he did.

★   ★   ★

It felt strange coming aboard a Tygerian war cruiser in chains. RomMen normally boarded to salutes and high praise. He wondered how Captain MyrAak was handling all this. He taught him just about everything he knew.

After RomMen was placed in a cellroom, he looked to see who else was on board. He thought he heard a female weeping. Strange, he thought, he didn't think there were any females aboard, but he could be mistaken. His cellroom was next to the entrance of the sickroom. There was a body on the table, but he couldn't tell what it was because it was covered.

The door opened and two Tygerians entered. They partially uncovered the person on the operating table to check on it's condition. *Well now, it appears I was wrong,* he thought. One of her breasts was uncovered. On the table in front of him was a Kaladonian female. She was of medium color, with similar features to the Earthling Carter, but with darker complexion. The doctor soon finished and he asked. "How's she doing?"

The doctor knew the prisoner who addressed him very well. And he welcomed the chance to talk to a captain he thought had been wronged. "Not too well, I'm afraid. She's very weak. She was wounded at the battle at Korinze."

"Battle, hell! It was a slaughter of unarmed people at a padport," a voice broke in loudly. They were both startled by the interruption from the female in the cellroom next to his. He knew prisoners weren't normally permitted to speak, but no one was objecting. Apparently the doctor was finished with what he was doing, because he quickly covered the body and left the room. Perhaps he just didn't want to argue with a hysterical prisoner.

"My name is RomMen and my cellroom is next to yours. Might I ask who you are?" There was no answer.

Finally, "my name is Shanza. And the person on the table is my good friend Dovina. I fear she may die." More silence. "We're Kaladonians and we certainly don't deserve to be here. Why are you here? Are you a criminal?"

"I suppose being in the wrong place at the wrong time makes me a criminal," said RomMen, wistfully. "You can't see me, but I'm a Tygerian. Shanza, is it?"

"Yes, and I don't have to see you, I could tell by the sound of your voice that you were a Tygerian."

"Don't judge all of us by the actions of others. I was the captain of a war cruiser just like this one, and I was blamed for the death of Lord GorDon's favorite nephew. In case you don't know who he is, he's the war lord of the Tygerian Empire and he probably ordered the attack you experienced."

"I don't want to talk anymore," she said.

"As you wish." Nothing else was said during the rest of the trip. In two days the Tygerian war cruiser landed in Calverone.

Five prisoners in chains were led off the war cruiser to a holding area nearby. All had received medical attention for their wounds in flight. This was apparent from the bandages on their bodies. Dovina was being carried out on a stretcher. They weren't sure if she would live long enough to get additional treatment.

"What a twist of fate," RomMen said softly to Shanza. "I delivered many prisoners here and now I too, come in chains." He was wondering if his old friend KorRak was here and possibly still alive. He also thought about Carter, and wondered where he might be.

"How is your friend doing?" asked RomMen.

"I don't know. They won't let me near her, but I'm afraid she's not doing very well at all. She needs better care than they could give her on this war cruiser."

"Perhaps they have better facilities here," said RomMen. "In fact I know they do," he added, remembering now. "There's a good hospital in the city and they have an excellent doctor."

"I sure hope so. What are they going to do with us?"

"Perhaps I shouldn't tell you, but you'll find out soon enough. This is the location of the prison arenas you may have heard about."

"Oh no, not here. I have heard about this place, but I thought it was just a story and never believed they even existed. They say nobody ever gets out of here alive."

RomMen could detect the fear in her voice as she spoke. *This place is enough to scare anybody*, he thought.

They were escorted off the spacecraft and led to a waiting area. A small flatbed vehicle came onto the padport next to them. Shanza stood helpless, watching Dovina being loaded on the back of the vehicle. She started to go with her, but the dwarf yanked on her chains and she fell hard.

Captain RomMen was reaching down to help her up when a dwarf hit him on the back of his head with a club. This knocked him to the ground and he could do nothing but lie there and try to shake it off. The Na'Reen in charge came over, stood over him, and said, "My, aren't we the gentleman? Perhaps your actions will be different the next time you have the opportunity to be gallant." He got up and went to stand by the rest, still shaking his head.

"I hope your friend will be alright," said RomMen, again trying to comfort her.

Standing there waiting for whatever came next, he looked up and spoke softly, "Carter, you don't know how many times I've regretted bringing you here." He meant every word he said.

"Who is Carter?"

"He's from Earth and if he's still alive he'll be in one of these arenas."

"Earth, where's that? I never heard of it."

They broke off their conversation when a vehicle loaded with individual cages drove up. They loaded RomMen and one other into the cages. As they drove away he was looking back at a very scared and lonely female.

"She looks pretty pathetic standing there, doesn't she?" Said Carznot. RomMen didn't reply, he just nodded.

★   ★   ★

"Who's your new patient, Doctor?" Carter asked, cheerful for a change. "Now don't you worry about my new patient," Zark said, as he paused a moment, then continued jokingly. "She's a female Kaladonian, if you must know."

"I've never seen one of those before, doc. What's she look like?" He was peeking around the edge of the door.

"Go see for yourself, she's in the room right next door on your left. She's probably still unconscious."

He went into the room to get a good look at her. *Hell, she looks like an Earthling with a good tan. Probably more like a Polynesian. She's really beautiful,* he thought. He went back to Zark and said, "Who is she, do you know where she came from?"

"No I don't. The Tygerians brought her, along with another female and two males from Krynta. There was also a Tygerian and I don't know who he is either. Nobody confides in me. I just get partial information here and there, then try to put it together. That one in there is in pretty bad shape. It'll take about two months before she'll completely recover."

A few days later as he was sitting next to her bed, she opened her eyes. "Hello, my name is Carter. I thought you might like a friendly greeting when you woke up. How are you feeling?"

"Not sure yet, give me a minute." She moved her body a little while looking around the room. She winced with pain at almost every movement she made. "Not too good, where am I?"

"A hospital, in Calverone."

"How'd I get here?" She asked, wonderment written all over her face. "I don't remember anything after the fight at Korinze."

"I'm sorry, I can't help you there, because I really don't know. I can't even tell you where you're going, because I don't know that either."

They exchanged some friendly conversation for a while and then he said goodbye. He told her he was leaving the next day for Harzzton.

★   ★   ★

"My Lord," said BryQat, "we received a message from Captain MyrAak. They just left Calverone and the message reads as follows: `The magistrate of Calverone confirms that Carter is dead, killed by DanKor in the arena, and he wishes you well.'"

"Well, that is good news. I'm sure we can persuade the magistrate to let DanKor go free the next time we deliver prisoners to him. Maybe he's learned his lesson and is ready to resume his place in our organization."

"I'm sure you're right, My Lord," BryQat agreed, chuckling to himself.

"More news, perhaps. What is the progress of that new spacecraft being constructed on Ra'Tor? Have we any reports on its progress or the expected completion date? We certainly contributed enough toward its construction. I don't trust Lo'Gon at all." GorDon seemed very concerned.

"My lord, we have a small network of agents working on that project as we speak. I'm expecting an update very soon. I will be sure to keep you informed of its progress."

CHAPTER 5

HAZZTON

About a month after his wounds healed, Carter finally made it to Harzzton. Had he stayed much longer the authorities would surely have been suspicious. He utilized the extra time well in learning the anatomy of the different aliens he'd have to fight.

Sitting by a window in the shuttle he saw the castle below. From his view point it appeared to be about the same size, but in fact it was much larger than the one in Calverone.

They went over the drawbridge and through the gate. The whole routine here was the same. The dwarfs, the chains, being escorted through the hallway, everything.

When he checked in they put him on the second floor. This irritated him a little, but at least he didn't have to put up with any Tygerians.

At his bunk on a neat pile he saw everything he'd need: a sword, clothing, and a small shield. The clothes seemed to fit a little tighter. He recalled passing a mirror downstairs, so on his way out he stopped to take a look. With all the training he'd gone through, his muscle tone must have improved. He hoped the food was better here; but he doubted it. The sword they gave him was about the same as the one he'd used at Calverone.

The warrior master was new at his job. He was the assistant training under Jackson, whoever he was. They said his name was Tarq. Word was, that the other warrior master was re-assigned to Calverone to take Dor'Gets' place. *I knew that,* he thought.

When he entered the arena, Tarq came over to him and yelled, "Carter! That is your name, isn't it? Do you know how to use that sword you're carrying?"

"Yes, sir, Tarq, sir, Carter is my name and I know how to use this sword, sir."

"Well now," said Tarq with a grin, turning around to face the rest. "I hope everyone was listening to his answer. That's exactly how I want everyone to answer me. Any questions?" he shouted, coupled with a mean stare. Everyone was very quiet. "We have some new talent here today. Anyone up for a challenge?"

An alien walked up to Carter, sneered at him, pointed, and said, "I want this one." His breath was as ugly as he was, and Carter told him so. His body was tan with small dark brown scales on his legs. He had round eyes, cauliflower ears and only three fingers on his hands. Ugly quickly drew his sword and came at Carter in a rushing rage. Carter side-stepped him at the last second and bumped him with his shoulder. It spun him around and he went sprawling in the dirt on his face.

Everybody started laughing, even Tarq. As Carter slowly drew his sword, the guy got up in a violent rage and turned to face him. "Perhaps next time you might think before you act."

"For that you die," the alien yelled.

This time he was a little more cautious, but not much. He came rushing at Carter again and ended up the same as before except this time he was flat on his back in the dirt. He had learned the anatomy on this one and all his vulnerability from the voice computer in Zarks' office.

The alien got up quickly and started shouting at Tarq while he pointed his sword at Carter. "I want him. I want him now. I want to kill him," he kept yelling in an embarrassed rage while hopping up and down.

"Well, Carter, what do you think?"

"You won't make any credits on this fight if one of us dies, will you, Tarq, sir?" Carter was trying to avoid the inevitable.

"I know," he said, with a broad smile on his face, "but this is fun, don't you think?" Still looking at Carter, he said again, "Exactly what are you going to do about this challenge?"

He knew he had to accept the challenge. If he didn't there would be hell to pay from the other warriors. He would be marked for cowardice and everyone would be after him. In reality, Tarq was doing him a favor. He stared at Ugly and said in a loud voice, so his translator wouldn't miss it, "I accept."

Instantly Ugly rushed him, swinging his sword wildly from side to side and hollering as he approached. *Speed over brawn, you imbecile*, he thought. He rushed in, Carter sidestepped the move again, turned, and swung his sword in a horizontal swipe. Ugly let out a scream, while holding his mid-section as he fell. He was lying on the ground flat on his back with a large gaping wound across his stomach, oozing thick brown fluid. *Poor soul, perhaps it's what he wanted,* Carter thought. It made him sick inside at having to kill him. He just stood there, looked over at Tarq, then at the body. Everybody was stunned at the speed of the fight. It was all over before it ever got started. The dwarfs hurriedly came out and removed the body.

"All right, that's enough for now. We'll resume tomorrow," Tarq said, breaking the awkward silence.

In the morning, just before the beginning of practice, Tarq held a meeting in the arena. "Warriors, and trainees, I have some information for all who are new here. This is the only arena with female warriors. They are here for the same reasons all of you are and they follow the same rules.

"If you're near a female and decide you might want to assault her, beware, she just might kill you. And if she doesn't, I surely will when I learn about it. You may talk to them only after you've earned warrior status. As long as you cooperate during your training and win your battles you may visit them, but only with permission from the female and me. Any violation of these rules will be dealt with severely. All right, that's enough talk, let's get started.

"Carter!" Tarq barked.

Man, this guy yells loud. You sure can't ignore him or say you didn't hear him, he thought. Carter briskly approached him.

"Yes, sir, Tarq, sir." He just stood there, staring at him.

"Carter, that's probably the shortest fight I have ever witnessed since I've been in the arena. Are you really that good or were you just lucky?"

"To be honest, sir, I'm really not sure. I know I can hold my own in most situations, but some of the fighting I do might be luck. You see, I was injured before I could be fully tested. I haven't been in too many fights yet, Tarq, sir."

"We don't know anything about you. All I was told is that you were good in the arena and you would be the least likely to give me any trouble. Is that true, Carter?"

"Yes, sir, Tarq, sir."

"I may never know the whole story on you, but I like the idea that you're cooperative. Don't create problems for me; do what you're told and we'll get along just fine."

"Thank you, Tarq, sir, I understand your policy."

The next day at the end of practice, he went to see Tarq before he left the arena. "Excuse me, Tarq, sir," he said. "I have a request, sir, if I may."

"What is it?"

"I would like permission to see a female named Shanza. I have a message for her from a friend who's in the hospital. She won't know me, nor does she know I have a message for her, but I'd like to deliver it anyway."

"That's a bold request from someone who just arrived. Are you crazy? I don't grant requests to anybody who hasn't been here at least three months. Don't bother me about this again," he said in a harsh manner. He turned and walked away.

Huh! So much for that, he thought, as he left the arena. When he entered the warrior quarters he felt calmer. Boy, this was a strange feeling, not at all like Calverone and those damn Tygerians. He must have impressed somebody with that fight yesterday, because the person behind the servant's counter told him he was being put on the first floor. He was instructed to find an empty room and move in. *That's much better*, he thought.

There were six empty rooms so he took the nicest one. It was the symbol 12 that he picked, and it was clean. After he moved in and got cleaned up, the evening meal was ready. Soon after that, he called it a day.

Two days later, after he finished the evening meal, one of the servants came to him. "Carter, Tarq wants to see you at the entrance to the arena."

He nodded, got up, and went to the arena. *Wonder what he wants*, he thought. When he arrived Tarq was waiting for him. "You need me for something, Tarq, sir?"

"Carter, I have arranged for you to meet Shanza."

"Huh? But you said—"

"Silence," he yelled. "I don't wanna hear it."

"Thank you very much, Tarq, sir." Shocked, but pleased, he was led through a rear corridor behind the arena to a double door. "Tarq, sir, how do I address the female warrior mistress? I mean, you normally don't say `sir' to a female."

Tarq laughed a little and said, "Yeah, I know what you mean. Use sem instead of sir. Here it means the same thing."

"Thanks, Tarq, sir, I really appreciate this."

"Yeah, yeah," he said, as he motioned with his hand for him to get going. The door opened to reveal a gruff, masculine sort of female looking at both of them. She eyed them suspiciously and finally said, "I am Sa'Gena. Come this way." She turned, and motioned for him to follow.

"Yes, thank you, Sa'Gena, sem."

She stopped short, which almost caused him to bump into her She turned around to look at Tarq. "I don't believe this. You've got a barbarian here with manners. I'm impressed." Ignoring her, Tarq pulled the door shut. It locked automatically.

It didn't smell bad in this arena either, he thought, being somewhat surprised at the cleanliness of the entire system.

Following behind her he noticed that both sides of the arena were identical, like a mirror image. They came to a small room that had a table, a couple of chairs and a small bed against the wall. She motioned for him to enter and she locked him in.

He sat there a few minutes before the door opened and in walked a female, wearing the same type of clothes he was. She was pretty, a lot like Dovina as far as the tan and the rest of her complexion was concerned. But that's where it ended. They were two completely different females, as he would learn soon enough. As a show of respect he got up when she entered.

"When I was informed you wanted to see me, I refused," she said softly. "The others told me it was to be a sexual encounter and I didn't want any part of that. I thought about it awhile, and I was puzzled by your request, because I knew we had never met. But then I remembered your name mentioned by someone when I arrived. It's Carter, isn't it?"

"Yes, it is," he replied. "I never thought anyone around here would know me. And you're Shanza. But who knows me?"

"His name is RomMen and he spoke very highly of you."

"Captain RomMen's here, on Na'Reen?" he was very surprised.

"Yes, at Calverone. But he isn't a captain anymore. He's a prisoner, just like us."

"I have a message for you from Dovina." Her eyes lit up and she even smiled. "She's improving and will have a complete recovery. She'll be sent here in about two months. She has no idea she's coming here and neither did I when I last saw her. How are you holding up? You look sort of down right now."

"Well, I certainly feel better knowing that my best friend, whom I expected to die and never see again, is alive and coming back to me. Otherwise, I'm afraid I'm not doing too well."

"May I ask what the problem is, physical or mental?"

"It isn't physical, because I've beaten most of my opponents and I've only been here about two weeks. I can't talk to anyone for three months. I'm surprised they let me talk to you. Maybe you're more important around here than you realize. Anyway I—, I just feel so lost," she said, stammering a little, a tear or two now running down her cheek. He offered his arms and she came to him. He gave her a comforting hug as she spoke, "I just don't understand what's going on or why I'm here." More tears began to flow. "I'm in a world I know nothing about and I certainly don't belong here. We didn't do anything to the Tygerians that would deserve being exiled to a prison arena."

"Boy, where have I heard that before."

She gently pulled away, "I don't understand, what do you mean?"

"Shanza, I'm an Earthling, and I'll probably never see my homeland again. I've also been put here against my will, into this unknown world. Hell, I didn't even know life existed outside the atmosphere of our planet. And even if I ever get out of here, I still have no place to go. I know nothing at all about Na'Reen or any other place for that matter. Now let me say one thing more. You have a very good friend in a hospital who's recovering from injuries. She's going to be counting on you when she gets here. Are you going to let her down and be more of her problem, or are you going to shape up and shake this self pity? Somehow you don't appear to be the self-pitying type. Then again, what would I know about a Kaladonian?"

"You seem to be very perceptive. I know nothing about your race either and I've never heard of Earth before I talked to RomMen."

"I suppose it doesn't really matter if you're an Earthling or a Kaladonian and it might be universal. But to me, it's what's inside that tells you what you're made of. And in my mind, that's what counts."

"How long have you been here?"

"I guess about nine months or more, by Earth's calendar. I don't remember; I seem to lose track of time," he gave out a sigh. "Like you, I'm just trying to survive here. But I'll tell you one thing you can count on, Shanza. I have no intention of spending the rest of my life here in this damn arena." She waited for the near-instant translation, then gave him a troubled look.

There was a knock and the door opened. "Time's up, Carter. Ya gotta go," said Sa'Gena.

Hell, that was short, seemed like only a few minutes, he thought. "Perhaps we can talk again," he said, with a smile.

"Yes," she said, her face lit up. "I would like that."

★   ★   ★

During the next two weeks Carter was pitted against some of the better warriors in the arena. While he won all his matches, he wasn't the quick winner like the first day and he could see by Tarq's expression that he was troubled by this.

One evening he was sitting at one of the tables in the warrior quarters when Tarq came by. "Carter, come with me." He got up and did as ordered. When they reached the arena entrance Tarq turned, and said, "I've been watching your progress lately and there's something I need to know. You seem to fight just good enough to get the win and you don't seem to be in any hurry about it. But when there's a grudge match you attack with much more ferocity. Explain," Tarq demanded.

"I guess when my life's on the line, I approach the matches a little more aggressively, sir. Nobody told me I was supposed to teach anybody else how to fight, so the less my opponents know about me and my style of fighting, the better off I am, sir."

Tarq's expression changed from a firm stare to a slight smile and finally said, "Get outta here, Carter."

"Yes, sir," he said as he turned and jogged left.

The next morning Tarq called Carter aside from the rest of the warriors and told him about a meeting he had the previous evening. They were to set up matches between two males and two females to evaluate the feasibility of promoting more variety in the arena. This training was supposed to be conducted in secret.

Tarq said both Shanza and Carter were selected as a pair and the identity of the other couple would be kept from them. The reason for Carter's selection was because they'd never seen his style of fighting before. Carter and Shanza were pleased to be able to spend the practice time together, and it helped pass the time more quickly. A strong bond was developing between them. The practice sessions continued for about two months while Shanza learned some of his techniques. After a few weeks of practice with Carter none of the other females even came close to defeating her.

About a week later it was big money day at the arena. The seating was sold-out for all events. Spectators were starting to like Carter and wanted to see more of him. They hadn't seen a constant winner like this since Jackson became a warrior master. He was the best they'd seen for a long time. The feature event pitted Carter against one of the best warriors. He learned who his opponent was the morning of the match.

It took about two hours for the preliminary matches, and three of them were with females. It was the first time he saw Shanza and Dovina fight. He wasn't concerned about Shanza, because he knew she could handle herself and it wasn't a stinking grudge match. In the stands, even the magistrate noticed Shanza's improvement. He also noticed how pleased the spectators were, even though her fights ended quickly. They liked her and cheered her on to victory. Carter was pleased to see how well Dovina did, especially after being hurt. Her style was different, but she was also very effective.

When it became Carter's turn, he walked over to the warrior he was going to fight. Then they walked to the starting area together. Tarq was waiting for them and the normally stone-faced alien was grinning at both of them. It was almost as though something was going on that Carter didn't know about. *Don't let them shake you*, he thought.

Standing in front of Tarq, Carter decided to keep an eye on his opponent, just to make sure there were no tricks. Something just didn't seem right. Tarq raised his arm, while holding his sword to give the signal to begin the match. *Well, here goes nothing,* he thought.

Suddenly, Carter's opponent turned toward him and swung at him while he was drawing his sword. "Hey," he said, "that's not a very friendly gesture at all." He was sure his opponent heard him, because in this arena the translators were kept on. If he hadn't been alert the alien might have killed him. But after he started his swing Carter moved out of the way just in time. Then knowing he was off balance, Carter made a quick countermove. He bumped into him, kicked his leg out from under him, and down he went. Before he could recover, Carter was on him with his sword at his throat. He laid there and looked up at him in disbelief, a sort of, "how'd you do that" look.

The crowd had never been so quiet. There was no cheering or boot rattling, the arena's form of booing. It was as if they were just as stunned by the match as Carter was. Tarq didn't know what to do. He looked up at the magistrate, sort of asking with his eyes what to do now. Obviously, the crowd was very dissatisfied. Up in the higher seat level, a boot rattle. Soon another one, then a few more. A short time later the whole place shook.

I didn't like it, but, hey, he thought, *I survived no matter what.* He turned and began walking toward the exit. The crowd became very quiet. The magistrate quickly sent a message down to Tarq. He read the note, looked up and nodded his understanding.

While Carter was walking toward the exit, he listened for the slightest sound behind him. He was wound like a coiled spring and furious that rules he had no choice but to live by were so easily swept aside. Then it came. He immediately jumped to one side, hit the ground, rolled over and got to his feet with his sword ready.

The guy was almost on top of Carter when he brought his sword up. The motion had stopped this new opponent's blow cold. He spun around and swung in a circle as hard as he could with his sword at a slightly upwards angle, knocking his opponent's sword from his hand. "Didn't know I could do that, did ya, you cheating bastard," he yelled. "Glad to have learned that from KorRak."

Then he noticed another approaching and heard Tarq yell, "Go get 'em, Carter, kill them if you can." He looked at Tarq to see the same smile he had worn at the beginning of the match. While parrying with this second opponent, he noticed the first going for his sword. *Better move fast and get this one before there are two,* he thought.

Carter rushed the second one and swung his sword at his leg. The guy jumped to the opposite side, but lost his balance. Then Carter drop kicked him and ran him through when he fell. Carter quickly turned to find not one, but two others walking slowly toward him. One of them was a woman. *Damn, this is getting a little crazy,* he thought. "Come on," he yelled, motioning with his arms. *Sure hope Shanza is watching this,* he thought. *Perhaps she could give me a hand. If they'll let her.* He circled, trying to keep the male between him and the female. He never dreamed he'd ever have to kill a woman and didn't know for sure if he could. Out of the corner of his eye he noticed more movement. Another figure was rushing toward them. Then he saw the woman move off to face the new threat. That's when he allowed himself a quick glance. To his pleasant surprise it was Shanza rushing toward the female warrior. *That sure makes my day,* he thought.

Carter moved in, confident now, parried a little, found an opening, and in a short time finished his opponent off. When he fell, Carter looked over to where Shanza was and saw the woman fall as she pulled her sword out of the body. She walked over to him with a smile on her face and said, "Hi, we have to stop meeting like this." The crowd was on its feet and going wild. *Did she enjoy this?* he wondered. *What have we become?*

Tarq and Sa'Gena approached Carter and Shanza from different directions. "Carter, I no longer have any questions as to how good you are. You and Shanza have just started a new trend for matches in the arena," said Tarq.

When Sa'Gena got to Shanza, she sheathed her sword and said, "Thanks, Sa'Gena, sem."

"Carter, I have never seen fighting like you displayed here in the arena today. All the other warriors are blood and guts, toe to toe, thrash and bash just to kill. Yours is more of an art, graceful, if you know what I mean. At your present level of fighting, I don't think anybody here could beat you."

"What about your better warriors, Tarq, sir?"

"You just beat them, you and Shanza."

Looking at her he said, "I'm glad you're on my side." *She sure is beautiful when she smiles,* he thought.

"Yeah, it went well, thanks to you," she said, laughing a little. "Next time we meet, could it be without your friends?" She waved her outstretched arm, pointing to the bodies.

He rolled his eyes. *Heaven help us,* he thought.

Shanza and Carter were now the main attraction at the arena. Their popularity grew and they were undefeated during their four months of fighting as a team.

There was more killing going on, but not as much for them. They were at the top in competition and didn't have to deal out death as often. Up and coming warriors who needed to make names for themselves typically killed.

The newer spectators liked the idea of a dominant female in the arena, but they also didn't want to see Shanza killed. They matched her against some of the males whom she soundly beat. Dovina was possibly their next favorite and they followed her progress also. She was slightly wounded twice while fighting males.

★　　★　　★

The season was finally over and it was time for some much needed rest. Carter was reading the notices posted on the bulletin board in the meeting area. All notices were printed in every language of those unfortunate enough to be represented in the arena. They were looking for volunteers to participate in the season ending tour. *At last,* he thought. *This is our chance.*

He met with Shanza that evening and told her she and Dovina must volunteer for the tour. It's the only way they'll get to Calverone. He didn't have time to explain his reasons, but he knew his urgency left her confident that he had an idea.

★　　★　　★

"What do you mean Carter's coming here?" Res'Itz growled. "I have no such notice."

"On my way in, one of your office staff mentioned it to me. He did well at Harzzton so they want to earn credits on him during the off season tour. Just who the Hell is this Carter?"

"Jackson," Res'Itz said coldly, "go back to the arena and keep the peace. Kick some ass, do something. Just—" He paused momentarily, scowling. "Just get out of here."

Well now, Jackson thought. *In a testy mood today, aren't we?* He turned and left. The two never did get along. The only warrior master Res'Itz ever liked was Dor'Get, because he was a "yes" man.

★   ★   ★

After the evening meal KorRak was still sitting at one of the tables. "KorRak," said one of the servants, "Jackson wants to see you by his quarters." KorRak got up and did what he was told. After all, you didn't keep the warrior master waiting. When he arrived he saw Jackson standing by his door, waiting for him.

"Do you know someone named Carter?" he said curiously.

"Yes sir, Jackson, sir, I do."

"Tell me, who is he, where'd he come from?"

"He's an Earthling, and—."

"He's really an Earthling?" Jackson cut in.

"Yes sir, Jackson, sir."

"Hold it right there." He stretched out his arm and pointed. "Come," he motioned with his finger. They walked out to the middle of the arena. "Okay, let's cut the crap, and no more "sirs", either. Let's just talk, you and me, man to man. Now tell me all you know about this guy Carter. Nobody is going to hear us out here, so get on with it."

KorRak hesitated, looking for clues that there wasn't some form of trickery. All he saw was a serious expression on Jacksons' face. "I'm not sure where to begin. I guess when I first met Carter here in the arena when he was learning to become a warrior. Unlike you, he was slow at first. I guess it was a matter of him being here against his will. He felt trapped, a prisoner forced to do something he wanted no part of."

"I can relate to that," he said, nodding his head.

KorRak continued by telling Jackson all he knew about Carter, about his adjustment problems and him being wounded by DanKor, who'd thought he'd killed him. And also about his transfer to Harzzton around the same time Jackson came to Calverone.

"There's probably only four people here in the arena who know he's still alive. Five now, counting you. Res'Itz doesn't want him here, because he's afraid of the Tygerians. If they find out he's still alive they'll probably send an invasion force here just to kill Carter."

"Christ, what'd Carter do that would get the Tygerian Empire up in arms against just one man?"

"He killed MarKor, Lord GorDon's favorite nephew, and his brother, on a spacecraft commanded by Captain RomMen. Both deserved to die, I might add. That's why RomMen's here, because he allowed it to happen under his command. From what RomMen said, Carter saved his life by killing MarKor. Don't ask me why a political officer would want to kill a war cruiser captain."

"All right, tell me. Is he going to be here with the rest of the warriors for the off-season features?"

"According to the rumors I heard, yes, he'll be here in a few days."

"DanKor's gonna love this," said Jackson, wearing a sly smirk on his face. "Thanks, KorRak." Turning, he walked away. *How do the warriors know these things before I do? After all, I'm the warrior master and I'm supposed to know first. Oh well, so much for the system*, he thought.

★   ★   ★

A few days later, about mid-morning, the warriors were practicing in the arena. Morris, as usual, was keeping watch on all that was happening. One of the warriors was looking in the direction of the arena entrance. He stopped and lowered his sword. Then another stopped and did the same. Soon they were all looking at the alien walking toward DanKor. His back was turned and he hadn't seen Carter yet. Wiping off his sword, he sheathed it, and turned around. His first thought was that he was seeing a ghost. "You're dead, how can you be here?" Without waiting for an answer, DanKor automatically grabbed for his sword, nearly in shock at who was standing in front of him.

"Hold, DanKor!" yelled Jackson, moving closer. "You can't challenge anyone who doesn't have a sword."

"Get him one, anybody, give him a sword," yelled DanKor, now back to his senses and ready for a fight.

"You took his sword, remember?" said KorRak, enjoying his confused rage.

Then DanKor shifted his gaze to Carter's right, as did the others when noticing movement. They became very quiet. A female, standing beside Carter, drew her sword slowly and handed it to him, hilt first. He took the sword, pointed it at DanKor, and said, "I challenge you, DanKor, to a grudge match." DanKor was all thumbs trying to unsheathe his sword so he could accept the challenge. As was the rule, Carter could make any challenge with someone else's sword if he lost his during a battle in the arena, but he couldn't be challenged. Finally DanKor got his wits together and shouted his acceptance for a fight to the death.

The match would take place at the next tournament, which was in three days. All females would be kept separate until after the tournament, with the exception of their practice sessions. There would be seven females available to fight by tournament day.

Carter walked over to KorRak and RomMen, who were standing next to each other a few feet away. "What a pair," he said as he approached them, shaking his head from side to side.

When he got close enough RomMen said, "Carter, it may not help much, but I want you to know I've always regretted bringing you here."

"Captain RomMen, and I realize you're not a captain anymore, you'll always have my respect as a professional, but as a friend, I can't respond to that right now." He turned to KorRak, then looked back at him and said, "I can't tell you how many times I cursed you for bringing me here, it's something I'm still learning to live with." They all turned and walked out of the arena.

As they walked by the forge, Ordak motioned for Carter to come closer. When he was close enough, Ordak whispered, "See me later. I have something important to tell you." Carter indicated he would see him after the practice session that day. Then they went down the stairs to the sickroom to see Doctor Zark.

"Ah, Carter, my friend, how are you? You certainly look well, I must say. I trust you used the information you acquired to your advantage at Harzzton. I mean you look very much alive."

"Yes, it was exceptionally useful, and I thank you."

"What are you two talking about?" said RomMen.

"Anatomy, my friend, anatomy," Zark cut in. Then he explained. "Many days and nights Carter studied the anatomical makeup of his possible opponents in the arena before he left for Harzzton. For a while I thought he wanted to be a doctor," he said jokingly. His friends were amazed that no one had bothered to do it before, but Dr. Zark had been the key. Carter briefly described the advantages, and how the knowledge had helped him succeed in the arena. All were pleased to hear of his success at Harzzton, and also about his "lady friend" Shanza, whom he mentioned only professionally. Soon they started back to the arena for afternoon practice.

Carter stayed behind for a personal request of his friend and tutor. "Doc, I need something else, sort of a favor, if you don't mind."

"What can I do for you?"

"I talked to Shanza the other night and we need to know if Earthlings and Kaladonians are compatible."

"I'll have to run a complete test on the both of you to be sure, which includes some blood work, uh, various organ scans and a host of other tests," Zark answered, thinking aloud. "It'll take some time, my friend, but you know I'll do it."

"I appreciate that very much Doctor, and thank you."

★   ★   ★

At the completion of the afternoon practice session, Carter stopped at the weapons forge to see Ordak. "Hello, my friend. Come in, come in." Ordak was very excited. Then he closed the door and locked it from the inside. That surprised Carter, Ordak had never locked the door for as long as he had worked with him.

He followed Ordak around to the far corner of the room. It was the same area they had gone to the day he showed him the metal he was working with. Ordak picked up a long piece of leather and started to unroll it, revealing to him what was now the finished product. "Behold, Carter, my completed masterpiece." He was just as proud as any artist.

Carter was a man changed by personal combat, for all he could do was stare at the object. "That's probably the most awesome sword I have ever seen." He took it reverently from Ordak's outstretched arms.

"It's yours. I made it for you to use in the arena. The sheath will be completed in a little while and you can pick it up tomorrow. You see, Carter, the sheath and grip looks much like any other of its kind. And no one will know anything about this sword until you use it. I seriously doubt anyone would attempt to take it away from you. Carter—, Carter, you hear what I said?"

"Huh, ah, yes, I heard you Ordak," The trance returned. He held the sword up to examine it more closely. He tested the weight, swung it and banged it on some wood. The cut he left was impressive enough, but the balance, the feel, was perfect.

"Here, let me show you," Ordak took the sword gently and heaved it over his head with the sudden wrath of a banshee and came straight down with the cutting edge on some chains. It didn't cut them all, but it broke through the first two links.

Carter looked at the blade carefully. Ordak was right, no nicks in the blade and no sign of wear. *Incredible*, he thought, *just incredible*. The sword was a little lighter than the one he used in the arena. It had a dull gray finish with a shiny cutting edge on both sides. The handle wasn't ornate, but it felt good in his hand. He could hardly wait to use it.

After the evening meal, one of the servants came to him and whispered, "Warrior Master Jackson wants to see you at the arena entrance right now."

He couldn't know about the sword; it must be something else, he thought. As Carter approached the entrance to the arena he could see a husky brown man waiting for him.

Jackson motioned for him to follow. They both walked out to the middle of the arena. Then Jackson turned to face him and said loudly, "Is your name Carter?"

Jackson was about four inches taller, but Carter looked him in the eye and replied, "Yes sir, Jackson, sir."

"Are you an Earthling?" he asked in the same tone of voice.

"Yes sir, Jackson sir." He replied, just as forcefully.

"Damn, Carter, how the Hell are you? I'm really pleased to meet you." His expression changed and he offered his hand.

"I'm sorry, Jackson, sir, I don't understand."

"Look, we're in the middle of the damn arena, nobody can hear us. And you stand there and tell me you don't understand. And cut the `sir' crap too," said Jackson. "You know Carter, it wasn't like this on a bird farm in the middle of the Atlantic."

"Christ all mighty! You're an Earthling and a damn swabby at that," he yelled, grinning from ear to ear and laughing as he shook his hand vigorously. "Hell, I was in the Air Force. You know, I heard your name mentioned many times, but I never made the connection, I mean, for you to be from Earth and all. I just never expected to see another Earthling way out here, and I sometimes wonder exactly where "here" is."

"Well, home's a very long way. That much I do know," Jackson replied. They talked well into the night, reminiscing about Earth and just about anything else that came to mind. Jackson told him he was from Philadelphia.

Carter said he was from Cleveland and employed by the Air Force as an agent investigating UFOs. They reminisced about football, baseball, and anything else that came to mind.

Jackson went on to tell him about his boss, Res'Itz and how upset he was when he found out Carter was coming here. "It must have slipped his mind, because he knew the off-season features were going to be held here this year. He really has a great fear of the Tygerians, and I can't say that I blame him for that. I guess we'd better get going. It's a good thing nobody's watching us because if they were, they'd either think we're crazy or get very suspicious." Carter agreed and they decided to meet again sometime later.

CHAPTER 6

THE REVOLT?

Gart Zordek was standing by his work table looking out a window at the city below. Sparkling reflections, caused by the setting sun, were bouncing off the windows. The weather had cleared from the early afternoon showers. *What a beautiful view,* he thought. In any event, his home would be a dreary place, perhaps for a long time to come. Dovina's absence played heavily on his mind. He had no idea where she was or if she was even alive. Many searched for her in every direction, but to no avail. A soulful sigh escaped his breath. *Governing would be easier if only my daughter was close. Perhaps, some day soon. Maybe never. I can only pray for her safety, wherever she* is, he thought.

The emperor was sleeping when a soft knock on his bedroom door awakened him. He knew it was night, because the security lights were peeking through the blinds. "Your highness," said Hoft, his servant, "I'm sorry to wake you at this early hour, but it's a matter of utmost importance!"

"Yes," Gart said, in a slight daze, "what is so important that you wake me at such an early hour?"

"General Wydorf is here to see you. He said it was very important that he talk with you," replied Hoft, in a whisper allowing his boss to shake the sleep from his body.

"Very well, Hoft, tell him I'll be there momentarily." *Doesn't he ever sleep?* he thought. Getting up, he put clothes on and went to meet with the waiting general. Just as he settled in his chair General Wydorf entered the room, his hat tucked neatly under his arm. The room was small, quaint, and comfortably furnished for his needs when not at the palace.

"Well general, what's so important to get me up at this hour?" The emperor wasn't angry, just concerned.

"We have a problem, sir, and I wanted to bring it to your attention as soon as possible."

"Go on," he said, still yawning.

"Do you remember that we sent an emissary to Ra'Tor?"

"Mmm!" He murmured, nodding his head. "Why do you ask? Was there a problem?" he was now fully awake.

"Yes, sir. We just received a partial message from Captain Centarkoh. It was broken up by interference, but it revealed that the spacecraft carrying our emissary was attacked and destroyed. There appears to be no survivors. The emissaries who went to Mylaar and Pendari arrived safely."

"That's certainly an interesting situation, isn't it?"

"Yes sir, it is." Espionage was a universal problem and the attack was too coincidental to be anything else.

"This certainly narrows the suspect list considerably. I'll brief General Sizdroz on this new situation."

"You may inform General Sizdroz that he may interrogate any senator he deems necessary or any of their aides as well," he said angrily. "I believe we are dealing with only one spy."

"I think you're absolutely correct. But what a clever spy he is, sir," said the general, wondering who it might be. All five people at the meeting had been loyalists for years.

"Perhaps soon he may outsmart himself." The emperor bared a grin. "Report back to me on anything new that develops and tell Sizdroz that no one else is to know about this."

"Understood, your highness. I have a meeting with him after I leave here. He will be in touch with you as soon as he learns anything. I'm preparing to leave for the Esterk Province; there seems to be some sort of unrest there that needs my attention."

"That's strange, they've always been very peaceful." He was surprised at the situation.

There was a knock on the door. "Yes, who is it?"

"General Sizdroz is here," said Hoft. "It's a matter of utmost importance."

"Let him in at once," said the Emperor, remembering his servant had used the same words moments ago. Upon entering he appeared to be very excited. "What is it, general?"

"Your highness, it's about your daughter."

"Yes, go on," ordered the Emperor, displaying excitement.

"One of our agents from Na'Reen has reported that she was last seen in the arena at Calverone. She was severely wounded at the battle on Krynta. But he is sure she has fully recovered and is doing fine. He doesn't know why she's at Calverone, because the arena at Harzzton is where they normally keep the women."

"How could this be?" said Gart, astounded by his words. "She must be a slave warrior in the arenas on Na'Reen. She could be killed. We must get her out of there. Perhaps I could buy her way out. How could she have gotten to the Ta'Rae solar system?" He asked, pausing for his thoughts to catch up. "It must have been those cursed Tygerians. It would do everybody well if we could rid the Tarn solar system of those marauders."

The two generals left the emperor and went directly to Wydorf's office. He wanted to discuss the conversations he had with the emperor before Sizdroz arrived.

"Sizdroz, conduct an electronic scan of the entire palace, including the emperor's quarters."

"It will be done immediately and the report will be on your desk as soon as it's completed," Sizdroz replied.

"Excellent," said Wydorf.

After Sizdroz left, he stayed in his office, preparing to depart for Esterk.

Captain Critz came in without knocking. He was short for a military man, with dark brown hair, a mild complexion, and an average physique. "General, I must advise you to delay your visit to the Esterk Province."

"Explain, Captain."

"Yes sir, General. As you know, a short while ago we sent a small contingent of warriors in response to a distress call for assistance, in a settlement near the border. This disturbance may be more serious than you realize. We haven't had any contact to verify casualties and all their equipment's missing too.

"Almost every week there appears to be some military aggression, either near our border or an outlying settlement in Esterk. A lot of people are getting killed."

"So what's going on in Esterk?" His frustration was showing.

"I'm not exactly sure yet, sir; we're working on it. A few more days should give us more valid information."

"It can't be just a small group of rebels that's causing these disturbances." He thought a moment, with renewed concern. *Organization meant bigger problems. And bigger problems usually had a name: Tygerians,* he thought. *No, it couldn't be. There aren't any reports of Tygerian activity anywhere on Kaladon.*

"Our agents will give us a full report in a day or so, sir. Might I encourage you to wait until then to make your decision?"

"Very good, Captain. I shall take your advice. As soon as you hear from our agents, schedule a meeting for all personnel with involvement on this issue."

"Yes, sir, General."

General Wydorf wasn't at all afraid, but he wasn't a fool either. *Observe, learn, think, and prepare. Then bust your opponent's ass. This has always been my approach to this sort of encounter,* he thought, displaying a grin.

In six days a meeting was re-scheduled in General Wydorf's conference room on the revolt in the Esterk Province. "The meeting will come to order," said Captain Critz firmly, quieting his colleagues.

"Who's leading this revolt? Who is this pain in my ass?" busted in General Wydorf, with a tone that demanded answers.

"I'm sorry to say, General, that we're not exactly sure yet." Critz indicated concern in his voice, because the general wanted answers he didn't have. "Sir, we have it narrowed down to a few possibilities. We also haven't been able to contact any of our agents since we last spoke. I thought we should have this meeting to bring everyone up to date."

There was a lull before Critz spoke again. "First of all, General, I think there is something very wrong with this revolt."

General Wydorf wore a puzzled look, then said, "explain."

"Well, sir, this disturbance isn't following any previous patterns I've ever studied on revolutions. It's as though this whole revolt is a sham, sort of a diversion or something to make us believe we have a very severe problem on our hands. Now granted, those warriors we sent there are definitely missing, and their equipment was either stolen or destroyed, but it doesn't make any sense, sir."

"Can you be a bit more specific, Captain," he demanded, proud of a junior officer who did his homework.

"Well, for one thing, sir, there is no military advantage for any action taken against the targets involved. We're talking attacks on civilians and destruction of homes and education centers. There are no demands for change, which is typical of a revolt. I just can't put my finger on it, nor can I prove anything yet, but it just doesn't appear to be the full scale revolution we're being led to believe it is. But I have found out one thing for sure, General; this revolt, or whatever we might call it, is being caused by outside intervention, perhaps the Tygerians."

The mere mention of involvement by the Tygerian Empire sent a low murmur throughout the room. "I have a few more facts to gather, and I know it's a little slow obtaining the information needed. But it's vital to our making the right decisions at the appropriate time. I'm positive, that for now, caution is the best procedure on our approach to this problem."

"As you suggest, captain, I'll depart another time. But I don't buy your theory about this being the work of the Tygerians. No one has mentioned them in any previous communications with the Esterk Province." The general hoped he was right, but they both knew it was a possibility.

★   ★   ★

It was morning, and Regent BryQat entered Lord GorDons' war room. The elder fighting man turned around in his chair to face his subordinate. "Have you heard any more on that new spacecraft they're building on Ra'Tor?"

"Yes, my Lord, that very issue is one of the subjects I wish to report on. We have learned that it will be operationally ready for space trials in a few days. It's anticipated that it could be ready for service in about three weeks."

"Good, very good." Lord GorDon allowed himself a smile.

"Also, my lord, Captain MyrAak has completed his assignment, as we expected. There are no survivors or any visible evidence remaining."

"Regent BryQat, transmit this order to Captain MyrAak: `Stay on location, new orders will follow in a few days. Well done on your last assignment.' Affix my seal and send it immediately."

Hmm, thought Regent BryQat, as he left. *That's one of the rare times Lord GorDon has ever complimented a captain on his success. He must be very pleased with his performance.*

★   ★   ★

The moonlight reflected its shining face on the surface of Buckondra Lake, the largest of many in this mountain range. When displaying its majestic snowcapped mountains and crystal-clear lakes, it had been said there wasn't a more beautiful place on the planet. Nestled in a deep valley in these Nuntark mountains was Plaxar, the capital of the Esterk Province and a fixture there for hundreds of years. In season the fresh clean air exuded the scent of the beautiful wild flowers on the hillsides, as they literally exploded their fragrances. At night, in the forests, one could occasionally hear the mating calls of various creatures, as well as howls and screeches of the larger nocturnal animals breaking the silent spell.

That night the provincial government chose to meet and discuss its future. Esterk was the largest of six provinces and possessed more then twice the population of all the others combined. Kaladon was changing and its people had to change with it in order to survive. Esterk's populace had little love for the central government, but their choices were somewhat limited.

The Tygerians capitalized on Esterk's independent spirit to create problems for the central government. That was of little concern to the majority of the ruling council. Besides, the central government wasn't powerful enough to deal with them anyway. As long as they didn't cause any trouble for Esterks' residents they showed little or no concern.

Esterks' industrial complex was primarily built to supply the central government, which included the sale of fighters and other military hardware. They already had forty of the latest and best fighters in stock, equipment that couldn't be bought anywhere at a better price. They had already sold 200 of the new fighters to the Na'Reens, who were going to pick them up in the near future.

It was obvious there was a council meeting that night based on the extra business at the club nearby. It was located on the first floor of a professional building near the center of the city and in the same area as the science and research complex.

"Nemarg, what do you think we should do about the settlement of Tygerians on our soil? I don't think we're strong enough militarily to eliminate them," said Epra.

"Perhaps you should leave those decisions to the men of the council, Epra." Females concerning themselves with provincial affairs didn't sit well with him.

"I don't think it really matters much, because the men on the council aren't making any of those decisions either." She left Nemarg's table to serve others. A short time later the door opened and in walked Nemarg's brother, Tobrak. He was a few years older than Nemarg, but one couldn't tell by looking at them. They both looked to be about the same age with a pleasant disposition. The main difference was that Nemarg was 40 pounds heavier and six inches taller than Tobrak. It was a common joke that Tobrak called Nemarg his little brother.

"Ah, Nemarg, why is it you're here tonight?"

"I wanted to talk to you about getting elected to the ruling council. We have some problems that aren't being corrected. I thought perhaps a little push in the right direction might help. When the Tygerians arrived they started causing trouble and everybody knew it, but the ruling council isn't too concerned.

"From the looks of the construction going on at the Tygerian settlement, it appears to have been the wrong decision. Their whole attitude toward our people has changed of late." He paused briefly. "I guess they don't need us anymore, nor do they think we can do anything about them now that they're well-established. I think they should go elsewhere to create problems."

"What you say may be true, but more concerned citizens are needed on the council, members who aren't afraid to take action. Unfortunately the older members don't see things as we do. We're short two members, so I don't think it'll be a problem getting you appointed. Perhaps you can help make a difference."

Three nights later Tobrak met Nemarg at the club to inform him of his approval for membership to sit on the ruling council. It was a testimony to Tobrak's influence. "We get together every week right down the street at the meeting hall."

"Thank you, my good brother. I'll be at the next meeting." His eyes expressed happiness for his approval to the council. He went to many meetings, but it seemed as though nothing much was ever accomplished. There was always bickering amongst the older members, and seniority was very important within the council. All he could do was watch and learn. He was discouraged by the slow progress as the Tygerians settlement grew rapidly.

Nemarg was already late when he stopped at Epra's house one evening to pick her up on the way to a meeting. She was going to wait at the club until it was over. This disturbed him and he was very upset with her, because he didn't like being late for council meetings. He was interested in what work the council was getting done for the communities and for the Province of Esterk. He was angry and suspicious because nobody wanted to do anything about the Tygerians. It was as if they weren't even there. Perhaps all the members were afraid. He made up his mind that tonight he would speak his mind. The Tygerian presence could no longer be ignored.

After he dropped Epra off he drove toward the center of the city where the council hall was located. Approaching he spotted a red glow in the sky. He started to hurry, because he feared something was wrong. The view he saw as he turned the corner set his stomach in knots. The windows of the council hall was belching multicolored flames and smoke. The heat was incredible and the stench of burning flesh was nauseating. The fire fighters were doing the best they could under the circumstances, but the fire spread too rapidly to save the building.

Nemarg jumped from his vehicle and ran toward the scene. One of the fire fighters stopped him from getting too close. "Easy, friend, easy," he said.

"What happened? How could this fire have started? Are any people still inside?" Nemarg wasn't letting the fire fighter answer any questions, due to his excitement. He finally ran out of breath and had to stop talking.

"Someone called in and reported an explosion, looked out their window and saw this building on fire. We arrived as soon as possible. The building was nearly destroyed before we arrived at the scene. You're Nemarg, aren't you?"

"Yes, is there something I can do? Anything to help?"

"I'm sorry to have to tell you this," he said. "There were a lot of people inside and none of them got out alive, including your brother. The roster of attendance was downloaded to another facility, so we have an up-to-date record of casualties."

The news of his brother's death sent him involuntarily to his knees. "No, not my brother," he sighed. This didn't make any sense. There hadn't been a fire for many years. The materials used for construction weren't even flammable. And there was nothing in the building that could have caused the fire.

Nemarg saw a woman on the other side of the road weeping. Composing himself, he walked over to her. "Were you the one who reported the fire?"

"Yes," she said. "I never saw anything like this before. I saw a flash of light that lit up the whole area, then there was an explosion that blew out our windows. When I looked out the building was nearly destroyed. What was left was engulfed in flames. It was just terrible!"

All Nemarg could think to do was comfort the woman as best he could. He knew her husband had been in the building. When he walked away his own pain began. Had he been on time for the meeting, he would have suffered the same fate. But something else accompanied the grief— resolve. Now he was the only surviving member of the council.

In a short time the people voted to replace all who had died. Most of the new members were younger, more energetic, and with good motives. But they were untested, and seemed to lack the ability or desire to counter the Tygerian threat.

One night at a meeting over which he presided, Nemarg said, "Members of the ruling council, I stand before you and demand quiet." This was the customary opening statement for the meetings to come to order. "It is time for us to make some changes in our society and the way we govern the Esterk Province." His speech went on for about an hour, outlining his ideas for the future. Surprisingly enough, about 90% of the council agreed to the majority of the programs he proposed. Perhaps their shortage of ideas had led them to accept his.

Now it was time for change. The technology their province possessed was always used for space travel and to bring peace to their agrarian culture. The arrival of the Tygerians in the Tarn solar system had changed all that. They had caused nothing but trouble since their arrival, and evidence of their treachery was all over the latest fire.

They would purchase raw materials from Moldarva (the fifth planet in the Tarn solar system) and use their science and technology to make newer and more improved weapons systems. With their existing industrial base they could create and build any weapons needed for their protection. The sword was always used to settle their differences in the past, but times had changed, and it was time to put away their swords.

Three more settlements had been attacked and destroyed in the last month, and Nemarg knew the Tygerians were responsible.

He became very active in provincial governmental affairs and got rid of those who served no useful purpose, who only wanted a free ride. He also cleaned out the nest of spies that were operating in Plaxar.

Word of Nemarg's activities had spread rapidly throughout the Province. His popularity grew and so did his followers. He called a special meeting of the ruling council and insured that his most trusted loyalists attended.

"Fellow council members; the time has come to take up arms. We must change from our old ways and look to the future. The Tygerians have taught us a valuable lesson. We must go forward and for the first time organize a military fighting unit.

"In a few more weeks we will have enough people trained to operate the war machinery we build for others. The first task for this new fighting unit will be the complete elimination of the Tygerian settlement." His voice getting louder as he spoke.

"If all are in agreement, I will appoint Engort as general of this new unit." A quick vote and the "ayes" had it— it was unanimous. "His first assignment is to organize this military fighting unit and complete the training of our young people. We can no longer depend on the central government to come to our aid; instead, the central government can come to us."

Near the end of the meeting Nemarg was voted in as `Lord of Esterk', Province of Kaladon. There hadn't been a lord in the province for many years. Slowly, Nemarg stood and looked around the room at the council members and his many friends. "I accept this appointment all of you have bestowed upon me." Everyone stood and gave a round of congratulatory applause for their new leader. *These Tygerians on our soil will not stand a chance, and there will be no mercy*, he thought.

A few weeks later, in the local club, Epra was busily working when Nemarg came in flanked by three armed men. After he sat down she came to his table. "Well, Nemarg, you have certainly surprised me of late. I never would have believed what they say you've accomplished in such a short time." She was beaming with pride. They hadn't been able to talk much in the last six weeks.

"You have organized an army. Esterk loyalists have been trained to fly the fighters we build and you have become Lord of Esterk." She made this last statement very respectfully, family or not. "You are the new leader of our people, and I suppose these are your bodyguards." She had her palm up in a pointing motion, emphasizing the three males standing near him.

"I guess you didn't know me very well did you, Epra?" he replied, smiling.

"No, I didn't know you very well at all, good brother. But, the Tygerians are still here. That much I know very well."

"Now, Epra, you must have a little more patience. Some of these things take time. Ask me about them again in a few weeks."

"I will do that," she said, with a sly grin, as she left to serve others.

Just before dawn 10 days later, forty fighters lifted off from a padport somewhere in Plaxar. Flying low, they headed in the direction of the Tygerian settlement. Twenty fighters went toward the western section to eliminate their communications and power generators. The other twenty fighters went to the eastern section to destroy their padport and any spacecraft that were there.

Upon completion of those objectives the pilots were directed to support the armored groups and warriors. The success of the fighters made it easier for the ground forces to complete their objectives. No communications were ever transmitted. That was objective number one. After a few hours of heavy fighting, the Tygerian settlement no longer existed. That was objective number two. Casualties for the new army were minimal and all Tygerian personnel were killed. But victory was seen as a threat to others who were observing the fight.

★   ★   ★

General Wydorf couldn't get to the palace fast enough. When he arrived he found the door open to the emperors' study, so he went right in. "Your highness, please excuse me for barging in like this, but we have a serious situation. There's an enormous amount of fighting in the Esterk Province. We're talking warrior movement of significant size, aerial combat involving fighters, explosions of large magnitude. And I'm sorry to say, we don't understand the situation at all.

"A few months ago we received reports of a revolt in the Esterk province. We were cautious at the time, because we didn't have any solid intelligence reports. The most troubling part is that we have an emissary in the foyer right now from the Esterk Province. And he's seeking an immediate audience."

"I'll see him at once, general." *Just what I need right now is a breakaway province,* he thought.

"Yes, sir, right away." Hesitantly the two men went to the throne room and the emissary was admitted.

"Your highness," said the emissary, making a customary bow. "I have come from the Esterk Province to negotiate an audience with you. My Lord Nemarg requests this to occur within ten days."

"Please be my guest for the night, and I will give you my answer in the morning," said the emperor.

"As you wish, your highness." The emissary bowed again as he was escorted to small but comfortable quarters.

"General Wydorf, I don't quite know how to answer this. It's going to take some thought. Contact Sizdroz, get him over here and maybe between the three of us, we can figure something out."

After discussing the situation well into the night, the emperor agreed to an audience with the Lord of Esterk, still not knowing whether he meant good or evil. He informed the emissary to relay the message to his leader. The emissary then left.

★　　★　　★

About mid morning eight days later, a shuttle sled landed in front of the palace. The small group exited and approached the steps leading inside. Four armed escorts met them and led them into the throne room.

Nemarg led the way across the throne room floor. He stopped at what he thought was an appropriate place and looked up at the emperor. Zordek got up, came down the steps to meet him. He went to the one who looked like their leader.

He gave a little nod of recognition. "My name is Gart Zordek, Emperor of Kaladon, and I welcome you and your group to Ozlonz."

"I am Rotz Nemarg, Lord of Esterk, Province of Kaladon, at your service," he said, bowing before the emperor.

Hoft motioned to an assistant servant to approach and softly ordered him to set up tables and chairs in the adjoining room for 20. "Forgive my servant, but we had no idea how many were in your group. They are setting up the other room so we can sit and talk more comfortably." *At least he included Kaladon loyalty in his title,* Gart thought.

Hoft asked, "Perhaps some refreshments, your highness?"

"Yes, Hoft, that would be fine."

Nemarg looked around the room and saw security guards at every exit. A few more stood near the throne. He had paid particular attention to the exterior security of the building when they arrived. Satisfied, he said. "I am pleased with the security measures you have taken on our behalf." *That should ease the emperor's fears,* he thought.

"We have come to discuss the future of Kaladon. We have solved one of your problems that you probably didn't realize existed. We were not pleased with the previous government, for it had many problems. We have learned about your new government and are very pleased with what we've heard."

"Well, I thank you for your confidence, and I plan on keeping an honest government in place as long as I am alive. Shall we move to the other room?" He motioned with his arm, and led the way. The group sat down around a large table.

Before everyone was seated, one of General Sizdroz's assistants came to him with an important message. He asked General Wydorf to be excused. "An important matter demands my attention," he said softly. Wydorf gave him leave and then went to the emperor to explain. The emperor nodded and then continued the discussions with Wydorf and himself.

"Lord Nemarg, you'll have to excuse General Sizdroz, my head of security, but something very important has come up that requires his presence elsewhere."

Zordek and Nemarg sat side by side, and Nemarg said, "Your highness, I want to enlighten you on what has happened in our province during the last eight days. I can understand your apprehension about the fighting you probably observed taking place. Perhaps you have intelligence agents in our province, perhaps not. If you did, I hope we didn't execute any of them. One of your problems was solved by the elimination of a Tygerian settlement in our Province." He paused to let that one sink in.

The emperor was visibly shocked that the Tygerians had set up a settlement on this planet without his knowledge. He looked at General Wydorf, who indicated he had no knowledge of this.

Wydorf was remembering something Captain Critz had said the other day about the Tygerians. He just sat there grinning, knowing full well that his young captain was correct.

The dramatic pause had worked. Nemarg now continued, "We also had a chance to test our newest fighter design in real combat. If you monitored some of the fighting in the last few days, you witnessed the impact of our newly formed army of the people under the leadership of General Engort." Lord Nemarg gestured toward him, and the general nodded in receipt of this recognition.

Nemarg pressed on. "It seems the Tygerians were causing both of us problems. You, because they made you think we had a small rebellion on our hands. Us by the attacks on smaller settlements, which until recently we were powerless to stop. We both lost many good people in our provinces until we figured out what was really happening. The Tygerians are known as a devious race which thrives on aggression. There were also some raids near the settlement of Ozlonz, I believe. They were getting close, your highness."

"Yes, I remember the raids being reported to me by General Wydorf. And you're correct. We thought it was your province."

"I inherited the Tygerian problem when I accepted the leadership position as Lord of Esterk," said Nemarg. "That problem has now been eliminated and all the Tygerians are dead." Lord Nemarg paused again and looked at the emperor. "Now perhaps you can enlighten us on your future plans for the central government, your highness."

Regaining his composure, the emperor told Lord Nemarg about all the changes in Ozlonz, at the palace, and their attempts to stabilize Kaladon. Toward evening Nemarg and his group agreed to spend the night and continue the next day. Gart told Nemarg about his missing daughter, and Nemarg told Gart about the death of his brother. They both relived their grief. The two generals enjoyed discussing military matters, each testing the other's loyalty, and both were satisfied.

The next day Lord Nemarg had one final item on his agenda, saving it for the right moment. "Your highness." Lord Nemarg stood, as did his entire party. "I pledge to you that the Esterk province will give our full support on any manner of assistance that would be requested from the central government. This also includes military assistance. And I would hope we can rely on your support as well." Diplomacy worked wonders when all the practitioners spoke the truth.

"The provinces of Kaladon will always receive assistance and have the support of the central government in any capacity that's requested," said the emperor, satisfied now that Esterk would not try to become a confederate province.

"I invite your Generals Wydorf and Sizdroz to visit us to discuss military matters and possible plans for the future," said Lord Nemarg. "And now, Your Highness, I bid you good day and ask your leave."

"Granted." The emperor stood and was sporting a broad smile of satisfaction on his face.

After the governing party from Esterk left, Sizdroz was waiting for the emperor by his throne and asked for an audience. "Your highness, I have learned that the previous information about your daughter was correct. She's in Calverone as a slave warrior, and Shanza is there, also. We've initiated negotiations to obtain their release as soon as possible."

"Thank you, General Sizdroz. Continue with the negotiations as planned. I want my daughter back at any cost and without delay." He was slow getting up, almost falling. The general reached out to help him. "Damn it, her well-being is not affecting my mind, but it's ruining me physically," he said in a rare candid outburst of emotion.

★   ★   ★

Regent BryQat walked hurriedly down the hall toward Lord GorDon's war room with a resolve that made people stand aside. "Come in, my friend. It's bad news again, isn't it?"

"Yes, my lord, very bad news." He was furious.

"Don't tell me it's that new emperor again."

"No, my lord, it's the contingent of warriors we had on Kaladon. All have been killed and their settlement was completely destroyed." Regent BryQat stood quietly with anger written all over his face. He said softly, "I had a brother in that group, my lord."

"Since this touches you greatly, my friend, what do you suggest we do about this massacre on Kaladon?"

"My lord, we both know we're not ready for an invasion. Perhaps in six months, but not now. I would consider an attack from orbit. We could send a battle cruiser to rendezvous with Admiral LanDok on the back side of Dynari, Kaladons' second moon. They could arm the capsules, move to Kaladon, and bombard from orbit. The destruction would take them at least six months or more to recover. But before then we could return and conquer Kaladon. The only problem we could have would be retaliatory action. But to be quite objective, my lord, I don't think Kaladon has any weapons in their arsenal that could be used effectively against us." He stood anxiously waiting for Lord GorDon's response to his suggestion.

"I agree with you completely. We think a lot alike, you and I." He allowed himself a very broad grin. "That's why we are so successful in our endeavors. I am confident Admiral LanDok's fleet will be adequate for this assignment. Inform him of our plan, and as soon as his supplies arrive he is to carry out his orders. The supply craft and battle cruiser will leave in two days. Put my seal on that and send it out. Allow the admiral's input to fine-tune the plan when he arrives at Kaladon, as we may not have anticipated every possibility."

"Yes, my lord." With a single conversation absent of much anger or emotion, the Tygerians were at war with Kaladon.

CHAPTER 7

THE ESCAPE

Carter got up early the day of the tournament and stopped by the forge to pick up his sword. When he walked into the arena to warm up, both KorRak and RomMen noticed the sword. This surprised them, because they figured he'd ask to use one of theirs.

"Where'd you get the new sword? The grip looks like it's never been used before," said RomMen.

"Hasn't," he replied, very alert, looking around the arena for his opponent. "It's new. Ordak made it for me." Still searching for DanKor. "It's a long story; I'll explain later. But I don't wanna draw it until my match with DanKor. KorRak, could you hide your sword outside the arena entrance somewhere until the tournament starts?" motioning with his finger. "I want Jackson to think I borrowed yours."

"Sure can." He turned and left.

It's great when friends don't ask questions, he thought. "RomMen, when do the spacecraft drop off prisoners? I mean, is there a pattern, or is it just at random?"

"I don't really know." He was a little puzzled by the question. *He hated it when a friend wouldn't tell you what was going on,* he thought.

When KorRak came back Carter asked him the same question. "I have no idea. Why do you ask?"

"I guess I'm just looking for a way outta here." *There it is, all out in the open. I hope the walls don't have ears. It just slipped out,* he thought.

"Do you really think there's a way out?" said KorRak, as excited about the idea as he was surprised at the suggestion.

"Somehow there's got to be a way," he said softly.

"Carter, do you have any kind of influence on Jackson? I mean, is it possible, with the two of you being Earthlings?"

"I don't know." His grin turned into a big smile at KorRak's insight. "It's certainly worth a try, isn't it? In the meantime let's check out the guards on the wall. We need to know their rotation times, if any would look the other way on a break, or if they could possibly be bribed."

"What about the doors between the passageway?" asked RomMen. "I know they're pretty thick and we have no key."

"Shh, here comes Jackson," Carter cut in.

"You men don't seem to be warming up. Overconfident, perhaps," said Jackson.

"I guess you're right, Jackson, sir," Carter said, not wanting to reveal too much. They immediately started practicing.

Jackson started walking away, then suddenly stopped and turned to face Carter. "Where'd you get that sword?" he asked.

"I borrowed it from KorRak, sir."

Jackson looked at KorRak, saw he had no sword, then returned his stare to Carter. Jackson didn't say anything, but he glanced at the grip on the sword. Then he went to the starting area.

"I don't think he bought that little story about borrowing my sword," said KorRak.

"I think he's right," cut in RomMen, not looking at Carter.

DanKor's entrance broke off their conversation. "All will remember this day," he said ceremoniously. "It will be the day of your death and my uncle will be proud of me again. Perhaps I will leave Calverone as a hero to my people. If my uncle wants me out of here he will come for me." DanKor turned sharply and walked to a different area in the arena to warm up.

The tournament began with a female match, followed by two matches with males. Soon it was time for Dovina's fight. Shanza and Carter kept a close watch during her match. *She will also be an asset if we ever get a chance to escape*, he thought. Next came Shanza and she was especially sharp today. "Excellent moves," he said softly, attracted both to her skills and Shanza herself.

At last, it was time for their grudge match, the reason the spectators were really here. All were well aware of their last fight, of how DanKor had driven his sword through the right side of Carter's chest and everyone thought he was dead.

The arena was sold out and the betting was the highest it had been for years. This was why the magistrates had these special touring groups; it made them wealthy. DanKor and Carter walked side by side to the starting area.

Jackson gave the signal to begin. They turned and started circling each other. When they were about 10 feet apart, they squared off for the match. DanKor slowly drew his sword while staring at his adversary. Carter stood straight, unshaken by the confident look on DanKor's face. He hadn't drawn his sword yet. *Surprise was better than over-confidence*, he thought.

DanKor slowly waved his sword back and forth, moving closer a little at a time. "You won't be so lucky this time. I won't run this sword through the wrong shoulder again." The arena was very still.

"DanKor," he said, with his hands on his hips, "I won't even work up a sweat. You'll be dead before you know what hit you." The crowd in the first few rows heard him and began to cheer.

Suddenly DanKor charged, swinging his sword back and forth as he closed in. He drew back to swing a haymaker. Carter stood still until he just about reached him. Then he stepped forward, blocked the swing with his arm on DanKor's, turned, elbowed him in the chest, used another karate move, and threw him over his shoulder like a rag doll. He went sprawling into the dust on his stomach, losing his grip on the sword. Carter quickly approached him as he rolled over and got to a sitting position, his face and chest all dirty. Carter swung and hit him with the flat part of his shield. "A little over-confident, are we?" he said, just loud enough for DanKor to hear.

DanKor rolled over and quickly leaped for his sword. He glared at Carter from about 10 feet away, a little dazed. He then became even more angry, and much more cautious. The crowd started laughing at DanKor.

Jackson must've liked the maneuver, because Carter caught a glimpse at the grin on his face. This was the first grudge match he saw Carter fight. DanKor, sword in hand, was slowly circling his opponent. He was shaking his head to clear out the cobwebs as Carter finally drew his sword.

Carter decided to do the opening warmup he had practiced. The crowd sat motionless during his routine, then cheered after he was through. *I guess DanKor got the message,* he thought.

DanKor wasn't sure what to make of it. He knew Carter had improved since the last time they fought, but he certainly didn't expect this.

DanKor glanced over at BriCon as if to signal something.

It was expected, now that his little charade was over and it was down to business. He cleared his thoughts of everything but this fight. After all, he didn't want to make any mistakes.

They started parrying a short distance apart. A jab here, a jab there, they began testing each other, and looking for a quick opening. DanKor came around with a wicked horizontal swing and Carter met it with an opposite swing of his own. When their swords crashed together, sparks flew and the impact stung DanKor's hand.

That really startled DanKor. One could tell by his reaction he had never experienced this before. The blow almost wrenched the sword from his hand. He quickly looked at his sword and saw a large nick in the blade. Carter quickly spun around, used another Karate move, and with his right foot kicked him on the left side of his head. The blow knocked DanKor off his feet and he flew backwards onto the ground. His sword went flying again. Carter was leaning on his sword waiting for him.

Jackson wasn't aware of Carter's previous fighting skills, but he knew he hadn't learned these moves here in the arenas. He just shook his head, knowing DanKor really didn't have a chance.

Carter glanced at his blade, noticing it was now silver in color and had a slight shine, instead of the dull gray it had been when the match first started. That's when he felt a tingle in his hand, not a delayed reaction from the blow, but something else. *No, it's not magic, that's for fairy tales*, he thought. It was a physical or perhaps a chemical reaction of some kind. He didn't care, because the more he used it, the more confident he became and the more powerful it felt.

Carter knew he had the upper hand and decided it was time to end it. He didn't care if they `boot rattled' him or not. The more aggressive he became, the more DanKor withdrew. Carter swung across the left side as DanKor came around with his sword. Much to everyone's surprise, including his, DanKors' sword was cut in half. After following through, he shifted his weight and came back across with another move, catching DanKor completely by surprise. Carter cut him open right across the lower chest area. He screamed as blue blood gushed from the large gaping wound. DanKor looked down and went into immediate shock, his eyes rolling back as he sank to his knees. He hesitated, slowly trying to look up at Carter, and then fell flat on his face in the dirt. The hilt half of the sword was still in his hand.

Suddenly BriCon came rushing toward the center of the arena. It happened so fast nobody had time to react. Shanza was a few steps too late. Were it not for Carter's keen sense of danger, he might have joined DanKor on the arena floor. A split second before BriCon got to him, he heard the footfall and moved by reflex only. It saved his life, because as he turned around, BriCon was swinging his sword toward his head. Carter had just enough time to react and block the swing. A kick he didn't expect sent him falling backwards into the dirt. There was time enough for him to be ready when BriCon came again.

Much to his surprise, BriCon was preoccupied trying to defend himself against the wrath of Shanza. Carter didn't know where she came from, but he was glad to see her. BriCon swung at her and missed. She gave him a drop kick and ran him through before he could recover. "Nice work," Carter yelled.

BriCon lay on the arena floor on his back as Shanza withdrew her sword from the right side of his chest. Everyone knew he was dead.

The whole audience was stomping their feet and cheering. It was the best fight the crowd had seen in a long time. Even the warriors came into the arena to cheer. Carter wasn't happy about BriCon's death, because he was just DanKor's puppet. Still, he had a sword and was just as deadly, so it couldn't be helped.

There would certainly be some questions to answer about his sword. Jackson came over immediately, but before he said anything he lightly kicked the sword from DanKors' hand and brushed some dirt over the two halves. Some of the warriors came out to congratulate Carter.

"Carter, where the hell did you get that sword? No, never mind, come with me, we have to hurry." Jackson led him quickly to his room, turned around, grabbed a sword of his own. "We've got to hide your sword. Here, take this one," as he handed the sword to him. "We'll hide yours in this locker."

When Jackson opened the locked door, Carter saw what looked like two weapons inside. "We gotta talk, Carter. Meet me in the arena after the evening meal and don't worry about your sword. It's safe with me. I only hope Res'Itz didn't get as good a look at it as I did. He was much farther away." He locked the door.

Without another word Jackson and Carter left the room and returned to the arena. The cheering had died down, and if they were lucky they weren't missed.

Shanza walked over to Carter and said, "is that the sword you were telling me about?" He gave an affirmative nod. "I've never seen anything like it before."

It was on everyone's mind right now. Perhaps he shouldn't have used it, he thought.

"Please, Shanza," he said, as earnestly as he could. "No more questions about the sword. I'll explain later, okay?"

Before she could answer, Res'Itz, with two armed guards, came over to where they were standing. "Carter, give me your sword, now." The two guards pointed their weapons at him. Slowly he drew his sword and handed it to Res'Itz, hilt first. Res'Itz took the sword, and as he turned to leave he looked directly at Jackson, pointed his finger, and said, "I'll see you first thing in the morning, in my office." Then he abruptly left the arena.

"So that's the infamous Res'Itz, huh?" Carter said.

"Yeah, that's the ass I have to deal with on a daily basis." Jackson really looked disgusted. "Hell, at times it's worse than when I was in the arena. At least there I knew what to expect, but with him you never know."

"Apparently Res'Itz didn't get here fast enough, so he doesn't know about the switch," said Shanza. They all mumbled and nodded in agreement. When the activity in the arena was over, the females followed Sa'Gena and the males went to their quarters.

★   ★   ★

The door banged open as Regent BryQat muscled his way through, walking briskly down the hall toward Lord GorDon's war room. He knocked and immediately entered. Lord GorDon looked up from his desk and saw a very angry regent approaching.

"What is troubling you, my friend? You look very disturbed."

"I am, my lord; I have most distressing news. We received a message from one of our agents on Na'Reen. Carter is not dead, as we were led to believe. And that's not the worst news. DanKor, your nephew, and his friend BriCon have both been killed in the arena by this Earthling."

The normally calm warlord jumped up from his chair and it flew back against the wall. "What are you saying? How can this be? Who's trickery is this?" He was as furious as his regent. "This contradicts all the information we have received from Calverone."

"My Lord, I have asked communications to make absolutely certain about these messages and they insist they're correct."

"Curse him," Lord GorDon yelled. "Can't anybody kill him?" Work stopped everywhere, as his voice carried through the halls. "What kind of fools does Res'Itz think we are? This is worse than that accursed emperor. Now I have two enemies with charmed lives." He was leaning on his desk with clenched fists. He whipped his head around. "What's the location of Captain MyrAaks' fleet?"

"Two days from Na'Reen, sir," said Regent BryQat.

"Perhaps we should pay this magistrate a visit and—," He paused momentarily, clenching and unclenching his fists by his sides. "Yes, we must make an example of him. I can't have this Earthling traversing the galaxy killing my nephews. He must be stopped. Perhaps I shall change his luck," said Lord GorDon. He stopped talking as a servant picked up the chair behind him. Sitting down, the careful strategist had returned from his angry fit. "BryQat, what's the status of the new spacecraft from the emperor?"

"My lord, they'll be fully re-supplied in two days, with personnel being assigned as we speak."

There was another pause as Lord GorDon slowly got up to gaze out one of the few windows in his office. He was sorting out his thoughts very carefully.

Abruptly, he turned. "Regent BryQat, send this message to Captain MyrAak in the Na'Reen solar system. `I'm promoting you to Admiral and elevating your status to fleet commander. Your first assignment will be commanding the new fleet I am forming in the Na'Reen solar system. In two days I'll send you additional spacecraft, including war cruisers, supply craft, and an adequate number of warriors to bring your command to full strength. Upon their arrival you may transfer your command to any spacecraft you desire, possibly the new larger war cruiser. Go to standby alert and await further instructions.' Put my seal on that and send it out immediately."

"Perhaps RomMen would have been the admiral of this new fleet." He looked at Lord GorDon after he made the statement and noticed a slight frown on his face. He knew Lord GorDon was having second thoughts about the way he had treated Captain RomMen. He also knew he was correct in his assumption, but decided he'd better let it rest. The last thing he wanted to do was anger Lord GorDon any more than he already was.

★ ★ ★

It was after the evening meal that Carter had a chance to go and talk with Dr. Zark. "I don't want you to think I'm pushy, doctor, but do you have the test results on Shanza and I?"

"I just finished them this morning and would like to say I hope you have many youngsters, but in these damn arenas it won't be possible. Yes, Carter, you two are medically compatible in all areas of anatomy. The few differences that exist are very minor and nothing to be concerned about. I did notice something rather odd though. If I didn't know any different I'd say you were both of the same race."

"Yes, that is odd," said Carter. "And my offer still stands, doctor. You coming with us?"

"I have certainly given it a lot of thought lately. I figure if we try and don't succeed, I can't be any worse off than if I stayed. I'd rather die trying to get out than live and work in these damn arenas for the rest of my life."

"KorRak and RomMen have some questions for you later, doc. I'd ask you myself, but Jackson ordered me to meet him in the arena. I'll see you later." He turned and left.

On his way to the arena he saw Ordak at the door of the forge. "Good to see you, Carter. I heard about your fight in the arena today. The more sunlight, the more powerful the sword is. Remember that and it will never fail you." They only had a short conversation because he had to meet with Jackson.

"Well, I guess we have a problem, don't we?" said Jackson, as Carter approached.

"Yeah, I think you're right about that. Did you check out the sword?"

"Yeah, but I didn't see much difference except for the color and perhaps it's a little lighter in weight."

"I don't know what to tell you," he said with a smile. "It sure works for me. Oh, that reminds me," a grin appeared. "I wasn't aware warrior masters were allowed to have weapons."

"You got that right," Jackson said, laughing a little. "I found them in the locker after moving in. I don't even know what they are for sure." The conversation stopped as they saw movement near the arena entrance. RomMen was slowly approaching.

"I have to ask you something before he gets here." He seemed a little reluctant.

"What's wrong? Something going on I should know about?"

"Well, I was just curious as to your intentions. I mean, are you happy in what you're doing here? Talk to me. It's very important," he said.

"I sort of feel like you did when we first met," he said. "I seem to be missing the obvious here. Just what is it you're trying to say? Or rather, what is it you want me to tell you?"

He sighed, then said, "how would you like a change in your lifestyle?"

"I think I'm getting you." he nodded his head. "Come with me." They went to where RomMen was standing and Jackson spoke first. "RomMen, is there anybody down the halls?"

"They're clear."

"Good, let's go." He gestured with his hand for them to follow. Before he opened the door to his quarters he said softly, "Don't say anything while we're in my quarters. In case they're bugged. I'm going to show you something and then we'll talk about it out there." He pointed toward the center of the arena. They both nodded as they went into Jackson's quarters. He opened the locker where the weapons were and showed them to RomMen one at a time. Handing them back to Jackson he locked them up again. Then they back went out to the arena.

All were quiet. It's as if they were waiting to see who would speak first.

"It's never been done before," said Jackson.

"We know," said Carter, "but there has to be a way. We just have to find it and make it happen. We've decided it's better to die trying than spend the rest of our lives waiting for someone to kill us. I'm betting you're going to throw in with us, because your military pride and your honor won't let you do otherwise. I also think it's almost possible to make it without you."

"RomMen, what are those weapons in my locker? I've never seen anything like them before," said Jackson.

"One of them is a hand weapon, fully loaded, but its range is somewhat limited. We could probably hit the guards on the wall from the arena with it. But the distance might be too far for any kind of accuracy beyond one shot. You'd have to kill three of them before they kill you. The other weapon is a blaster. It'll bust a big hole in whatever you're aiming at. It's accurate up to about 40 meters. It'll wreck a structure of moderate size at perhaps 150 meters. I think Carter can attest to the destructive force from what he saw on Earth." He looked at Carter and a slight affirmative nod answered his question.

"The problem is this: the one you have in your locker is old. It should probably be on a scrap pile. If we can't get it tested and find out if it's functional, we'd do better with Carters' sword. And that's no joke."

"I wonder if Ordak knows anything about blasters?" said Carter.

Jackson and RomMen sort of looked at one another indicating they didn't know either. Finally Jackson said, "I suppose it's worth finding out just how much Ordak knows about weaponry."

"I can ask him in the morning," Carter said. After a few more questions, they all agreed to let it rest until they could meet again.

★   ★   ★

Life was a little easier during the off season when they were on exhibition at other arenas. That meant a slower pace than at home. RomMen, KorRak and Dr. Zark were discussing various escape plans as Carter walked in from visiting Ordak.

"Well, gentlemen, it seems as though Ordak knows something about blasters," Carter said, happily. "Ordak claims all weapon systems are basically the same. The majority of scientific research went into space travel and not weaponry. That's why weapons on spacecraft seem somewhat primitive."

All looked to RomMen for his report. "About all I can find out about the transfer of prisoners is they always arrive during late morning, but on no specific days."

Next was KorRak's report. "The guards on the wall rotate at different times each day. They don't even know their schedule until early in the morning of the day they're on duty. They aren't issued translators, which prevents them from talking to prisoners or being bribed."

Dr. Zark didn't have anything to add.

"Doc," Carter said, "you'd better have your bags packed because if an opportunity comes our way, it'll be quick and we'll have to act fast. I'm going to meet with Jackson and Shanza tonight. So we'd better be ready for anything."

It was early evening when Carter walked out to the center of the arena, now a favorite meeting place of theirs. Jackson was already waiting for him. Approaching, he could see a new resolve on his face. "We gotta find a way. I'm in 100%, I'll do whatever it takes to get out of here, or die trying."

Grinning, Carter said, "the first thing we've got to do is get that blaster to Ordak and have him check it out. He knows quite a lot about them."

"I had my meeting with Res'Itz this morning. I don't trust him at all. I've never seen him so angry before. He threatened to have me killed, but he has to have the approval from the majority of the magistrates in order to do that. I think he's going to try something during the next exhibitions."

"We'll just have to be careful. We also haven't made much progress in our escape plans. Everything seems to lead to a dead end. But sooner or later there will be an opportunity and we have to be ready when it happens. I just hope it's before we leave for Ratoon."

It was early evening when he went to see Shanza. The news from Dr. Zark distracted him more than any homesickness ever could. He was hoping to make love to the beautiful Shanza for the first time. They were both very much in love, but it was a forbidden love, until now. This was the strangest feeling for him. He felt like a teenager again, meeting his sweetheart to make love for the first time. But this time it made him even more nervous. Imagine, a woman from another world. It just seems so bizarre. She could sure fill the empty void in his heart and eliminate the longing for Earth.

When she came into the small room where they always met, she could see he was very happy. "Well," she said, "you're in a good mood tonight. Anything I should know about?"

"I talked with Dr. Zark today." He was really nervous now. She sensed this and reached out to hold his hand. "He told me we're compatible in every way. There are a few differences, but they won't be a problem for us."

"That's wonderful," she said, almost jumping into his arms. They embraced a few moments and then animal instincts took over. Nothing else mattered at this time. The arena, their predicament, it all seemed so far away. It was hard to conceive that anything so beautiful could occur in a place as cold and deadly as this. They would always remember this night, which only belonged to them.

In two days there would be another full round of fighting. They had so many top warriors, both male and female, it was very difficult to pick an easy winner. And that meant more credits for the arena, because a lot of people were betting without knowing the true odds or the skills of the warriors.

Res'Itz was eager for this day to unfold. He had a plan that would see Jackson go down. *That arrogant fool,* he thought.

It was mid-afternoon, an unusually hot and sunny day, and Carter still didn't know who he would fight. It was usually posted on the bulletin board in the warriors' quarters the morning of the match, but an opponent's name was not next to his.

Dovina and Shanza won their matches easily, almost too easily for the spectators. KorRak and RomMen also won, but RomMen had a very difficult time this day. He wasn't nearly as good in the arena as he was on the bridge of a spacecraft.

There's something wrong, Carter thought. *I can sense it, but I can't put my finger on it and I don't want to ask.* KorRak had the same feeling, and he had already conveyed it to RomMen. This unnatural suspicion made them more alert than ever.

"RomMen, did you notice there's only one guard on the walls?" said KorRak.

"Yes, I did," he motioned for Carter to look on the walls, and the shortage of guards didn't escape him, either.

"Carter," said Shanza inquisitively, "why is Res'Itz coming down the steps to the arena flanked by two guards?"

Res'Itz had a portable microphone with him. He turned and spoke to the spectators in a loud voice. "Quiet, quiet please," he said again. "I need your attention." Everybody quieted down to hear what he had to say. "My fellow citizens of Calverone. I have an important announcement. Today's final match will be to determine if the warrior Carter is really as good as he appears. Since we all know our warrior masters are supposed to be the best, my announcement should send you back to the wager booths," he said, smiling. "I'm going to match warrior master Jackson against Carter. This will be the battle of the Earthlings, to the death!" Res'Itz yelled with a raised hand and an evil smile. "Now, all of you have plenty of time to place your bets before the match begins. All the agents will be eager to accept your wagers." The spectators started to cheer at the news of this match and headed for the betting booths.

When Jackson looked at Res'Itz he also saw the two guards, one standing on each side, with weapons pointed. Jackson slowly walked over to KorRak and dropped a key in his hand. "Ordak fixed the blaster and returned it this morning. The problem is, the weapon only has four shots. If this is our time, use them wisely." He then walked over to stand near Res'Itz.

Observing what was going on, RomMen went over and stood in front of KorRak to act as a shield. KorRak quietly told RomMen what he was going to do and left. He returned to the arena entrance, gave the handgun to RomMen, and kept the blaster along with Carter's sword. The blaster was an old model for sure, and small enough to hide it behind his shield. It almost looked like a toy in his large hands.

He then made his way to Jackson and Carter as they were getting ready to fight. Soon all the spectators had made their wagers. Res'Itz turned around and signaled for the match to begin. They drew their swords and positioned themselves about ten feet apart. Standing very near each of them was a guard, poised ready to fire, to ensure both of them would fight well.

As Res'Itz turned around and started to ascend the steps to his booth he heard an explosion off in the distance.

"Attention. We have an emergency. Attention everyone, this is an emergency," came the word over the public address system. "Two Tygerian war cruisers have landed at Calverone and their warriors are heading for the arena. They are killing anyone who shows the least bit of resistance. Another war cruiser has destroyed our fighters and Tygerian warriors have taken over the military base. This is an invasion and we ask you to make an orderly exit from the arena and go to your homes. This whole area will soon be under the control of the Tygerian Empire."

Res'Itz wasted no time. He turned around and pointed with his finger. "Kill Carter!" But his was the surprise when he saw RomMen raise a weapon. He picked off the guard on the wall just before he could follow Res'Itz's order, then turned his gaze to Res'Itz. The other two guards were already lying on the ground. He couldn't shoot at Res'Itz because of too many spectators.

"How could this be?" Res'Itz yelled. "I curse these damn Tygerians. I curse them all." He turned and ran up the stairs, weaving in and around the spectators, pushing everyone that got in his way. Shanza picked up a weapon one of the guards dropped and Dovina got the other one.

They heard the noise of a blaster. On the other side of the wall fiery sparks flew through the air. "Get Zark and Ordak fast. Let's get the hell out of here," he yelled. Everyone knew they had to hurry, because those blasts meant the Tygerians were in the other side of the castle.

"RomMen," yelled KorRak excitedly, "shoot the control box for the fence." He pointed to the electrical box hanging high on one of the poles. "Carter," he yelled again as he threw him his sword, "the gate latch."

Carter slammed his sword into the metal and it shattered the latch. By then dozens of enslaved warriors were scrambling out through the gate to what they hoped was freedom.

Some stayed behind because they were afraid. With the blasters the Tygerians had they knew there wasn't much time to get out. Carter was wading through panicking spectators, some yelling, some screaming and stepping on each other, trying desperately to escape. Others had already been trampled to death in their attempt to get out of the castle.

Three more guards were near the betting booths and office area of the castle, but between Dovina and Shanza they were also killed. Carter grabbed one of the weapons and Carznot got the other. Carznot blasted the lock of the small weapons cabinet in the hall and had to hurry out of the way. The melee for everyone to get a weapon prompted his decision.

They were being very systematic in their escape, moving as fast as they could and being very careful as they approached the castle entrance. There was no sign of Res'Itz anywhere nor any resistance either, only spectators crowding through the large door at the entrance to the castle running in every direction.

A few warriors were covering the rear as they went out into the countryside and on toward the settlement. All looked to Carter for leadership. He was surprised not to find any Tygerians at the main entrance of the castle.

After breaking into the rear of the castle Captain SenKez said, "Admiral, according to their drawing the warrior quarters are on the other side of that wall," pointing as he spoke.

"Blast it," he ordered. A fiery blast left a gaping hole in the wall with stones flying everywhere. There was a large hole in the upper floor of the warrior quarters.

Captain SenKez ordered his warriors to advance and capture any and all inside. They obeyed, but found only the small group that had remained behind.

Admiral MyrAak stood in the middle of the arena, looking up at the seating area. He saw many bodies lying around, but where was Carter? "Admiral," said the captain, "we found 35 warriors that remained. Some are dead and a few of them are wounded. Carter and the rest of the warriors are gone. They went out through the gate in the fence and escaped among the fleeing spectators." Captain SenKez gestured as he spoke.

The Tygerians moved on into the office area. "Captain," the Admiral said, "search this whole area. I want to make sure we don't overlook anything."

"Admiral," said Captain SenKez, as he came from an office opposite the betting area, pulling on someone's shoulder.

"Well, what have we here?" said MyrAak as he turned around. "And what's your name?" Not waiting for an answer, he said, "Is the name on this door yours?"

"Who wants to know?" said Res'Itz defiantly.

Captain SenKez backhanded him, which sent him reeling into the wall next to his office door. Sliding to the floor, somewhat dazed, he shook his head and looked up at the person who just hit him. Very pale green colored fluid was pooling at the corner of his mouth.

SenKez looked Res'Itz right in the eyes and said, "The last thing you want to do is anger me. Now, shall we try this again? Is your name Res'Itz?" He raised his voice as he tapped a claw on the door next to the nameplate.

"Yes sir, it is, sir," said Res'Itz, meekly this time.

"Take him to my craft and put him in a cellroom. Be quick about it. The arrogant fool won't be alive long otherwise."

"Captain, I'm going back to the padport. I expect you to find Carter and bring him to me, so I can present him to Lord GorDon personally. Is that understood?"

"Yes sir, Admiral," replied the Captain, with renewed confidence. "I will have this elusive Carter in short order. "Communicator," said SenKez, grinning. "Contact Captain TenKot. If the military base is secure, he and his warriors can converge on the city from the padport. I think perhaps we'll have this Earthling in a neat little trap."

All the warriors with Carter were starting through the city. Another explosion from the castle told them their trackers had just blasted a hole from the courtyard into the warrior quarters. It wasn't hard to figure out, since there weren't many places you needed a blaster in the castle. All were crouched low and mingled with the crowd as they walked.

Some of the people got into vehicles and sped away, while others just ran into the city. It was an interesting mismatched group they had here, comprised of many races.

When they started into the city all looked to Carter for the next move. "Anybody have any suggestions?" he asked. "Perhaps the padport. Maybe we can capture a spacecraft."

"No," said RomMen excitedly. "That's the wrong way. All the war cruisers will be on alert. We wouldn't even get close."

"Go through the city," Dr. Zark yelled. "We have to get to the science complex. That's where the transporter is. It's the only way out for us and the fastest way is through the city."

As they walked briskly toward the middle of the city, all seemed quiet. "I don't like this," said KorRak. They were searching for any movement.

"I seem to remember something about this city when passing through on my way to the castle," Carter mumbled softly. Then it hit him. "The windows. Everyone get off the road quickly. Hug the walls, let's go, move, move, move." His voice got louder and more excited with every word he spoke.

They had no sooner gotten off the middle of the road when shooting erupted all around them. The residents fired from their windows as the escapees dove for what little cover there was. Someone gave out a low cry of pain, and then another. Their group became smaller with every shot fired. A hand with a weapon was sticking out of a window. Shanza used her sword and cut it off. Someone screamed and quickly pulled it back.

"KorRak," he yelled. "Blast them. Use all the shots if you have to. If something isn't done soon, none of us will get out." KorRak fired down one side of the street. When the fireball hit, it blew out glass, ripped up walls and left the fronts of five buildings in flames. The empty casings dropped to the pavement with a clinking noise, shattering as it fell.

Carter looked down and remembered where he had seen those before. They were the same metallic looking casings he had found on Earth.

KorRak turned slightly, and fired a second time on the opposite side, with the same devastating results. He swung around to blast into the direction they were traveling, but he didn't have to. The resistance stopped. "I guess they had enough," Carter said softly. They quickly moved on through the city with no more incidents.

When they heard weapons firing behind them, they knew the Tygerians were not far away. They could not afford to lose any more warriors, as they'd already lost a quarter of their group.

Approaching the newer area of the city they came to a group of large buildings. The center structure was the tallest which resembled a metallic-like tower surrounded by eight shorter towers protruding out of the top in a near-perfect octagon pattern. There was a high fence around the entire complex.

"In there," pointed the doctor. "I'm sure glad I treated a patient here last month or I never would have known about it."

As Dr. Zark spoke, Carter hacked through the gate with his sword. They didn't want to use the weapons because of the noise. They came to a door which was a lot more secure than the gate. RomMen had to use his pistol to blast the door lock.

They entered a hallway that led to three more doors. Zark pointed to the right one and what they saw, after forcing it open, made them more hopeful than at any time during their escape. It looked like it was some kind of control room.

Its occupants didn't have any visible weapons, but that didn't mean there weren't any hidden somewhere. They became very nervous at seeing two armed Tygerians entering the room.

They already knew about the attack on Calverone, but nobody seemed to know why. Incredibly, they agreed to help transport everyone to Ra'Tor.

An individual led them down a hall through a door to two large elevators. They piled on and went down to another level. They stopped at an open hallway that led to a vehicle of some kind. Forty-eight of them got on each vessel and strapped themselves in. The guide went out and the door closed automatically. They felt a slight vibration and an upward movement. The `G' force was trying to drive them through the floor. Other then the momentary surge at the beginning it was a smooth ride. In about fifteen minutes the door opened. Getting out they walked down another open hallway and entered what seemed like the same two elevators. Everything looked identical to the building they just left. Upon opening the door they instantly knew this was not the same place.

CHAPTER 8

FREEDOM AT LAST

They must have looked awfully strange to the group who greeted them as they came through the door. Carter's sword was sheathed, he had a handgun tucked in his belt and immediately asked to speak to the person in charge, trusting they all wore translators. Their rugged group was not expected, to say the least. But they weren't disarmed or imprisoned either. He took it as a good sign.

Deep concern was written all over the faces of the crew that operated the transporter capsules. The presence of Carter's group signaled a monumental change on their home planet. Quickly, as if shaken back to reality, one stood and motioned for him to follow. Carter could tell he was not at all happy that a Tygerian carrying a blaster followed right behind him.

As KorRak and Carter followed this person down a corridor, he noticed Shanza also fell in line. Turning left, they went through an open doorway into a large room. Desks, various drawing boards, and a variety of worktables cluttered the room. Numerous diagrams and schematics crowded the walls.

Upon entering, the activity that seemed to be a normal part of this environment stopped. The inhabitants displayed faces of shock, fear, and anxiety as they slowly tried to back away. They approached a person sitting on the edge of a desk with his back to them. He was talking to three others who were staring at them.

"Lo'Gon, I want to introduce you to, ah, I didn't catch your name, sir," looking at Carter. Lo'Gon turned around, dropped what he was holding, and joined the others in shock at what he saw.

"My name is Carter, this is KorRak, and this is Shanza. She's a Kaladonian and KorRak is a Ty ..."

"A Tygerian." Lo'Gon cut him off. And then almost in a whisper, "A Tygerian with a blaster, no less."

Gradually Carter sensed the target of their concern was armed and dangerous. It wasn't him or any of the others—they were watching every move KorRak made.

Wow! He really has them rattled by his presence. I might as well play this through, he thought. "There's also another armed Tygerian out in the other room." Motioning with his thumb. He looked at Carter, with contempt in his eyes. *Heh, nothing personal*, he thought. *I need an advantage.*

★   ★   ★

Captain SenKez knocked on Admiral MyrAak's open door aboard one of the Tygerian vessels. He looked up and said, "Speak."

"Admiral, I took the liberty of ordering the immediate departure of all spacecraft but one. Forgive me, Admiral, but I thought it imperative to get after Carter as soon as possible."

"What do you mean get after Carter? Where is he?"

"He's on Ra'Tor, sir, moon of Na'Reen."

The admiral was shocked by this captain's words. "But that's impossible. Ra'Tor is over two hours from here. How could he possibly be on Ra'Tor?"

"Unknown to us Admiral; they had transporter capsules in Calverone at their science complex, for transporting personnel and equipment to and from Ra'Tor. I felt the faster we moved on this situation the better." The captain was trying to recover from his lack of success. "We would have lost valuable time had I reported to you first. I also ordered Captain TenKot to destroy the transporter."

"You were correct in the orders you have given on my behalf. Just be sure you don't exercise too much authority in the future. If you're wrong it could cost you more than you realize … get to your vessel. We must leave immediately."

"Yes, sir, Admiral," he snapped to attention and departed.

After traveling in space for awhile MyrAak, left his quarters for the control room to check on their progress. Upon entering, all snapped to attention. "Progress report, captain?"

"Helm, report."

"We're more then half way to Ra'Tor, Captain. Power plant is operating at 110%, and we'll arrive ahead of schedule."

"Very good, captain." said MyrAak, not letting the captain relay the report.

★   ★   ★

"And to what do we owe the pleasure of your company here on Ra'Tor?" Lo'Gon said.

"It doesn't take a military expert to see that we escaped from the arena. Now we're looking for a way to freedom." Lo'Gon waited for the translator. English had probably never passed through these devices before.

"I see, well, I agree with what you said and—."

"Lo'Gon," interrupted the communicator, in a loud voice. "The Tygerians are destroying Calverone. They crushed our military base and are on their way here." He looked to his boss. "They will arrive in less than an hour." His voice got softer toward the end of his sentence, until you could hardly hear him.

"One hour," said Lo'Gon loudly. How quickly his mood had changed. He displayed the same face of fear as when he first saw KorRak. "What would the Tygerians possibly want here?" They had managed nicely to avoid any run-ins with the brutes, but that was apparently about to change. "It couldn't be you people, could it?" He turned his attention back to Carter. "You can't be that important to the Tygerians, can you? If not, what would they—?" Suddenly his voice faded. His eyes got wider as he snapped back to reality. In a loud voice, said, "No, they can't have that, never!" Lo'Gon strode to the communications station. "Put me live on all channels, including the construction station, now!" he yelled."

"Yes sir." He handed Lo'Gon the microphone.

"All personnel, this is Lo'Gon. We have an emergency. Authentication code 31, confirmed. Prepare for the immediate evacuation of the construction station. Tygerian war cruisers, number unknown, are on their way here. We must leave as soon as possible. Those of you who stay can return to Ra'Tor on the spacesleds. The rest can join us as we escape on the spacecraft." After the announcement he turned to the communicator and said, "Sound the alarm. Contact Captain Za'Dor and tell him I said to make all preparations for immediate space flight." The alarm sounded and flashing red lights came on.

Lo'Gon turned to Carter and said, "Sorry we can't get to know you better. It was a pleasure, but we have to go." He hurriedly ducked past them toward the exit.

Before Carter could react he was nearly out of the room. "RomMen, grab him," he hollered, pointing to Lo'Gon so he knew who he meant without waiting on the translation. RomMen snatched him as he passed through the doorway. Carter gave him a thumbs up, so he knew he had the right one. *I'm sure glad RomMen studied a lot of our customs while on Earth,* he thought.

Lo'Gon was against the wall, with his feet dangling. RomMen had picked him up by the front of his garment. Tygerians were a strong race, as Carter found out the hard way. Everyone froze as they saw weapons being pointed at them from every direction.

"Now everybody relax for a second," he said, in a loud voice, motioning with his hand for RomMen to lower Lo'Gon to the floor. "Nobody leaves until we get some answers. I'm sure we have that much time, don't we?" He gave Lo'Gon a firm look. Lo'Gon raised his eyebrows, cocked his head to one side, gesturing, "Okay, but don't take too long."

"Now what's so damned important here, or with that spacecraft at the construction station?"

"They want the spacecraft we're building there."

"Go on," Carter said angrily.

"It has the most advanced technology of any spacecraft ever built. We must hurry, time is of the essence." he said nervously.

"I think he's right about the Tygerians wanting that new spacecraft." RomMen cut into the conversation. "I remember Lord GorDon talking about it for the last year or more."

"Just where is this construction station?" Carter asked.

"It's in orbit around this moon," said Lo'Gon, pointing upward with his thumb and getting more impatient. "Our time is limited; it doesn't take very long to get here from Na'Reen. There's much to do to prepare the spacecraft for flight and get a jump on the Tygerians. Time is running out."

"Do whatever you have to do, Lo'Gon," said Carter. "We're all in the same situation, wanting to escape from the Tygerians. So we'll help you all we can. But remember this: one of us will be watching you. And, since we came from the arena, you must know that any one of us is just as deadly as the other."

"Hmm, how refreshing," said Lo'Gon, sarcasm in his voice.

★　　★　　★

It was mid-morning and the emperor was busy in his office. He figured it would be a slow and uneventful day when his servant came to him with a different situation. "General Wydorf contacted the palace requesting an audience with you and General Sizdroz," he bowed slightly. "He said it was important."

"Hoft, tell the generals I will meet with them in my study." They were waiting for him when he arrived. "Well, what's so important today that needs my attention?"

"It's about your daughter, sir. We just received information from one of our agents on Na'Reen," said General Sizdroz. "The arena at Calverone has been destroyed by the Tygerians in a surprise attack. They also destroyed a large portion of the city. Many thousands have died as a result of this bold attack. Our agent is lucky to be alive herself, and she hasn't been able to learn anything about your daughter. But she does know some of the warriors escaped. She has no idea who, how many, or where they could have gone. She also knows that any escaping warrior who is re-captured is automatically put to death. There's much confusion there and it's a wonder anybody knows what's happening. Since your daughter was a combat prisoner, she may have fled."

"We're sorry to have to bring you the sad news, sir, truly sorry," said General Sizdroz, showing concerned. "There is yet another item we must discuss. We have identified the spy."

"Who?"

"Your good friend, Tak Byrrok."

"What? You must be mistaken." But he knew better, even as he spoke.

"Search your mind, your highness, and you'll know we are correct. Everything points to him. He's the only one it can be. The only difficulty we're having is figuring out how he gets the information to the Tygerians."

"How can it be, after all these years?" He paused, deep in thought. *Betrayal is nothing new when ruling an empire. Take control,* he thought. Shaking a finger, he continued. "You are correct, now that I think about it. He wasn't harmed at the padport on Krynta. There were only five of us at the meeting to send an emissary to Ra'Tor. The electronic scan of the palace was negative, and there are a few more instances I'm sure I'll remember if I think about it later. And your suggestions are?"

"Since we don't know how he communicates with the Tygerians, I suggest we hold off on the arrest. We need more time to gather additional evidence. We'll just have to work harder," said General Sizdroz.

After the two generals left, Gart sat there alone with his thoughts. He'd never understand how Tak could be a spy. And there was his daughter to worry about, too. He would not sleep this night. Too much to think about. Perhaps she escaped somehow. "Resolve!" he said softly. "Chuvorac, the ancient philosopher, had once said, "Adversity tests leaders. Those who prevail, lead better. Those who don't were never leaders." He would lead.

★   ★   ★

Lo'Gon told Carter they could transport 48 people at a time. In case of treachery, they'd insure warriors were on every flight. They left the room through a doorway and went down a corridor to a door that led outside the building. Once outside they passed through a clear domed walkway. It was about five meters in diameter and made of some type of clear substance. As Carter looked out he could see the landscape on the moon, but it was the planet of Na'Reen up in the sky that got his attention. *Trouble's coming,* he thought.

On one side there were odd looking buildings visible, including the octagon shaped structure a short distance away. This was an atmospherically controlled environment, totally enclosed and self-contained. On the other side one could look out onto an uninterrupted lunar surface. All that was visible as far as the eye could see was barren soil.

They entered a smaller building, walked through to the other side, and came to a corridor that led to the spacesleds. As they entered, they were a little surprised to find rows of seats, two deep on each side with twelve to a row. Everyone found a seat, sat down, and strapped themselves in. RomMen, Shanza, Dovina, Ordak, and Carter were on this flight along with Lo'Gon and 18 others. KorRak, Morris, and Dr. Zark decided to follow on the next trip. The rest would arrive on later flights.

Most of the people on this flight were in engineering and technical fields. The rest just wanted to stay alive. All had skills in one field or another or they wouldn't be here.

Shanza sat next to Carter. "This is the first time I've had any real hope of ever getting out of this alive. And I'm starting to feel good about it," she said.

"Yeah, I guess our freedom gets closer all the time," he said, smiling. "It looks good so far." He felt good about his relationship with Shanza. He wasn't sure how Kaladonian females conducted themselves with males in public, but so far, she wasn't letting him out of her sight. It was like she watched his back and he was expected to watch hers. In the hostile environment they'd been living in for the last year or so, it was very comforting to know she was always there.

The door closed and he could hear a hissing noise, perhaps air escaping. There were monitors in front of the seating area that all could watch as the spacesled took off. The roof of the rectangular building opened and they could feel a small surge from the thrusters. In no time at all they were on their way.

The monitor pointed to the rear of the craft and showed the buildings getting smaller. Soon the captain switched the monitor forward and within five minutes the construction station became visible.

Carter wasn't aware of much on his first space voyage, but this one was different, since he wasn't in a cellroom. He struggled to control his anxiety.

Now that they were getting closer, he could see how large the construction station really was. It was a long cylindrically shaped tube that had thousands of lights all around it. He couldn't even venture a guess as to its length and diameter. Size and distances were very deceiving in space. On one side were three platforms and they were headed directly for the middle one.

A large circular array of blue lights came on as they were approaching the platform. The lights shined on the spacesled and guided them in.

After they landed, a circular tube raised and attached itself to the side of the sled. The door opened and they exited the sled through a small corridor to an elevator. Leaving the elevator they stepped onto a moving sidewalk, which was enclosed in a familiar clear circular tube. They stepped off the sidewalk as it passed through a large room. A few meters away was a row of open cars that held 12 people at a time. There were no visible tracks or wheels under the cars, just blue lights on the bottom shining down on two wide stripes. There were others getting off to return to Ra'Tor. *Bad move*, Carter thought.

One of Lo'Gon's assistants said, "We're going to the docking control area at the end of this clear enclosure tube. We will go by the spacecraft so you can partially see what it looks like. We will board immediately upon arrival."

Sure enough, through a clear tube Carter was looking at the most magnificent spacecraft he had ever envisioned, given his limited experience. To think these people built this, the technology involved must be astounding. He wondered what RomMen was thinking.

Sitting there in awe, it was difficult to explain what he saw. There were two platforms protruding outward from the side and swept back about 15 to 20 degrees, each with a different sized spacecraft fastened on it. The rear platform was larger and therefore had the largest spacecraft attached to it.

It was difficult to see very much, because their view was partially blocked by the spacecraft on the platform. This one had about four levels and curved under to a tube of some kind. Below the platform it curved under as well.

There were some protrusions in various places on the outside of the vessel. He had no idea what they were for. As they moved on toward the rear of the spacecraft he could see the stripes went all the way across to the other side. There appeared to be tracks of some sort coming out of covered tubes on the bottom. *I wonder if they carry any fighters*, Carter thought. Both spacecraft had the tubes with tracks also. He glanced back at RomMen and noticed him staring at the spacecraft.

After arriving at the main platform of the docking area they made a 90 degree turn to go across the rear of the spacecraft. The docking area alone had to be eighty stories high, chock full of work shops and offices. The other end of the construction station had a huge double door, pressurized and sealed, that allowed for departure into space. They were going to board and head through those doors, escaping to what, he didn't know. He looked back, and noticed others coming to board.

As they approached the rear of the spacecraft he saw what looked like the exhaust of six main engines, three on each side horizontally installed, about 11 to 12 meters in diameter. As they walked across a gangplank onto the platform, he looked down. It was a long way to the bottom. Walking another twenty meters they came to a huge steel-like door. It was open about three meters so they could get through. Apparently humans and other aliens were all within a certain height, making spacecraft construction almost universal.

They walked into a large, three-story rectangular room with walkways around three sides on every floor. The ceiling glowed with a solid light; below on the deck, six spacesleds were anchored to the floor. Again his curiosity overwhelmed him.

RomMen stopped a few times to look around. *He probably feels at home now, by the look on his face. I'm sure he's in his glory,* Carter thought. He wasn't missing much either, but there was an enormous amount to see. *Geez, it would take a lifetime to even try and learn everything,* he thought. He almost bumped into the side of the elevator, by not watching where he was going. How many decks they had gone up, he had no idea.

RomMen turned to Lo'Gon as they got off. "Take us to the bridge. I want to meet with the captain as soon as possible, Tygerians chasing us and all."

"I don't think you understand. You can't go on the bridge."

"Lo'Gon," Carter said angrily, "I think it is you that does not understand. If you don't take us to the bridge now, and I mean right now, you might not appreciate the end results of our immediate action. Since time is of the essence I don't plan on discussing this. Do I make myself clear?"

Lo'Gon stood there for a few seconds, looked at both of them in anger, and said, "Perfectly." He turned and hurriedly led them down a different corridor. Before they arrived on the bridge Carter thought he should say something to Lo'Gon on the way. "We're not looking to hurt anyone, but we're on the run. I'm sorry you're caught up in all this, but you're escaping danger too. Why the hostilities?" Lo'Gon ignored him.

After numerous turns and two elevator rides later, they arrived at their destination. They walked over a security grid, turned right, and passed an unmanned security station. Carter started gawking again and RomMen went straight toward the captain. Captain Za'Dor caught sight of RomMen as he approached and almost fainted.

"What's he doing here? A Tygerian doesn't belong on my bridge. Security, get him out of here," Za'Dor said in a loud voice. Carter searched the room to see where resistance might come from. At that moment someone a few feet away, who looked like a security guard, was grabbing for a weapon.

Quickly going over to him Carter said, "Don't even think about it," as he pointed his handgun directly at the guard's head. "That would be the last thing you'd ever do in this lifetime." In spite of his resolve, he really didn't want any trouble. He turned to see if there was another guard only to see Shanza poised to shoot the other guard.

"Not today," the guard said. Just then the door opened and in stepped KorRak and a few more of their group. "Well, that's all we needed right now, a Tygerian with a blaster," said Captain Za'Dor.

"I guess the Tygerians got here sooner than you expected, Lo'Gon." Captain Za'Dor said softly.

"These are not the Tygerians I was referring to."

"Then just what are you talking about, Lo'Gon? This is a Tygerian isn't it?" Pointing to RomMen, Lo'Gon nodded yes. "And there's one over there with a blaster in his hand, right?" Again Lo'Gon nodded, indicating he was correct. "Then what do you mean these aren't the Tygerians you're talking about."

"I know what you're saying, but it's too complicated to explain right now. Forget these two, they're not the problem. It's the Tygerians on their way here that we're going to have a problem with. We have to get this vessel out of the docking bay as soon as possible."

"Captain," said the communicator, "docking bay reports all personnel are aboard, sir."

"Very well. Shut all hull openings, zero atmosphere in the docking bay, check all indicators and report when everything is completed," ordered Captain Za'Dor, nervously, now returning his attention to the immediate problem.

"Don't let my presence here intimidate you, captain," said RomMen. "I can help if you need it. Our situation is the same, we all want to get away from those marauders." Lo'Gon stared at RomMen, eyes wide and almost in shock, never thinking he would ever hear a Tygerian talk that way about another of their race.

"Captain, helm and engineering reported ready for space flight," said the operations officer.

Lo'Gon noticed the captain's nervousness getting worse. He wasn't making decisions fast enough. Something must be done and fast or they'd never get out of here on time. "Captain Za'Dor," said Lo'Gon, "is there something wrong?"

"How do you expect me to get anything accomplished with all this pressure? If it isn't this Tygerian badgering me, it's you. Now will all of you just shut up and leave me to my work?" That's the last thing Lo'Gon wanted to hear, knowing the captain wasn't being badgered. Lo'Gon thought the real problem was with Za'Dor himself. To take the spacecraft out on trials was one thing, but to be in a critical situation, that was another.

Carter moved closer to Lo'Gon after hearing the outburst. "Lo'Gon, I see your captain seems to be having some difficulty right now."

"Yes, he is," answered Lo'Gon softly. "At the rate he's going we're never going to make it."

"Do you have anybody else on board that's qualified to fly this thing, er, spacecraft?"

Shaking his head no, he said, "The crew on the operating stations know their jobs, but I have no experience. I don't know how to run it. I can build them, but operating them is another matter completely. That takes a war cruiser captain." He paused. "And I know of no one on board qualified. This thing's not like taking a spacesled around the planet a couple of times."

"Lo'Gon," he said, "if you back me and help direct us, we'll make it outta this docking bay just fine. What do you say Lo'Gon? We together on this?"

Pausing a little and wondering what he meant, he said, "yes, go ahead."

"KorRak," yelled Carter, "I'm taking charge. You're the new chief of security on this vessel. These two guards will take orders from you." He turned his gaze to them and both nodded in agreement. "Za'Dor, I relieve you of command. You are no longer captain of this vessel, because I have weapons and you don't. If you cause any disturbance I'll have you shot, but I'd prefer you stay and help." The captain stared at him for a second, then looked at Lo'Gon, who just shrugged his shoulders. After seeing no support from him, he conceded.

"RomMen, I name you interim captain of this spacecraft. Lo'Gon will assist you all he can. Captain RomMen, your first order will be to get us out of here and take her—," shaking his head, "I don't care where."

"Yes, sir, Carter," said RomMen, smiling. "I have command."

The operating stations didn't seem to mind that a Tygerian was running the show. They were just happy someone was competent and could project authority while giving orders. It gave them confidence as well. Captain RomMen and Lo'Gon conversed about the preparations in between barking orders to the crew.

"Lo'Gon, how much time do we have?" Carter asked.

"It's hard to say; I'd estimate we have about a quarter hour at best. After that it's anybody's guess as to when the Tygerians get here."

"Do we have anything to fight them with?"

"Well, yes we do. We have very powerful weapons, but nobody aboard has ever fired them."

"What?" Carter said. He quickly lowered his voice, not wanting to alarm anyone. He glanced at the weapons station, only to see it unmanned. "You're telling me that this high-tech spacecraft has never had its weapons tested?"

"You forget, Carter, this vessel hasn't completed all its flight trials yet. It's not even totally operational for space travel. And this is somewhat of an unscheduled flight. The weapons crew decided to stay on Ra'Tor. The only things that are 100% tested and operational are engineering, communications, the reflector device, and hull integrity systems. The four spacecraft on the platforms that travel with us have also been tested and are 100% operational, but we have no crews or captains to command them. Even the sleds are ready, but they won't do us any good against war cruisers."

"Hell, we might have been safer back in the arena," he said, laughing softly. Lo'Gon even chuckled at that.

"Captain," said the communicator, "the construction station reports zero atmosphere in the docking bay."

"Carter, we're ready to go," said RomMen.

"Get the docking bay doors open," Lo'Gon whispered softly.

"Remove the docking restraints and get those docking bay doors open, now," ordered Captain RomMen.

A moment later the communicator said, "Captain, construction station reports: restraints removed, doors energized and are beginning to open. They are vacating the station. They also report that the Tygerians will be here in ten minutes."

"Very well," replied RomMen.

"Carter," said Lo'Gon excitedly, "I think we're going to make it. It'll take about five minutes to open the doors and then we're out of here."

Three minutes later, Captain RomMen ordered, "Helm, put main engines on line, ahead 5% normal speed."

"Put main engines on line, ahead 5% normal speed, aye," replied the helm. A minute later the helm reported, "Captain we're starting to move."

"Very well," replied the captain.

"You're cutting it very close," said Lo'Gon.

"I know," said RomMen, "but if I remember correctly, it'll take a minute or two for a spacecraft this large to start its motion."

"You're right about that, Captain." Lo'Gon was somewhat impressed by the Tygerian's knowledge.

"Lo'Gon," Carter cut in, "I neglected to tell you that Captain RomMen was probably the best war cruiser captain in the Tygerian fleet."

Lo'Gon glanced at this Tygerian in his element, then back at Carter, cracking a smile, he said, "I guess we got the right one for the job."

"There's no doubt about it," said KorRak, also sporting a grin.

The nose of the spacecraft stuck out of the construction station before the doors were open all the way. RomMen was going to get every second he could out of the time they had left.

"Captain, docking bay doors open," said the communicator.

"Very well." The spacecraft was slowly picking up speed as it came through the opening and out into space.

"Captain, we're clear of the construction station," said the communicator.

"Very well," said RomMen. "Operations, energize reflector device. Helm, ahead 20% normal speed, bring her about by 180 degrees."

"Captain, reflector device energized." A few seconds later, an observer looking from the outside would see a vehicle the size of several football fields slowly disappearing from view.

"Captain," said operations, "I'm picking up two spacecraft on our sensors. They will arrive at the construction station in three minutes, sir."

"Understood," said RomMen, happier to escape this time than fight.

"Helm, make light speed," ordered the Captain. "Head into open space, until we come up with a destination." They could feel a slight forward thrust as the spacecraft increased speed.

"Captain," said Lo'Gon, "You can't go to hyperspace until the energy level of the reflector device is at 75% or it will shut down the system and make you visible again. The power conversion factor is critical during that time period. It takes a few minutes to build up enough energy to heat the exterior mechanism. The reflector device utilizes an electronic holography system, but it has difficulty functioning during start up at absolute zero."

"Thank you Lo'Gon, I appreciate that bit of information."

A few minutes later, Wooz, the operations officer, said, "Captain, reflector device energy at 75% power. Holographics functioning normal."

Captain RomMen nodded, then picked up the mic and said, "Construction crew and warriors, this is Captain RomMen, we are now clear of the Tygerian threat, and are traveling at light speed into open space."

Then the cheering started as all on board were relieved to hear that the warriors from Calverone were free at last.

"Well, Shanza, we made it."

"Yes, we did." She smiled, giving him a kiss and a big hug.

CHAPTER 9

ADJUSTMENTS

Dovina was thinking about her father and going home. She certainly missed both. *How worried he must be,* she thought. Mortal combat in those horrible arenas could change anybody's character. It was as if she had finally grown up.

Was her father well? Had he succeeded in his efforts to form the new government? So many questions about home and no answers. She would go to Carter, ask him what was in store for them, and when they might get to Kaladon. Right now, the most important thing to her was going home and getting on with her life.

After everyone was assigned quarters and obtained some much needed rest, they decided it was time for a meeting. Input was needed from everyone in order to set goals, formulate plans for survival, and look to the future. They were free now and wanted to make the most of it.

★   ★   ★

An intermitting shrieking noise bellowed from the loud speakers. It was a call to battle stations on the Tygerian war cruisers as the construction station appeared on their monitors. "Signal on all channels. Open the docking bay doors or suffer the wrath of the Tygerian Empire,'" said Admiral MyrAak.

"No response, Admiral."

A gruff noise emitted and he said, "Weapons, fire one blaster cannon at each of those big doors," pointing a claw at the visual display.

All heard the faint sound of the blast, as the fireballs streaked through space. They hit the middle of both doors with an explosion that easily blew them off their tracks. The huge metal doors; smoldering from the heat, rapidly floated to the opposite end of the docking bay, slamming into the main platform, smashing walls behind it, shattering glass, and destroying everything in their path.

Hmm!, he thought. Quickly realizing the station was empty. *Strange, we didn't pick up any contacts on our approach.* "So where is the spacecraft?" he said out loud. "Send a message to Captain SenKez: 'Fire at will, destroy the construction station.' Captain RynGar, after completing our business here move on to Ra'Tor and contact me then; I'll be in my quarters." *Perhaps Ra'Tor will produce better results,* he thought, as he turned and stomped off the bridge.

In ten minutes the construction station was destroyed, with debris floating in space and falling out of orbit toward Ra'Tor. The menacing duo now turned their attention toward Ra'Tor. "Signal Captain SenKez to open fire on the settlement at once," ordered Admiral MyrAak. The two war cruisers started firing on the defenseless colony.

The first building they hit exploded with scattered debris floating back to the surface. It was the only warning that the inhabitants had of impending aggression. Small groups of people could be seen scurrying around on the surface, falling and gasping for air. The largest building housed the transporter and was located in the center of all the structures. It was the first one targeted for destruction.

A signal was sent from the surface of Ra'Tor pleading for mercy, but the Tygerians reply was only more destruction. In a short time all that remained on Ra'Tor were ruins. After MyrAak signaled Captain SenKez they headed for Na'Reen.

★   ★   ★

Carter decided to get up early and discuss their situation with Captain RomMen. He hoped KorRak and Jackson would be around, because their input was needed, too. They were flying blindly from the Tygerians with cargo aboard he didn't want, namely some of the construction engineers and company employees. Carter bungled his way to the bridge and found RomMen in command as usual. He looked up as Carter approached him and said, "well, how are you feeling now that you're free again?"

"To tell you the truth, Captain, I haven't felt this good in a long time. It doesn't stop here, you know. We have a lot of work to do and only a short time to accomplish it, my friend." He looked RomMen in the eye and offered his hand. He shook it eagerly and the cloud between them dissipated.

"I sure hope nobody catches us with our pants down, if you catch my meaning," said Captain RomMen cheerfully but with the seriousness of the situation still in his voice. He had learned many expressions during his time on Earth. "When do we get started? You're calling the shots. And, as far as I know, KorRak feels the same way."

"I don't know how the others feel about that. And what about Lo'Gon? I mean, after all, he designed and built this thing. In reality, he'd probably be considered its owner. Anyway, we're having a meeting in the crews' lounge. I think somebody is waking everyone to make sure we're all present. You all right here Captain, or do you want a relief to attend?"

"I'm fine right here. You can cast my vote in your favor, and brief me when it's over."

It was decision time again, for the hundredth time, and all were present. Shanza was standing by Carter and Dovina was nearby. Jackson was on one side of the room and KorRak on the other. Everyone was still armed. *Good,* Carter thought. Fellow warriors from the arena were scattered all around, watching everyone in case of trouble. There were a lot more people from the construction station than he had realized. He was sure they were wondering what was going to happen next, just like the rest of them.

Carter moved to the middle of the room with his arms raised. "Okay, quiet everybody, quiet please," he said. "I want to say a few words before we begin. Don't let these weapons intimidate any of you." He held up his pistol. "We all have a stake in this, and I want everyone to speak their minds here and now, before this meeting is over. All of you who volunteered to come along from the construction station have as much right to be heard as anyone. I'm sure this is new to all of us, but the Tygerians play like this all the time. For those who only came along to escape from the Tygerians, I want to say this: we can drop you off at the nearest friendly place and arrange for your return to Na'Reen. Lo'Gon, I'd like to hear from you first."

Lo'Gon stood and looked around the room. "I'm not sure where to begin," he said, with a serious look on his face. "I realize I built this vessel, but I think that's about as far as it goes. This is a difficult time for everyone and we have to make the right decisions, here and now. You'll forgive me if my thoughts are divided. My whole world was destroyed back on Ra'Tor and the same goes for many of you. And I never thought I'd be standing in a room, talking calmly with a Tygerian standing nearby holding a blaster. This certainly proves there's good in all races.

"Anyway," Lo'Gon continued, now looking at Carter, "I think you're amazing. Brash, too, but amazing. I almost envy you. You have all these aliens of various backgrounds from all over the galaxy standing here and looking to you for leadership. Blind obedience without fear, just respect. I must admit I feel very similar. When my company built this spacecraft, we had no customer in mind." He paused, quickly looking around for any reaction from the group, and seeing none, he continued. "I was certainly not going to sell it to the Tygerian Empire. I would have destroyed it first. My thoughts were to have something powerful enough to combat their destruction, as it seems force is the only thing they understand. Before they came along, we had peace in the Tarn and Na'Reen solar systems. And I don't mean to offend the Tygerians present."

"None taken, Lo'Gon. Go on," said KorRak.

"Carter, I would like to see you lead our group. Perhaps we can straighten out a few things in these solar systems as we travel through them. If it weren't for you and Captain RomMen we wouldn't have the luxury of standing here and having this discussion." After Lo'Gon was finished all in the room voiced their approval.

As Carter stood, he had goose bumps all over his body. Even though he didn't buy everything Lo'Gon said, it did make him feel good. "I thank all of you for your vote of confidence and I accept the position of leadership for this group. My first order is to designate RomMen as permanent captain of this spacecraft. I also need someone for record keeping and office work." Phi'Lik immediately got up and volunteered.

"Lo'Gon, I'll meet you on the bridge in about a half-hour. Dr. Zark, I'd like to speak to you in your office right after this meeting." He looked to his side and told Shanza he would meet with her and Dovina in the officers' lounge as soon as he could get free. There were some questions from a few in the group, some of which he couldn't answer, so he informed them he would get some answers as soon as possible and would respond privately.

Everyone seemed satisfied, so he went over to the interphone to call the bridge. "Bridge, Carter here."

"RomMen here, go ahead."

"I've been voted in by the majority as leader. I have officially appointed you as permanent captain of this spacecraft. You're to take orders only from me. Is that understood?"

"Yes, sir, Carter. Understood."

He hung up, and said, "we can go now, Doc." He followed him from the crews' lounge to the sickroom. *I'm glad he knows the way*, he thought.

"Now, what can I do for you," said Zark.

"I want to see if we're thinking the same way on a few things. It's in reference to job assignments for the prospective crew. First I need to ascertain their level of competency in order to qualify them for certain job assignments. Based partly on their medical history along with your recommendations. That means full anatomy, including me," he said.

"Yes, I understand," said Zark, softly, "I brought all the files of the warriors from the arena." He held up a small floppy disk. "Upon completion of the files on the newer aliens, I'll submit a report to you for review."

He's been in this position before. I almost feel a little ridiculous asking him, Carter thought.

"I'm a little excited about this sudden turn of events, and the fact that we're free again. Never thought we'd pull it off, I'm just elated, thanks to you."

"I understand," Carter said, pleasantly. "I'm just glad to see you so cheerful. Also, doctor, if you find any qualified medical assistants, hang on to them. Just let me know who they are, okay?"

"I will and thank you. Oh, one more thing before you leave. We have the capabilities to implant new and updated translators through minor surgery for every member of the crew."

"Excellent, doctor. Make it an option and see to it as time permits." Carter turned and left. "Permission to come on the bridge."

"Permission granted," was the immediate respond from RomMen.

He walked over to where RomMen and Lo'Gon were sitting. "How's it going, captain?" he asked.

"Well, so far, so good. But this group on the bridge needs a relief from their watch stations. Any suggestions on where we're going to get more qualified people?"

"That's exactly why I'm here. Dr. Zark is compiling medical histories for everyone on board. I hope we can assemble some sort of a crew out of the few we have. Captain Za'Dor could fill in for you off and on so you can get some rest."

"Do you have any suggestions, Lo'Gon?" Carter asked. "Are there any more from the construction station qualified for any of these watch stations?"

"I believe we can get a few more, but probably not a full watch section. Where I can help is determining what areas must be staffed and what we can temporarily do without. I can also cross-train some for similar duties," said Lo'Gon.

Jackson had been sitting by the helm observing his routine. He'd been there the better part of two hours. He had asked some questions and learned a lot. When he saw Carter arrive on the bridge, he got up and went to join him.

After they talked about the prospective crew, Jackson cut in saying, "I'd like to relieve Tarsh on the helm for a while. I think I know enough to handle it. That is, if it doesn't get too complicated. At least Tarsh will have a break to get some rest."

"I don't think we'll have a problem as long as the reflector device is energized. It's all right by me." He glanced over at Carter with an inquisitive look.

"Don't look at me, Captain. It's your command. If you're comfortable with it, do it."

Now he knew exactly where he stood with Carter, as far as the command and his own status was concerned. "I guess what we need most right now is time," RomMen said.

"Captain, since you and Lo'Gon are here, I think we should discuss where we're going."

"Oh, that's easy," Lo'Gon cut in, "Kaladon. It's in the Tarn solar system. We have to pick up 200 fighters that belong to us."

RomMen looked at Carter, and noticed an affirmative nod.

Huh, I guess that answers any questions I had about fighters on board,

Carter thought.

"Helm," said the captain. "Set course for Kaladon, lets get to hyperspace. Operations, check long range sensors, I want a clear path."

"Captain, long-range sensor check indicates all's clear ahead," said Wooz, the operations officer.

Jackson pushed a few odd-shaped white buttons with black symbols on them, turned a few switches and said, "Course set for Kaladon, transiting to hyperspace."

"Very well," replied the captain.

"How long to Kaladon, Captain?" said Carter.

"Helm, time to Kaladon?"

"Time to Kaladon, helm, aye," Jackson said, displaying an inquisitive look. Tarsh made another adjustment on the console and checked his indicators. Jackson nodded that he understood.

After Tarsh left, Captain RomMen stepped over to the helm. "You fit right in here. Were you in the military on Earth?"

"Yes, sir, I was an operations officer on what we called an aircraft carrier." He then gave him the time to Kaladon.

RomMen seemed pleased and went back to his captains' chair which Carter was standing next to. "Estimated time to Kaladon, 21 days, nine hours, 23 minutes, ah, Earth time."

"Earth time. Yeah, right, I wish."

Ronous was sitting at the communications station while monitoring space traffic when Carter approached him. "Ronous, I thought your expertise was in operations?"

"I'm sort of an everywhere officer," he answered, returning Carter's smile. "I'm qualified to handle any watch station on the bridge, including captain on a temporary basis. The only doubts I have about my knowledge would be weapons. Have you seen what we're carrying?"

"Interesting," Carter replied. "No, I haven't been to the weapons console yet."

He turned around and approached Lo'Gon. "Will you and the science staff meet me in the officers' lounge in a little while?"

"Sure will," said Lo'Gon.

Carter left the bridge and went looking for KorRak. He found him in the crews' lounge talking to the five members of security.

"KorRak, could I have a word with you? I'll be brief."

He excused himself from the others and they went to a corner table and sat down. "KorRak, how would you like to be chief of security of this vessel, on a permanent basis?"

"Whose orders do I take and who would I answer to?"

"You'll take orders from me or Captain RomMen, no one else. I just gave him complete authority over this spacecraft as captain, answering only to me."

"Sounds good to me. And, thanks." A smile appeared. It was difficult to observe a facial expression because of all the fur.

"From now on you'll be Lieutenant KorRak, chief of security. One more thing. We have an officer's quarters with a lounge on this vessel. That's where you will be staying from now on. Go grab yourself a stateroom without a name on the door and move in. I would also like you to familiarize yourself with every space and compartment on this vessel as soon as possible. Learn everything you can, paying particular attention to location. Anything you're suspicious of, see me, or RomMen. I'm really counting on you," he said.

"Not to worry, I won't let you down." He got up and left the lounge with the security detail. Those five were all he would have to work with for a while.

When Carter entered the officer's lounge Shanza and Dovina were waiting for him. "Is it really true that we're going to Kaladon?" said Dovina.

"Yes, it is."

"We heard the rumors but just couldn't believe they were true. Dovina's very happy she's going to be reunited with her father again. He probably thinks she's dead," said Shanza.

"We'll be there in about three weeks," said Carter. "Why don't each of you pick out a stateroom here and move in. Now, I'm afraid you'll have to excuse me, more things to attend to."

He went over to Lo'Gon and said, "Would you be the science officer? I know you were heavily involved in the construction, but I don't know what your technical knowledge is."

"I'll give it my best effort. I'm not up on military procedures, but between you and RomMen I'm sure you'll give me the guidance I need."

"I'd like you to set up a training program and teach the rest of us all you can about this spacecraft." he seemed happy to be asked. "And finally, I've saved the worst for last. Who's the weapons expert on this spacecraft? That's my next project."

"Well," Lo'Gon said with a slight frown. "I think we have a problem there. We don't really have a weapons expert on board. They all stayed behind on Ra'Tor."

"Well, at least we have plenty of help in engineering," said Carter.

"Yes, we certainly do," he answered, taking Carter's cue. Everyone in engineering came along. And believe me, they're all well-qualified. They work under a staffer named Ri'Zar. Have for almost a year."

★   ★   ★

"My Lord, we just received a message from Admiral MyrAak, and I'm afraid it isn't good."

"Well, let's have it, good or bad." He had a somber look on his face that came from years of leadership.

"The admiral reports that the new spacecraft wasn't at the construction station, but he found some stragglers on Ra'Tor. He has no way of telling if Carter and the escapees from the arena were among them."

"What did he do about it?" asked an anxious GorDon.

"It says here he completely destroyed the construction station and the small settlement on Ra'Tor."

"Good. It wasn't exactly what we planned but at least it wasn't a total waste of time. They won't be building any spacecraft on Ra'Tor for a long time." He was somewhat pleased by the news from the admiral. He looked at his regent and said, "Did the new spacecraft and supplies leave for the Tarn solar system yet?"

"Yes sir, my lord, a short while ago, and they should be there in a little less then a month. They're going to make the rendezvous and transfer on the back side of Syntok, one of Kaladons' moons."

After Regent BryQat left his office, Lord GorDon sat there thinking, as was his habit when circumstances changed. *Perhaps Carter is finally dead.*

Huh! I don't think so.

★　　★　　★

A knock on the door. "Yes?" said General Wydorf, as the door opened and Captain Critz stuck his head in.

"General Sizdroz to see you, sir."

"Send him in." The general appeared, his uniform perfect in spite of the hours he'd put in recently. "Come in, Sizdroz, come in," Wydorf said pleasantly to his colleague. "Have you found out anything more about Dovina?"

"I'm not sure if it involves the princess or not," replied Sizdroz, frowning. "I was on my way to the palace to see the emperor, and I thought you might want to join me."

"I'll get my coat." They chatted briefly on the way and in a few minutes they were in the palace waiting to see their boss.

"Well, my generals," said The emperor, cheerfully. "To what do I owe this visit?"

"Your highness, I have some news about the situation on Ra'Tor. We learned a little while ago their orbiting construction station was completely destroyed. The settlement on Ra'Tor was also targeted for destruction. Only the Tygerians could be this daring."

"This is the second incident we've heard about the Tygerians," said the emperor. "The aggression in the Tarn and Ta'Rae solar systems was caused by them, no question. But this, well, it's proof. This is open warfare." He paused, "I guess there's no hope for my daughter anymore, is there Sizdroz?"

"We can only keep hoping she's still alive and well, your highness."

★　　★　　★

Hmm!, that's an interesting bit of news, thought Ronous as he listened intently to incoming space traffic. "Captain, I just picked up a message a moment ago you might be interested in. It seems as though we'll have to deal with someone else for our fighters when we get to Kaladon." He handed him the message.

He read the message and said, "Phi'Lik, get this to Carter immediately. He's in the officer's lounge.

"Yes sir, Captain." He left the bridge, message in hand.

"Captain," said the operations officer. "I recommend a course change. Long-range sensors indicate an object will cross our path in a few minutes. Two points dar will make the necessary correction. Probably an asteroid, sir."

"Make the correction, when clear, return to course."

"Helm, aye." A moment later, "Captain, course corrections complete."

"Very well, helm."

A few minutes later they passed an asteroid. At 60 meters across, it would have splintered anything it struck. A few moments later they returned to their original course.

Carter returned to the lounge and saw Shanza and Dovina sitting at a table. He sat with them and talked awhile, figuring he needed a break from his vigorous schedule. A short while later he got up and called the bridge.

"Bridge, Ronous."

"Carter here, is Ordak there?"

"Yes, sir, he is."

"Good, have him come to the officers' lounge."

"Will do, Carter. Phi'Lik is already on his way. We just picked up a message from space traffic we thought you might be interested in."

"Understood, and thanks." He no sooner sat down than Phi'Lik walked in and handed him the message. He nodded a thank you and accepted the message.

As Phi'Lik turned to leave Ordak entered the lounge. He got up and they went to a more quiet table in a corner of the room. After their lengthy discussion Ordek got up and left.

Carter reviewed the report he had from Dr. Zark and after his interview, he decided that Ordek was not suited for the position of officer-in-charge of the weapons department. He then picked up the message from Phi'Lik and read it. "Hmm," he mumbled softly. Getting up he walked over to join the inseparable twosome sitting nearby. "Dovina, are you comfortable in your stateroom?"

"Yes, of course," she said, puzzled by his question.

"I can offer you better accommodations to fit your status. We have an area on this vessel for dignitaries. And if you prefer, you can occupy one of those suites." He paused, "Princes Dovina."

"What?" Shanza interrupted. "Why did you call her princess?"

"I just wanted you two to know that I'm honored to be the first to acknowledge the Princess Dovina Zordek of Kaladon." He was smiling from ear to ear.

"You're not joking, are you?" Dovina said, regaining her composure.

"No, I'm not. Gart Zordek, your father, is the new emperor of Kaladon. And he will have his missing daughter home soon." He handed her the message.

"Oh," she said, almost covering her face. A tear running down her cheek.

"Congratulations," he said, as he got up. "I'll leave you two alone for a while. I'll be on the bridge, if you need me."

Coming off the elevator and about ten feet away was a counter for a security guard to sit. Behind and below the counter was a control panel. It had a handrail making a 90 degree right turn onto the bridge. Just before the 90 degree turn was a metallic looking grid on the floor, clearly marked to indicate where the bridge area started. They could keep track of all personnel coming and going on the bridge for security reasons. There was a force field in the grid and an arched doorway above it to protect all personnel on the bridge in case of an emergency. The force field was controlled by security. At the time there weren't enough personnel to man the station.

"Permission to come on the bridge?" said Carter.

"Granted," RomMen replied.

"That is the routine I suggest we use for everyone coming on the bridge from now on, Captain."

"Agreed."

"We have a lot of training to do and not enough time to get it done. Lo'Gon said the support craft on those platforms are completely operational. Could you operate one of those?"

"Yes, I'm sure I can. Once you know the basics you can operate any vessel. Some spacecraft are arranged differently and perhaps some controls will be in different locations, but that's about all," said RomMen.

"How long would it take to learn how to operate one of those spacecraft out there?" Carter asked, pointing to the general location.

"That depends on the individual and their background. For you it might take a little longer because you're not familiar with most of our technology, and you should learn that first. But then again, you're not the average person, so you might have no trouble at all."

"We need four more captains and I'm not sure where we're going to get them. I have two in mind, but they're untested. The other two, I'm not sure about. Za'Dor or Li'Zit can run the spacesleds, but we have two carriers and two war cruisers to be manned. Geez, this thing is huge. Perhaps we can get some volunteers from Kaladon."

"Lets hope so," said RomMen.

Carter went over to where Lo'Gon was standing and said, "is there anyone on board who can make clothing? I'm getting tired of these arena uniforms."

"We do have apparel facilities on board. But no need to make them. We have a storeroom full of clothing. Maybe now we can get rid of that bad odor on the bridge," Lo'Gon replied, grinning. Carter had to laugh too.

★   ★   ★

"Your highness, Generals Wydorf and Sizdroz would like an audience with you," said Hoft.

The emperor nodded he heard him. When he got to his study they were already waiting. "Well, my generals, let's have it."

"We have just completed construction of our new electronic scanning device. We installed it in a strategically positioned satellite in a low orbit for optimum reception. Perhaps now we can catch this elusive spy in the act."

"What's the effective range?" asked the emperor.

"It'll cover about one fourth of the planet with excellent accuracy," General Sizdroz replied.

"Your highness, I have a message for General Sizdroz. He is wanted in his office right away," Hoft interrupted. Sizdroz excused himself and left the palace.

Arriving at his office, he immediately said, "Captain Critz, what's so important that you had to interrupt my meeting with the Emperor, and where is Captain Saroutt?"

"General, we've just picked up a signal from space. We can't tell where it's coming from but we do know where it's being received. Captain Saroutt had a vehicle accident, sir."

"Sorry to hear about Captain Saroutt's problem. Let's see if we can catch us a spy," said the General, smiling.

They left his office and went to the roof of the government building. The captain walked to the edge of the roof and pointed to a building off in the distance. "That roof over there." He referenced a few key objects near the roof he was looking at.

But there's nothing there. You must be mistaken."

"General, I agree there's nothing there, and I can't explain it until I investigate further. But allow me, sir. Since we know the instruments are correct, there can be only one conclusion: what we are looking for is not visible to us at this time. And I stress visible at this time."

"Hmm, point well taken, and you might be correct. There must be another possibility." Old generals enjoy new mysteries. He was giving this some serious thought.

"You don't suppose they could've installed an electronic holoshield, do you, general?"

"That certainly is a possibility. But I thought they were still in the experimental stages and not perfected yet."

"That's what I thought too, sir, but I don't have any other explanation at this time."

"What's in the building and who's the owner, Captain?"

"From memory, sir, the building has a few shops, an eatery, some rental dwellings on the upper floors." Critz flipped through his notepad for the rest. "It's operated by Marrok, a management enterprise, which is owned by, ah ... ," he paused to check further. "Tak Byrokk, sir."

"That's him," said Sizdroz, excited by the name. "He's our main suspect. Keep a surveillance on the building. I shall inform the emperor at once. Captain, while I'm gone I want you to make arrangements to get some photo equipment up here and cut the power to that building."

"Your highness, General Sizdroz is requesting another audience," said Hoft with a slight bow. It was the third time that day.

"Tell him I'll meet with him, as before."

When the emperor came into his study the general said, "Your highness, I'd like to arrest Tak Byrokk for treason."

"I presume you have some solid evidence."

"Yes, your highness," said Sizdroz, glowing with confidence. "I think we have everything we need to make the arrest. We must check out one more piece of evidence and then everything should fall into place. I think he's using some type of electronic holoshield to disguise the equipment on the roof of his building."

★   ★   ★

"Yes, may I help you?" said the woman behind the counter in the shop on the first floor.

"I'm from the utility company and I've come to investigate an electrical problem we think is in this building." The utility man went to the rear room of the building, and to his surprise, he also found an emergency generator connected to the electrical system of the building. He disabled the generator first and then disconnected the power distribution circuitry. It happened as they expected. Power to the whole building shut down, including the electronic holoshield. From the roof of the government building, military personnel photographed the elaborate array of equipment and components mounted on the roof of the building.

★   ★   ★

About mid morning of the next day Sizdroz and four armed security staff entered the Senate building with relentless strides through protesting staffers, then went directly into the Senate meeting room. The group was in session and its members were clearly startled by this rude interruption. The senate secretary raised his hand for quiet while leaders inquired about the disturbance. General Sizdroz walked up to Tak Byrokk and said, "Tak Byrokk, Secretary of the Senate, I arrest you for treason against the government of Kaladon."

Captain Critz loved to see a high official go down.

All looked in shock at General Sizdroz and Tak Byrokk. He stared at his accuser and said, "General, I demand you leave the senate building immediately. You have no authority here."

"You will come with us peacefully or I'll remove you by force." Sizdroz motioned to his security force. They surrounded him and placed restraining devices on his wrists, ankles and attached them to his waist. A senator stood up and demanded that the security detail leave the building. Soon another stood, and then another. One of the senators who stood up raised the common objection. "The emperor is going to hear about this immediately." For an instant all was quiet.

Then a voice from the back of the room. "The emperor already knows. And anyone interfering with security in the performance of their duty will also be arrested," said the emperor firmly. "The general has complete authority over any and all security matters, answering only to General Wydorf or me. If there were no evidence against Tak Byrokk, General Sizdroz and his security force would not be here making this arrest. I have seen the evidence myself." He pointed his finger at Tak Byrokk, raising his voice. "He is spying for the Tygerian Empire against the government of Kaladon. Neither I nor the people of this senate are above the law."

A security staffer attached a resistance chain to the restraining device Tak Byrokk had on his wrists and led him away. As they walked by the emperor, the two men exchanged glances. Gart said, "Why my friend? Why did you do this terrible thing?" The sorrow in his expression was evident.

"I'm not who you think I am, Gart, and you've never been my friend." To have hit the emperor with a club would not have hurt him as much as Tak Byrokk's statement did.

CHAPTER 10

DESTRUCTION

After two weeks en route to Kaladon, Carter was sitting in his lounge chair thinking about the progress the ship and crew had made. He was awestruck by the prospective destructive power at his fingertips. *Check that. Someone else's fingertips. I haven't a clue,* he thought. In a few minutes Lo'Gon, Ordak and Jackson would meet with him in the officers' lounge, which was fast becoming his favorite planning place.

Jackson and Ronous were spending numerous hours on the bridge, absorbing as much knowledge as possible about the operation of the spacecraft. Lo'gon and the engineers from Ra'Tor were conducting classes on various systems and components. These included structural integrity, compartments, and various holding tanks. Carter was trying to attend as many classes as time would allow. He was bouncing back and forth between the sickroom with Dr. Zark and the officers' lounge with everyone else he had to interview. But no matter how it stacked up, there just weren't enough hands.

Disgusted, he got up and left his stateroom. *This kind of thinking's going nowhere,* he thought. Shanza and Dovina were just finishing lunch in the officers' lounge when Carter arrived. Pouring a fruit drink of some kind, which he had long since given up asking what it was, he went over and sat down beside Shanza. "Well, we should be on Kaladon soon."

"Yes, I'm started to get anxious," Dovina said.

"A lot more than I am," Shanza cut in, happily. "But I'll be glad to get home too."

"Planning to stay on Kaladon when we arrive, or are you coming with us?" Shanza knew what he wanted her to say, just by his expression. The discussion had not come up before.

"I don't know yet. I thought I did. But now," pausing, "I'm not sure. I ... I'm just not sure what I'm going to do yet. I need more time to think about it. We've been through so much in the past six months. I have to be sure it's the right choice. It's a decision I'll have to live with the rest of my life."

"When you decide, I'd appreciate your letting me know," he said, staring into her beautiful eyes. "Your decision is very important to me." She glanced away momentarily then their eyes met again. Hers were teary now. She squeezed his arm, got up, kissed him on the cheek and then walked briskly to her room.

"I'll see you later." Dovina got up and followed her.

Carter was sitting at a table when Lo'Gon entered and sat down across from him. "What's on your mind, Carter?" he asked.

"How've things been going for you the last few weeks? Have you given the job offer we talked about much thought?" He noticed that Lo'Gon didn't appear to be his usual grumpy self.

"As a matter of fact I have, Carter. I think I'd make a good science officer." He allowed himself a smile.

Standing up, Carter said, "I'm glad you're going to accept my offer, because we can use your knowledge of this spacecraft on the bridge, Lieutenant. No hard feelings about our introduction, I hope." Lo'Gon didn't answer as he turned and left.

Jackson walked in just as Lo'Gon was leaving. "As I walk throughout this vessel I see happiness and pleasant people abound. You never realize just how good freedom is until ya lose it. I've been spending most of my time on the bridge, trying to increase my knowledge of this spacecraft, especially the operations on the bridge. I never knew there would be this much to learn," he said with eagerness in his voice.

"I'm glad you're working hard to acquire the knowledge you'll need, because I have something to discuss with you."

"Okay, what's up? And whatta ya mean I'll need?"

"You had a lot of carrier experience, didn't you?"

"Yes, sir, I spent six years on a carrier in the Atlantic. The last two as operations officer."

"Anyway, the reason I asked you to meet me here is to offer you a job."

"Oh yeah? Wha'cha got in mind?" he paused, then quickly said, "sir."

Taken by the man's loyalty, Carter grinned and said, "how'd you like to be the captain on one of those carriers sitting out there on the platforms?"

His face suddenly turned very serious.

He hesitated, perhaps in shock. Then his grin faded as he sobered up. "You're serious, aren't you?"

"I have never been more serious," said Carter. "I believe you can handle the job or I wouldn't be asking you. Lo'Gon and RomMen will help you all they can. We have an excellent training facility in the CCC; you'll be trained by the best."

"Yes, of course, I accept. I have an awful lot to learn. But as you said yourself, we have the best training facilities right here on this spacecraft."

"Good, then it's settled. From now on you'll be Captain Morris Jackson."

"That's why you're having me learn as much as possible about this spacecraft, isn't it?"

"You'll do just fine, Captain." Carter got up and went over to the interphone. "Bridge, Carter here. Could you send Ronous to the officers lounge when Jackson gets there?"

"Will do, Carter," said RomMen.

Ordak came in just as Carter sat down. Jackson having left a very happy person. Yet after his second interview with Ordak, Carter was not so pleased, but his choices were somewhat limited.

A few minutes later Ronous walked in. "Say, you know Jackson was really happy about something. I've never seen him this way before."

"Perhaps it was something I did or said to him during our conversation," said Carter.

"What can I do for you, sir?" said Ronous.

"I've been observing you ever since our escape. I'm very impressed with your attitude and your apparent knowledge of this spacecraft. We're on our way to Kaladon and we'll be there soon. I was curious as to your intentions upon arrival."

"I'd like to stay on board and be a permanent part of the crew if possible. There's so much to learn. This is really a challenge. I've been assigned to every thing that flies in the military, even commanded some, but this, it's an incredible feat of engineering," he said, raising his eyebrows as he glanced at his surroundings. "I wasn't doing much of anything on Kaladon anyway. The military sent me to Krynta in an advisory capacity. I was hitching a ride back to Kaladon when the Tygerians hit the padport. That's how I got to Harzzton."

"I was talking to RomMen the other day and he spoke very highly of you. I guess what I'm trying to say is, I need a captain for one of those carriers sitting out there on the platforms. Would you like to give it a try?" Carter watched him carefully to observe his reaction. He was looking for a positive sign and getting one.

Ronous seemed to be speechless for a moment and then answered, "Yes, of course, sir. I certainly would like to be one of your captains. I'll have to thank the Captain for speaking up for me. And I want you to know, you can count on me, sir."

"I'm sure you're aware that we have a shortage of crew members. Perhaps when we get to Kaladon you might help us do some recruiting."

"Yes sir, I just might know a few we could use." Now he was beaming with confidence.

"From now on you'll be Captain Ronous. You'll take orders from Captain RomMen or me." Getting up, Carter said, "come on, Captain. Walk with me to the bridge. By the way, Jackson is the captain for the other carrier and he's going to need some help."

"I'll help him all I can, sir," he cut in before Carter could finish.

"Permission to come on the bridge," Carter said.

"Permission granted," said RomMen.

"Captain, I think we're finally starting to get a crew together. Ronous and Morris will command the carriers. Za'Dor and Li'Zit will run the spacesleds. Lieut. Lo'Gon accepted the job of science officer, Lieut. Wooz will be operations, and Lieut. Tarsh will head up navigation. We already know Ri'Zar is the engineer and I still haven't been to engineering yet. We don't have anyone to command the war cruisers." He gestured with his thumb toward the outside of the craft. Do you approve of these appointments, Captain?"

"We already had lengthy discussions about most of them. And I must say the rest seem very appropriate. I think with the proper training they'll do well." RomMen shook his head, then said, "It's still not enough. We need more crew members."

"We also need a name for this spacecraft, got any ideas?"

"Nothing right now, how about you?" said RomMen.

"Yeah, how about *Star Wolf*."

"Huh ... what's a wolf?" he asked.

After Carter explained what a wolf was, RomMen remembered something about them during his stay on Earth. Although most of what he saw were coyotes, he still thought it might be a good name at that. So *Star Wolf*, it was.

Before arriving at Kaladon they sent a message about the fighters. Carter finally met Ri'Zar and was very impressed by the engineering spaces. The crew trained hard and everyone was exhausted. All were looking forward to a break. Some knew why they were pushing so hard. Others only knew they were running from the wrath of the Tygerians. That was enough. The crew didn't realize they had to load fighters as soon as possible and head out into space to train even more. To get the semblance of a qualified crew out of what they started with would be just short of a miracle.

"Lieut. Wooz, scan ahead for coming out of hyperspace, energize shields," said the captain.

All was clear ahead as the *Star Wolf* came out of hyperspace and slowed to 10 percent speed. Everyone on the bridge was watching as they approached. During the speed changes Shanza came on the bridge while Princess Dovina prepared for her return to Kaladon.

"Lieut. Tarsh, initiate normal orbit of Kaladon."

"Lieut. Wooz, de-energize the reflector device."

In a few moments a normal orbit was achieved and they set the orbiting watch stations. This situation left the operations station, communications, and security stations manned with one qualified captain on the bridge.

"Communicator, contact launch control, prepare a spacesled for a flight to Kaladon." Launch control acknowledged and in a short time a sled was standing ready for a spaceflight.

"Captain, are you clear on the orders while I'm gone?"

"Yes sir, perfectly."

"I'll contact you if we have a problem." Carter turned and left the bridge.

"We get to wear our new uniforms to visit the emperor," said Carter, smiling, as they were getting on the elevator.

"It sure felt good to get out of those arena clothes," said KorRak. "They were starting to smell pretty bad. I disintegrated mine."

The new uniforms were mostly dark blue, highlighted with black and silver. Carter had his sword, pistol belt, and a knee length cape. The landing party arrived at the launch station and boarded immediately. The side door closed and in a few minutes they were on their way to Ozlonz.

Dovina, Shanza, Ronous, Phi'Lik, KorRak, and Carter were making the trip, along with two members of their security detail. They didn't expect any trouble, but they brought their weapons anyway.

* * *

"Your Highness, we have some visitors arriving at the palace very soon," said Hoft. "We have no idea who they are, but the request for an audience came from someone named Carter."

"Hoft, get General Sizdroz and General Wydorf here right away," said His Highness. "Do you know how many there are?"

"Yes, there are eight of them, Your highness."

In a few minutes the two generals arrived and Sizdroz asked, "who are these people?"

"I'm not sure who they are, General," His Highness replied. "Hoft said the request came from someone named Carter."

"Carter." he said, a little shocked at hearing his name.

That caught the emperor's attention. "General, do you know this person named Carter?" Sizdroz just stood there, deep in thought.

"Sizdroz," the emperor repeated, a little louder this time.

"What? Oh, ah, no sir. I don't know him, but I've heard about him. His name came up more than a few times from our agents on Calverone during our inquiries about Dovina. He's the one who led the escape from Calverone and allegedly made off with that new spacecraft from Ra'Tor."

"He apparently gets things done, doesn't he?" said Wydorf.

"Perhaps he knows where Dovina is," Gart replied.

* * *

The two security guards that met them in the foyer were shocked to see an armed six-foot Tygerian coming into the palace. He was hard to miss. They were led to the steps in front of the emperor without being asked to disarm. During the approach the indoor security force also saw KorRak. This group was not as diplomatic. Two of them started to converge on the small band, weapons ready. It was not every day they saw a Tygerian, blaster in hand, coming into the palace. The emperor put his hand up for the guards to stop their approach.

"Your Highness," Carter said, making direct eye contact with him. "My name is Carter." He bowed before him. "I have the distinct honor of being the first to introduce the Princess Dovina Zordek of Kaladon." He motioned with his arm toward their small group. There was a hush over the crowd that had followed them inside. Carter's group moved aside to let the emperor's daughter walk slowly toward her father. She was teary-eyed, for this was one of the happiest days of her life. She wore a beautiful flowing gown, befitting a princess. A seamstress on board *Star Wolf* had made it for this special occasion.

The emperor, never much on formality walked toward her with open arms. They embraced. She could not hold back her tears of joy that came from a reunion neither had ever expected. In a few minutes the emperor turned to Carter, saying, "How can I ever thank you for returning my daughter safely to me? Come, let's move from these formal surroundings." They went to a smaller room and he turned to Hoft. "Some refreshments, please."

General Sizdroz still had the same shocked look on his face. Seeing this, Carter said, "Do not be concerned. You have nothing to fear from us."

"I'm General Sizdroz, in charge of security on Kaladon. I wasn't afraid, but I certainly am shocked. I didn't realize Tygerians ever got this tall." He nodded in pleasant recognition. "He's the only Tygerian I've ever gotten this close to. But I thought the whole race was much shorter."

KorRak nodded recognition in return and chuckled to himself.

"Perhaps you two have more in common than you may think, General. KorRak here is chief of security on the *Star Wolf*."

"So that's what you named the spacecraft you absconded from Ra'Tor," said a smiling general.

"General, who's in charge of the Esterk Province?"

"Lord Nemarg. Why do you ask?"

"They have 200 fighters that belong to us and we've come to pick them up. I'm sure Captain Jackson and Captain Ronous can make the necessary arrangements for delivery."

While the two captains went with Captain Critz, KorRak, the two generals and Carter went to join the others. When they entered the room he noticed two empty places next to Shanza. They joined her as the generals went to sit next to their emperor.

"I want to go with you," she said softly, as he sat down beside her. "That is, if you still want me to."

"Of course I do." Carter was pleased that she had finally made a decision. "I love you very much." She responded that she loved him too, then giggled a little.

The next morning Carter called *Star Wolf* to check in with RomMen. "I've heard from our captains, Carter. They have plenty of volunteers to fly the fighters up to *Star Wolf*. But in order to load the carriers, they have to be launched."

"Do you have enough personnel for that?"

"Yes, sir. Captain Za'Dor will relieve me on the bridge and I can launch one carrier at a time and proceed with the loading." "Very good, Captain. We'll be leaving for *Star Wolf* later this afternoon. Carter out."

It didn't take long to load the fighters and even with landing beam technology they still had problems. Six fighters were damaged during the loading process, a small price to pay for inexperience.

Dovina and Shanza were saying their farewells on the padport at one of the military bases in Ozlonz. "I'm going to miss you," said Shanza, now teary-eyed herself. "We've sure been through a lot together this past year, haven't we?"

"Yes, we have."

"They're ready to go. Come and visit soon."

"Every chance I can." Choking back a few more tears, Shanza turned and boarded the spacesled.

Carter noticed this spacesled was full and saw two others had already left for the *Star Wolf*. Perhaps Captain Ronous was responsible for this.

"*Star Wolf,* spacesled five, request permission to board," Carter said.

"Hold up, spacesled five, we're still clearing a busted landing beam from the alignment track. Switching to auxiliary control." A few minutes later, he could see the rear door open and the blue landing beams come on. "Spacesled five, launch control, okay to board."

After acknowledging Carter could hear the other spacesleds request permission to board as well. After all the spacesleds landed the large door came down to hermetically seal the room. In a few minutes the atmosphere normalized and the people exited the spacesleds.

"That was a very respectable landing for your first time, Carter. You can certainly operate a spacesled."

"Thank you for the compliment, Captain Za'Dor," pleased he wasn't holding a grudge.

"Permission to come on the Bridge," said Carter.

"Permission granted," said RomMen.

"Captain, let's get out of here, I think we've been exposed long enough."

"I certainly agree with that. Energize shields, secure from standard orbit, make 20% normal speed and head for open space," ordered Captain RomMen.

"Shields energized."

"Secured from standard orbit, making 20% normal speed, heading into open space."

"Very well, on all reports."

"Lieut. Lo'Gon, do you know a good place to conduct weapons testing without interruption?"

"Hmm! Perhaps Minto, moon of Moldarva. It should be quiet there, because it's not inhabited."

"Sounds good to me," said RomMen.

"Then let's do it," Carter said, figuring he'd finally get to see the firepower this craft was capable of delivering. "When you're ready for weapons testing, call me, I'll be in my quarters."

"Yes, sir." said RomMen. He turned toward Tarsh, "Set course for Minto, 80% normal speed."

"Course set for Minto, 80% normal speed," replied Tarsh.

"Very well."

When he arrived at his quarters he thought he would relax until they called him. The beautiful Shanza was sleeping in the other room. He couldn't ask for a more wonderful woman. When Kaladonians choose a mate, it was for life. They had a small ritual before they left.

He removed his clothes and laid down beside her on the bed. She moaned a little at his sensitive touch and turned over to face him. A smile appeared and her eyes opened slightly as she put her arms around him and gave him a passionate kiss.

★   ★   ★

A while later the inter phone buzzed. "Carter here."

"We'll be ready for weapons testing in about ten minutes, sir," said RomMen.

"Thank you, Captain. I'm on my way." Time for a reality check. He thought there for a while he was in heaven. She always made him feel that way when they were alone.

Nobody carries their weapons anymore, but most of them still kept in practice. It was probably something they'd never get over. The crew was starting to knit, and Carter was glad to see it. They had to rely on each other for survival. All the construction people and anyone else that wanted to stay behind, they left on Kaladon. Each had to make their own decision.

"Permission to come on the bridge," said Carter.

"Granted," replied security.

"I hope you slept well, Carter. Nobody's heard from you in a while," said RomMen.

"I guess I slept most of the time I was in my stateroom. I really needed the time to myself. Haven't been able to relax much lately."

"During your absence we conducted take-off and landing drills for the carriers and fighters and it went extremely well. Captain Ronous worked overtime in his recruiting effort. Most of the people from Kaladon had previous military training and were eager to join us. We can now man 80 fighters with trained pilots. They were all assigned to the carriers which made them completely operational with full crews except for warriors.

"I guess you noticed another change here on the bridge. I felt security should handle the movement of personnel going on and off the bridge.

"Four of the six fighters damaged during initial loading have been fixed. The other two will have to wait until our return to Kaladon. We have nine females and five males who want to train for watch stations here on the bridge. My only concern remains in weapons proficiency. That concludes my report, sir."

"Very good, Captain. I congratulate you on all you have accomplished. And I agree, security can handle that assignment. When we get to Minto, perhaps we can test the weapons systems on *Star Wolf* first, and give the crews on the carriers some rest."

"Agreed," said RomMen.

"Captain, how long has it been since you rested?"

"It's been a while, sir."

"I know how important weapons testing is to you, so perhaps I could relieve you. Captain Ronous is here in case I need help. Carznot has operations, so that leaves you free for now. You could get some rest and we can train here on the bridge for a while. If anything comes up, I'll be sure to summon you."

"Sounds good to me. Security, Carter has the bridge."

★   ★   ★

During the next eight hours they conducted station training and he interviewed others for specific jobs. Shanza came to the bridge shortly after RomMen left. She took the helm. *Amazing woman, she is,* he thought.

After extensive discussions and recommendations from Captain RomMen and Captain Ronous on an earlier day, they both agreed on a choice for captain of one of the war cruisers. Carter went over to the communications console and said, "Carznot, I think you should consider being a war cruiser captain."

"I was hoping you'd ask me, sir. It's been a dream of mine since I was young. I've always wanted to command a war cruiser. Thank you for giving me this opportunity."

"Captain Ronous, that person you told me about before, the one who's an authority on weapons systems?"

"Yes sir, she's in the officers lounge."

"Have her come to the bridge. RomMen is due to return soon and I want her here when he arrives."

"Yes sir," said Ronous.

In about an hour, RomMen came out of his quarters and gave a greeting to those few by the captain's chair.

"Security, RomMen has the bridge." Seeing an affirmative nod Carter got up from the captains chair and Ronous stepped forward with his guest.

"Carter, Captain RomMen, this is Myena Zyene, weapons expert from the science department on Kaladon. Myena, Captain RomMen, commander of *Star Wolf* and Carter, our leader."

She was a petite woman, about five feet tall. It was obvious she was a Kaladonian, even before the introduction. She reminded him a little of Shanza, in her complexion, but about four inches shorter. *I hope her intelligence makes up for her size,* he thought, chuckling to himself.

Ronous turned to Captain RomMen. "Shall we proceed?" They walked over to the weapons station where she sat down.

She hesitated, scanned the console, and then said, "This is the most advanced weapons systems I have ever seen." She flipped a few switches, adjusted some knobs and depressed a button or two. A variety of touch pads began to illuminate and small square white lights with black symbols etched on them came on. About 15 seconds later she looked at Captain RomMen and said, "weapons batteries are fully loaded, all systems positioned and appear normal. Weapons ready for testing, sir."

Lo'Gon watched her, then said, "Captain, the information she relayed is correct. The computer says so. I'm impressed." He turned to Carter, smiling. "Before the weapons crew left they said everything was fully loaded and operationally ready."

"Operations, what's the power level of the shields?"

"Shields at 100%, captain."

"Very well, Lieut.," said the captain.

"You don't need the shields energized for weapons testing, captain," Lo'Gon said softly. "Computer says it's not necessary. Well, suit yourself."

After the second remark, Captain RomMen looked at Lo'Gon with a firm cold stare and said, "I killed the last person that tried to disrupt my authority. Do you want to be next?"

Lo'Gon was visibly shaken by RomMen's words. It was written all over his face. And anybody on the bridge that heard what he said knew without a doubt who was captain of the Star Wolf.

The captain looked back at the monitor above the console, completely calm, and said, "See that cluster of boulders on the moon's surface in the middle of your monitor?" He pointed at the screen. "Fire the left forward battery when I give the order."

"Aye, Captain," said weapons.

"Fire." Zyene touched the diagram on the left side of the console that looked like a cannon protruding flame. The low noise of the weapons firing could be heard. Two streaks of concentrated flame lit up the darkness. Almost instantly there was a fiery blast on the surface of the moon and a few minutes later the dust settled. There was a large hole about 70 meters across and 25 to 30 meters deep.

Carter was amazed at the size of the hole on the surface of the moon. Sure they had nukes on Earth, but no gun that could fire with that kind of destruction. He wondered what else this spacecraft had that they don't know about. Nobody said anything; they just stared at the monitor showing the moon's surface.

In a few hours the weapons testing was complete. Both carriers and war cruisers were launched in order to complete their weapons testing and everything went well. The war cruisers weapons weren't as powerful as the carriers and Star Wolf's, but according to Captain RomMen they were the most powerful weapons he had ever seen on a war cruiser.

"Carter, excuse me, sir," Carznot cut in. "We're receiving a message on space traffic from Princess Dovina, sir." He quickly handed the message to Carter. "Message is as follows: Under heavy attack from space. Ozlonz sustaining severe damage. Please help."

He turned around, and on his way back to where RomMen was standing he said, "Captain, get us to Kaladon as quickly as possible." When he was close enough, he handed him the message.

"Set course for Kaladon, scan the area en route, if clear, get to lightspeed."

"Long range scanners indicate path is clear. Increasing to light speed, Captain."

"Lieutenant Tarsh, time to Kaladon?"

"The orbital position is to our advantage. Time to Kaladon is 56 minutes, sir." The distance to Kaladon was too close to travel in hyperspace. They'd never be able to stop in time and would overshoot the planet.

★　　★　　★

Forty fighters headed skyward from the Esterk Province to engage the enemy, all recognizing they were Tygerian spacecraft. They didn't have much of a chance, but they were valiant in their effort. They did some damage to two of the war cruisers, but it was minimal.

Menk Frokst was yelling for the evacuation of the Senate building as he heard explosions going off all around them. One hit the senate building as Frokst had expected; he was knocked to the floor and was partially buried in rubble. He looked to the other end of the building and could see bodies everywhere. *Must have been a direct hit,* he thought. *Hopefully some had escaped.*

General Wydorf was with the emperor as they ran for the rear of the palace to get to a shelter. All communications were cut off. Before they got to a rear door an explosion went off in front of them, killing both almost instantly. A few moments later the palace lay in ruin. The emperor's last thoughts were of his daughter.

General Wydorf had tried to communicate with the military base commander before he died, but he was cut off as he heard explosions coming over the speakers. Tak Byrokk escaped during the siege and was on the roof of his building in downtown Ozlonz cheering as he watched the destruction of Ozlonz. Then there was an explosion near him and he fell, tumbling over and over down into the midst of building rubble. During the transition to semi-consciousness before his death, Tak's thoughts drifted back to his earlier years on Kaladon.

Ozlonz was being obliterated, and it wasn't letting up. The palace was gone. The Senate building nearby was leveled and a good portion of the city was destroyed with it. Their defense wasn't very effective because of its shortage of spacecraft. All the forces of Ozlonz could do was stay under cover and wait for it to stop. They had a few blaster cannons, but they were destroyed soon after the first shot was fired. That one blast might've struck a spacecraft, but nobody could be sure. Kaladon was not very well prepared for this type of attack. It was a one-sided battle from the beginning.

★   ★   ★

"Admiral LanDok," the captain said. "Captain MatKon is signaling you."

"On screen," said the Captain.

"Admiral, a good part of the city is destroyed including the palace. Their military facilities are useless against us. We have destroyed all but about 12 of their fighters. If we had our full invasion force with us, Kaladon would be ours."

"Very good, Captain MatKon. I agree, but it's not."

"Admiral, we've been at this for almost an hour. Shall we continue or direct our attack at another target?"

"Shift position, Captain, and move the battle cruiser to the Esterk Province. Concentrate your efforts on destroying their science and manufacturing facilities, including the military bases as well. This will eliminate their capability to rebuild before we return to conquer the planet. Two war cruisers will accompany you."

Captain MatKon left his shields de-energized while he moved his craft toward Plaxar. There wasn't any threat in the vicinity to make him think otherwise. Kaladon's defenses were eliminated and he was protected by the war cruisers.

★   ★   ★

"Lord Nemarg," said General Engort, "our sensors indicate three Tygerian spacecraft moving in our direction. We'd better seek shelter in the emergency command center under the palace."

"You're correct, general, this way please," said Lord Nemarg as he gestured for all to follow.

Three fighters were flying toward the bottom of a Tygerian war cruiser.

They all fired at the same location. Captain Centarkoh and his two friends were determined to inflict more than minor damage. The captain thought it might work because the underside of a war cruiser was the most vulnerable part. Just before impact they veered off in three different directions in a circular flight to return to the surface of the planet. If this didn't work there was nothing more they could do.

The small war cruiser became engulfed with electrical arcs that encircled the vessel, as it began tumbling toward the planet. "Captain, we're having electrical problems throughout the vessel," said the operations officer, with fear in his voice. "Main engine control has failed."

"Captain, we have an emergency," said the engineer on the war cruiser, now showing deep concern. Suddenly it exploded.

Another war cruiser fired on the three fighters before they could get out of range. Captain Centarkoh opened a channel the enemy used and said, "That was for my brother."

Before they could get out of range one of the fighters erupted in flames as it entered the atmosphere.

Captain Centarkoh's flight took him over Ozlonz, and what he saw sickened him. He turned toward the padport in the Esterk province and saw a brilliant flash of light in space. There was a huge fireball where the Tygerian battle cruiser had been. A few seconds later nothing remained.

CHAPTER 11

STOP A KILLER

"Helm, make 50% normal speed," ordered Captain RomMen as they approached Kaladon.

After coming out of light speed the navigator reduced to 50% normal speed and reported, "Making 50% normal speed, Captain."

"Very well," said RomMen. "Perhaps they'll be preoccupied on our arrival. Let's get to battle stations."

Lieut. Wooz re-positioned a switch on his panel, BONG, BONG, BONG, BATTLE STATIONS, BONG, BONG, BONG, ALL PERSONNEL TO YOUR BATTLE STATIONS, the voice computer sounded. It could be heard throughout the vessel. Since the carriers were now fully operational, battle stations were meant for them as well.

"Captain, *Raven* and *Vandor* reported, battle stations ready," said Carznot. *Raven* was the call name of the carrier under the command of Captain Jackson. *Vandor*, the name of a very large bird native to Kaladon, was commanded by Captain Ronous.

"Captain, all departments reported battle station ready. Shields energized, reflector device operational, holographics normal," said Lieut. Wooz.

"Very well."

This, being my first opportunity to observe Captain RomMen using his skills at battle, should be interesting, Carter mused.

"Weapons, locate the largest target and prepare to fire forward batteries. Do not, I repeat, do not lock weapons. All stop," ordered the captain. They used reverse thrusters to slow the vessel and adjust their position. Everyone was tense.

That thing's a killer, we have to stop it, he thought. He waited a moment, then, "Weapons, lock on target."

"Target locked," said Lieut. Zyene. The Tygerian battle cruiser was on their visual.

★   ★   ★

"Captain, someone has locked their weapons on us."

"What?" he said excitedly, as his head snapped around. "That's impossible. Scan it's origin."

"There's nothing there, Captain."

"Energize shields, contact the admiral at once."

"Admiral, message coming in from the battle cruiser." He's energizing his shields," said Captain VirQex.

★   ★   ★

"We're in range, Captain," said the weapons officer.

"Fire," barked RomMen. She depressed the firing button on her console and a near instant display of 20 feet of concentrated flame broke the vacuum of space. These traveling fireballs hit the battle cruiser dead center. The vessel exploded, leaving debris drifting in space and burning up as it fell into Kaladon's atmosphere.

"Captain," Carter cut in softly. "I don't think we should fire again. They're obviously not sure what has happened and I don't think we're quite ready for a battle such as this might be. We both know that the battle cruisers' shields weren't energized and there are still five war cruisers close by. They're probably aware there's another spacecraft in the area, possibly with a reflector device, so they'll be looking for our cannon flashes this time for sure. A mistake now could be enormous. Perhaps we can fight another day, when we're better trained." All this was in measured tones so that the more war-like RomMen would reason.

RomMen looked at Carter with a thoughtful stare. Taken with his words a grin slowly appeared. "I think you're absolutely correct. The aggression has stopped and yes, there is confusion. Agreed," he said, "we'll just observe them for a while."

★   ★   ★

The shock wave shook the two Tygerian war cruisers in the immediate vicinity. "Admiral LanDok, it's gone," yelled Captain VirQex, excitedly. "There's no visual." Admiral LanDok could grasp the severity of this situation by the tone in his captain's voice. "The message said they were energizing their shields and then it exploded. There wasn't any indication of a malfunction, nothing," continued VirQex, excitedly. "It just exploded."

"I agree with what you say," replied the confused admiral. "Get it together, Captain, now. Signal all war cruisers, scan the entire area. I want an immediate report."

A few moments later all the Tygerian war cruisers reported in. "Admiral, no contacts observed anywhere, said the captain.

"All spacecraft make light speed," ordered the admiral. Now also visibly shaken. "Rendezvous at the predetermined location. In a short time all the Tygerian vessels disappeared.

★　　★　　★

"General Engort," said Captain Centarkoh. "This is flight captain Centarkoh."

"Captain Centarkoh, General Engort here."

"It's gone, General," the captain cut in, a little out of character.

"Explain, Captain. What's gone?"

"The Tygerian battle cruiser, General. It just exploded; it's like thousands of flares falling from orbit. There's nothing left but debris, it just exploded inexplicably."

★　　★　　★

The crew on the bridge of *Star Wolf* jumped for joy and let loose an uncharacteristic cheer. They had sent the great Tygerian fleet running scared with a single shot.

"Navigator, status of the Tygerian fleet."

"They're in hyperspace, Captain and fading from our long-range sensors," replied the navigator.

"Let me know when they're out of range. I want to be certain they don't double back while the shadow device is de-energized and surprise us."

★   ★   ★

General Sizdroz and a small group of military personnel were visiting the leaders of the Esterk Province in Plaxar with Princes Dovina tagging along. When the attack was over they came out of the palace and Dovina said, "What's happening, General?" General Sizdroz nodded, indicating the same question.

"Captain Centarkoh reports that the Tygerian battle cruiser has exploded. The Tygerians have withdrawn, Your Highness," said General Engort. "They've disappeared in hyperspace."

"It's Carter," said Dovina happily. "I knew he'd come."

"I beg your pardon, Princess, but our sensors aren't indicating any spacecraft in the entire area," said General Engort. They walked out of the palace and looked up, seeing a bright clear sunny sky.

"They have a reflector device, General." She said, grinning. "What do you call those?" She pointed with her out-stretched arm at the activity that just became visible in space. "Is that another attack?" A hint of pessimism was in her tone. High above they saw five fighter groups in formation.

"General," interrupted Captain Moratz as he came running out of the palace. "You won't believe this, sir, but a very large spacecraft became visible and immediately thereafter, the skies were full of K-1 fighters." He stopped long enough to catch his breath. "We also picked up a space sled that's going to land somewhere in Ozlonz." He paused. "It must be Carter, sir."

Shortly after the survivors saw the fighters, they watched a transport sled land near the palace. Its purpose was to take Princess Dovina and her group to Ozlonz. "Oh no!" she said. "In the excitement I completely forgot about my Father. Please, get me to the palace as soon as possible." A new sick feeling replaced the worry she'd felt for her own safety.

★   ★   ★

The spacesled from *Star Wolf* landed in front of what had been a beautiful palace. Emperor Zordek, General Wydorf, Captain Saroutt, the entire senate and thousands of others had died.

KorRak and the others exited the spacesled, spread out, and started looking around. Zark and his limited medical staff lent immediate assistance. Before landing, they knew all about the damage Ozlonz had sustained. Fighter reconnaissance had given them a full accounting.

Captain Critz was approaching KorRak, unable to hide his feelings. Carter saw this and decided to move closer. "Captain, there's been enough killing for one day, don't you think? I'd hate to see you added to the statistics as well." Captain Critz looked at Carter, and then KorRak. Abruptly, he turned sharply and left.

Medical personnel were loading bodies into vehicles and taking them to a medical facility, or what was left of it, for treatment or burial.

KorRak looked up when he heard a small shuttle approach. It circled and then landed. As soon as the skids made contact, princess Dovina stepped out. Shanza ran to stop her from going into the palace debris. "Dovina, it's too late." She grabbed her and pulled her aside.

"My father," she cried, fearing the worst.

"I'm sorry, sis." At times like this Dovina needed a closeness to someone, and they were truly like sisters.

"No, not my father," she cried, unable to hold back the tears. "It can't be, not that."

Another shuttle landed in front of the palace rubble near the other two. Lord Nemarg stepped out and approached the princess. He offered his sincere condolences and the use of his palace until hers could be rebuilt.

In about a half hour Dovina regained her composure and started taking charge. She began acting like a princess again. "I want to talk with Carter," she said to General Sizdroz.

"Your Highness," said Carter, as Princess Dovina and General Sizdroz approached. He bowed, not sure what else to do.

"Carter, what are you going to do about this?" She gestured with her arm toward the palace and the immediate part of the city that lay in ruin behind it.

Cautiously, he asked softly, "What do you want me to do?"

"I know what I want you to do. But I don't think I have the right to ask. Right now all I can think of is revenge for the death of my father and all these people. However, it's impulsive and may not be the wisest choice at this time. I will put Kaladon's needs first. It is befitting of a princess."

"Correction," he said with a straight face, "it's Empress Dovina Zordek now." She looked a little shocked at first, but she knew he was right. She was now ruler of Kaladon.

"I'll tell you what our problem is, your highness. We have a lot of training to do on *Star Wolf*. And until that's completed we're not a very effective fighting unit. Oh sure, we can destroy a bombing cruiser with no shields while hiding behind a reflector device. But in a real fight, well that's another story. We have two spacecraft we can't even operate, due to the lack of personnel. We have no warriors and are short on technical staff, which is especially true for weapons." Speaking firmly and as an equal to an empress was something few people could get away with, even though he was speaking the truth.

"Perhaps I can help you with that problem." She turned to General Sizdroz, who snapped to attention. "First, I'm going to promote you to Brigadier General, in charge of the 'Army of the People' on all of Kaladon. You can name your own successor, subject to my approval, of course. I want you to put out a notice that Admiral Carter," she smiled as she turned and looked at him, "needs volunteers for assignment on board *Star Wolf*. They're to go with him and become permanent members of his crew. See what you can do."

In a few hours, things started getting more organized. He glanced around and saw close to two hundred Kaladonians standing on the padport nearby. General Sizdroz and Empress Dovina were approaching him and Shanza as they stood next to their spacesled.

"Carter," said the Empress, "We have a few volunteers."

Wow, he thought. *This is better than I had hoped. This may be all we need for a full crew.* "Empress Dovina, I thank you for the volunteers."

"You should be safe during this cleanup," said Carter. "But this action by the Tygerians was just the beginning. If I were them, I'd send an invasion force as soon as possible."

"What do you mean? Why would they?" she asked.

"I'm positive the Tygerians are planning an invasion. This was just an attack to knock out your defenses and assess your ability to defend yourselves. No offense Your Highness, but you flunked. If they can conquer

Kaladon, they'll be able to control this whole sector, including this solar system and beyond."

She looked at General Sizdroz, and then KorRak. Their facial expressions confirmed Carter was correct. "We'll be back in a few months. Then perhaps we can talk more about the future," he said, trying to lighten the mood. "If you need help, call us. We won't be far away." He gave her a brief hug, which she responded to. "Let's get going. We have a lot of work to do." As they turned to leave he saw the expression on the general's face, conveying that nobody hugs the empress, at least not in public.

While they were talking, the last group of volunteers were boarding spacesleds to be taken to *Star Wolf*. As their group boarded Shanza and Carter turned around and acknowledged Empress Dovina. She waved as they left. *She'll make a fine empress, if she survives*, he thought. *Hell, will any of us survive?*

After everyone got over the initial shock of losing their emperor and the entire senate body they had a month-long mourning period for all of Kaladon. The lords of all the provinces and their family's attended the burial ceremonies. Dignitaries from Krynta, Pendari and Mylaar attended to express their condolences.

★   ★   ★

Regent BryQat walked down the hall to Lord GorDon's office, with messages in hand, and walked right in.

"Well, my friend, bad news again?"

"Yes, my Lord," as he handed him the message.

As Lord GorDon read the message, he paused briefly to grasp its meaning. "This doesn't make any sense. Battle cruisers don't just explode for no apparent reason." He paused again to study it further.

"My Lord, we also have a message from the emperor," said Regent BryQat, a little more excited.

After reading the second message he said, "well my friend, this certainly is good news." He even cracked a smile. "The emperor is sending Admiral ZynTak to us with a new fleet, unexpectedly ahead of schedule and with enough warriors for our invasion."

"Do you know this Admiral ZynTak, my Lord?"

"Yes, my friend," he said, displaying a slight frown. "I know him well. He's the emperor's favorite. He's also the uncle of Captain ZynTak, who is under the command of Admiral MyrAak."

"Do you know what this means, BryQat?" Not waiting for an answer, he continued. "Our invasion can begin much sooner than we anticipated. We must start planning immediately. I want you to send a vessel to Kaladon. Have it manned by Bendoatiis so no one suspects us of spying if they're captured. We must find out all we can about this new spacecraft. Also order Admiral LanDok to return with his command craft, but not the rest of his fleet. I want our technical people to check out his computer banks."

"Yes, sir, my Lord, I'll see to it at once." Observing the confident smile return to his boss's face, he left the room.

You shall know how you are beaten, Carter. I shall sneak up behind you soon with my agent from Ra'Tor. He's probably aboard with you already. I'm surprised I haven't heard anything from him yet. I can only assume he can't contact me without giving away his position, GorDon thought.

★　　★　　★

"General Sizdroz, we have to upgrade our defense systems as soon as possible. We were helpless during that last attack. Like Carter said, we flunked. Understand this General, I'm not blaming you. It's just that we weren't very well prepared. Things have changed with the coming of the Tygerians. Lord Nemarg probably lost the majority of his fighters, and our blaster cannons were totally useless."

"Your Highness, I hate giving you excuses, but we never had time to really establish any defenses for Ozlonz."

"I wonder," she said, "was it a false sense of security or perhaps a lack of vision on General Wydorf's part?"

"Lord Nemarg's people are in the process of replacing our blaster cannons with new and updated models, but it takes time."

"How much time?"

"Lord Nemarg has informed me he will have 20 of the latest, more powerful, cannon emplacements completed and installed around Ozlonz in less then two months. He also informed me he has begun construction of more fighters and will continue around the clock until the Tygerians attack. He estimates he should be able to complete at least 30 each month. I realize that fighters aren't supposed to be very effective against war cruisers, but the attack Captain Centarkoh carried out against a Tygerian war cruiser made us think differently about their effectiveness. Especially with more powerful weapons. We do know, however, that they're extremely effective against ground forces.

"We have been informed by Pendari that the war cruisers we ordered will be completed within a month. There's a slight delay, because of the new weapons system we requested. We haven't heard from Mylaar, even though I've requested an update."

"That sounds better, General. Thank you for your report."

"One more thing, Your Highness. I'm not sure if you're aware of this, but since we don't have an active senate to represent the people, your word is absolute law on Kaladon. This includes the provinces as well."

"Thank you, General. And no, I wasn't aware of that law. That's why I have a general I can trust and keeps me well informed." She gave him a friendly smile.

★　　★　　★

Two provinces, Harket and Gentar, were shipping ammunition for blaster cannons to the central government on a weekly basis. Neither had been touched by the Tygerian attack. All of the provinces had begun training armies.

Ozlonz was making excellent progress in their recovery. Many craftsman were employed constructing a new palace for the empress. She liked the old one, but wanted a few changes. One of which was a shelter beneath the living quarters.

★　　★　　★

Carter was in the CCC to see if he could find out anything about additional weapons in their arsenal that he wasn't aware of. Since he was blocked by access codes he decided to study the basics on structure and compartments. Maybe he could find his way around better. After spending a few hours on the computers he went to the bridge for some personal contact. While looking around he noticed Lo'Gon wasn't on the bridge. He went over to where RomMen was standing and stood there quietly for a moment.

"Learn anything, Admiral?"

"Yes, I did. I'm starting to understand the layout of this vessel much better. You know, I really get disgusted by Lo'Gon's continual denial of knowledge. I mean, listening to him you'd wonder who really built this vessel. I don't trust him and I know there's something wrong with this whole scenario, but I have no proof. And that little speech he gave shortly after we left the construction station, well! That was a joke."

"Yeah, from what I've heard about it, I agree with you."

"I did learn something of interest from the computers, when I wasn't blocked by security codes. We have sensory probes installed on every spacecraft. I think we should launch at least 100 of these probes as soon as possible. Some in an array around Kaladon and the others off into deep space in every direction."

"That's a good idea, I'll get captain Carznot on it."

"Good choice— his crew's well trained. Have him see me in the CCC before he shoves off," Carter said.

A short while later Captain Carznot came into the CCC. "You wanted to see me, Admiral?" The eager captain asked.

"Yes, I wanted to discuss exactly what your orders are before you leave. We need an early warning system for Kaladon. I want you to place an array of sensory probes in space to give us just that." After Carter explained the details from the drawings in the CCC, Carznot left. He assembled his crew, boarded the spacecraft and was on his way.

★   ★   ★

Carter was on the bridge the next evening reeling from a full day of training when ... *Carter.* He raised his head to respond. No one was looking at him. "Captain, did you hear anything, anybody call my name?" *Carter!* "There it is again."

"Are you feeling all right? Too much training, perhaps?" RomMen said jokingly. "Maybe you could use some rest."

"Maybe you're right. I'm going to my quarters. See you in a few hours," he said, as he left the bridge.

Alone, at the table in his quarters, he said softly, "Guess I am a little tired after all." After a good yawn he headed for bed.

"Carter."

He looked around and without thinking, he said, "What, who are you? What do you want?"

"Carter, I need your help."

*   ★   ★   ★

Captain RomMen looked up as Carter returned to the bridge. "Captain, is Shanza qualified to go out on one of the war cruisers with a trained crew?"

"I think it's a little premature. We should give her a few more weeks of training before she'll be ready."

"I'll use one of the carriers then. Have Captain Jackson make ready the *Raven* for space flight."

"Aye, Admiral," he replied, obviously wondering what was going on. Carter's explanation didn't help him much either.

After they left *Star Wolf* he gave Jackson the coordinates on the far side of the moon.

"What's down there?"

"To tell you the truth, Jackson, I'm not sure myself. I just know someone or somebody is in trouble down there."

"Captain," said operations, "I have a small contact on the lunar surface."

"Operations, launch six fighters for cover. When we land, cover us like a blanket," said Captain Jackson.

He received an affirmative nod from the operations officer.

In a few minutes they set down near a small spacecraft. They suited up for the short walk on the lunar surface. The side hatch on their spacesled opened and formed a ramp to the surface.

As they emerged, Jackson said, "Well, I'll be. How'd you know this was here?" About halfway up the side of the vessel it split open and a ramp slid down to the surface of the moon.

"Don't ask. You wouldn't believe me anyway."

"Try me sometime."

Going inside, they found a doorway to the rear compartment and went through it. Carter looked at the side of the craft and much to his surprise he could faintly see the outside. It was as if he was looking through tinted glass. He then looked at what appeared to be a metallic container sitting on the floor in front of them. It was about six feet in length, four feet high, and four feet wide. On each side of the room was another container.

"Carter, please take this container to the Star Wolf and all will be fine."

"Captain, did you hear that voice?" Carter asked.

"Huh? What are you talking about?" He looked at him in a strange way.

"Never mind. Like I said before you wouldn't believe me if I told you." Carter had a smile on his face. "There's no danger here, I'm sure of that."

When they were airborne they retrieved the fighters and returned to *Star Wolf*.

After landing Jackson asked, "What's in the box, Admiral?"

"Not sure myself, but it certainly won't hurt us. Put the container in the middle on the docking bay deck, will you, I'm going to call RomMen and then we'll open it."

"Bridge, Carter here." The captain walked over to Ronous on the communication console when he heard his voice. "Well, I guess you're not crazy after all."

"I brought a metal box on board. Least I think it's metal. Anyway, it's sitting in the middle of the docking bay, on the deck. I have it sealed off from the rest of the vessel. Just don't ask me what's inside, because I'm not sure yet. Have KorRak meet me in the docking bay and then we'll open it."

"Understood, he's on his way."

KorRak came through the air lock and into the docking bay.

Carter heard the voice again. It said, *"Carter, have everyone stand back and I will open it, soon."*

"Stand back, everyone, the container is going to open." It started to glow slightly. They heard the click of a latch, and a hissing sound, like an air lock being vented. The lid slowly opened to a vertical position. It had a large piano hinge on the rear of the lid which couldn't be seen until it was fully opened. A fine mist floated out and dissipated as it hit the floor. There wasn't any odor from the mist, but they could feel the dampness.

"*Carter, please don't touch me until I am out of the box. I require no assistance.*"

"Stand back, everyone, and don't touch him," said Carter.

"Him?" somebody said.

"Shh," said someone else.

In a few minutes he was out of the box and standing on the floor. *He looks sort of frail, about five feet tall,* he thought. *Bet he doesn't weigh more than 100 pounds.*

"*One hundred and two in your measurements, to be exact. I suppose I should talk audibly when I communicate with you. That way your subordinates won't think you're, ah, mentally ill, is it, when you answer me.*"

"*Thank you,*" Carter thought back.

"*You're welcome,*" he thought to Carter.

"This is a strange conversation," Carter said out loud.

Then out loud he said, "I am called Pyzor. I come from a distant planet we'll call Pyzentarri in your language. It's millions of light years hence and won't be on any of your charts. I've been in this container for the equivalent of 12 years," as he pointed to the container. "My parents and I were banished from our home planet. The authorities did not put us to death because killing had been abolished in our society for nearly five hundred years. Evil forces caused this to my family. I'm sure it resulted in civil war and the end of peace on Pyzentarri as we knew it."

"Pyzor, I know this might sound strange, but you look tired, like you need some rest." Carter said.

"Not so strange, but true. I will need time to adjust."

It appears he's just happy to get out of that container, he thought. Picking up the interphone, he said, "Sickroom, Carter. Send a wheelchair to the docking bay, please."

"Zark here, wheelchair's on its way."

Carter was assessing him while he spoke and noticed he was wearing a tan one-piece outfit. He had small ears, shaped like an elf's and his eyes were slightly larger than a human's. His mouth was shaped like he had a slight grin and he was rather slender. KorRak pushed the wheelchair and Carter walked beside it. When they arrived Carter introduced him to Zark. "Pyzor, I'll have some questions to ask you later, perhaps when I return."

"Yes, that would be fine. I shall wait for you here in the care of your physician. Then I'll answer all your questions."

Zark asked him to lie down on an examining table. "My health is fine, Doctor. After I get my strength back you can ask me anything you want about my anatomy. Would you be so kind as to put two heat lamps above me, one at each end? I'm chilled from the long stay in my container."

Good to know some manners are universal, Carter thought. "KorRak, I'm going to the bridge and update Captain RomMen."

A short time later Carter arrived on the bridge. "Well, what was in the magic box?"

RomMen sounds more Earth-like all the time, he thought. "It was an alien named Pyzor. I'll say one thing about traveling in space and hanging around you people. I never know who or what I'm going to run into next." He had to laugh. It must have been catching because everyone else laughed too. After Carter had a discussion with RomMen about Pyzor, he left for the sickroom.

"Captain, I'm picking up a message from Carznot. He says mission completed, but he picked up a contact, fast approaching Kaladon."

"Very well."

"Sickroom, Zark here."

"Dr. Zark, bridge. Is Carter there yet?"

"Hold on, he just walked in."

A few seconds later, "Carter here."

"We have an unidentified contact that dropped out of hyperspace and is approaching Kaladon at light speed."

"Have Carznot intercept. If it's hostile, I want him to take strong offensive action. Let me know the results."

"Understand and concur. RomMen out."

As he hung up the interphone and stood there. *Now it begins,* he thought, *It was just a matter of time.*

CHAPTER 12

THE SENTRIES

Sifting through the rubble a few blocks from the palace, a cleanup crew found Tak Byrokks' body. Normally more reserved, even General Sizdroz chuckled at the news and said, "That's one spy we won't have to worry about again." The smell of decay only speeded the demolition and cleanup crews in their work.

It took weeks to clear out the rubble where the palace once stood and start construction. The work progressed well under the watchful eye of the empress.

General Sizdroz was ahead of schedule in gathering an army for Kaladon's defense. The pending attack had galvanized the planet. He picked 40 of the most qualified young people and sent them to Esterk for fighter training.

Lord Nemarg's engineers were installing newly constructed cannon emplacements and the construction of fighters progressed at a rapid pace.

★   ★   ★

Carter returned to the sickroom to see the strange alien was lying on one of the examining tables. Dr. Zark turned off the heat lamps and Pyzor sat up. "Glad you're back. Now we can have a talk about me. Dr. Zark and KorRak, please join us, that is, if it's alright with you, sir?" He spoke audibly now.

"It's okay with me," he nodded.

"Good. Doctor my strength is returning. Your heat lamps did the job. Let me start by saying it was difficult to communicate with anyone early in my exile. The back side of any moon is not a frequently traveled area, and the range of my communication power is somewhat limited. If you had not come here for your weapons testing, I'd still be stranded on the moon."

"How did you know to contact me?" Carter asked, expressing curiosity.

"I tried to seek out a leader. And I chose to communicate with you," Pyzor said confidently.

"I will tell you my story in a way that you will understand. We crash landed on the moon about a year ago. My father already died, but my mother and I were well.

"We were attacked by two war cruisers and they damaged our vessel. While trying to escape around the back side of the moon we realized our power was draining. Between the gravitational pull of the moon and our power loss, we had a rough landing.

"Fortunately for us, the aggressors didn't investigate to see if we survived. I suppose they were happy just to see that we crashed. Their scanners couldn't detect any life forms on board because the containers have their own protection mechanism and couldn't be scanned for contents. The impact disrupted mother's life support system and she died later. The `Container of Life' can sustain us indefinitely when they're working properly.

"When I opened my container I noticed a problem with the operating mechanism as well. Apparently, it had also been damaged during the landing, but the malfunction on my container was in the start-up sequence, not life support. This simply means it can never be used again.

"We have to go down to the surface of the moon one more time, if you please. There are some things I need to get from the spacecraft that are very important to me," Pyzor said earnestly.

"I'm sure we can arrange at least one more visit to the moon's surface if it's as urgent as you say," said Carter.

"Now, how about some anatomy?" cut in Dr. Zark. "Why don't you go over to the computer and fill in the blanks, so to speak." The doctor motioned with his hand where to go.

"Yes, sir," His long slender fingers moved rapidly over the keyboard and in a short time he was finished. Turning around, he looked at Zark with a grin and said, "Anything else?" KorRak and Carter just looked at each other.

"When you've completed your work here, KorRak, I'll see you on the bridge." Carter got up and left.

Arriving on the bridge he walked over to Ronous who was sitting in the Captain's chair. "Have you seen Shanza?" He asked, looking around the bridge for her.

"Yes sir, Admiral, Shanza's in the training room on the tactical computer for war cruisers. She's been getting some very high marks and her practical operating abilities are equally as high. She's going to be a fine war cruiser captain." Carter was beaming with pride for his sweetheart.

"I presume Captain RomMen is resting."

"Yes, sir, he's in his quarters. He's due on the bridge," he said, glancing at a time piece on the bulkhead above the main viewing screen, "in about three hours."

"How's the training program going with the new people from Ozlonz?" he asked.

"Very well," answered Ronous in a pleasant tone, "it's going better then expected, but there are some problems. We've gotten help in some key areas, but still not much in weapons. RomMen is pleased with their progress even though about a quarter or so will wash out. He expects we'll have a fully trained crew very soon and *Star Wolf* will be operational in nearly all respects."

"Best I can hope for," said Carter. "Where are we weak?"

"Experience," he answered. "Battle experience."

And time, Carter thought. *Hell, occasionally I still take a wrong turn on the way to my quarters, and I run this operation.*

Ordak was doing better since the pressure of officer in charge was lifted. He was happier working under Lieut. Zyene.

"Captain, contact engineering and tell them I'm on my way. If anybody needs me that's where I'll be," Carter said.

Engineering was the highest security area on board *Star Wolf*. It was a necessity, because it was the most vulnerable. It wouldn't take much to destroy the vessel from engineering.

An armed alien he had seen in the arena stood by the door. But unlike their exchange in the arena, he smiled and gave him a friendly greeting. Between him and the force field behind him, it would be tough for any unauthorized access. It was de-energized and the door slid open from both sides. He was welcomed by Lieut. Ri'Zar.

A few hours later Carter thanked him for the tour and left, his head spinning from everything Ri'Zar had told him. Carter told him he'd return later for a more detailed discussion. Ri'Zar indicated he looked forward to it.

Carter returned to the bridge as Captain RomMen came out of his quarters. "You're to be congratulated on the progress you've made toward getting this crew ready," he said. "Captain Ronous informed me you expect to attain that goal very soon."

"I have every reason to believe that schedule is attainable. However, in all candor, I do have doubts about battle readiness."

KorRak escorted Pyzor to the bridge. They went over to where RomMen and Carter were and introduced him to Captain RomMen.

"Pyzor, let me introduce you to Captain RomMen," said KorRak.

"So you're Pyzor," said RomMen as he stuck out his hand. "Welcome aboard." They shook hands. Pyzor seemed puzzled by this greeting, but didn't make any comment.

"Perhaps I can perform the duties at some of the watch stations and make myself useful."

RomMen looked at Pyzor for a moment and then at Carter. A strange feeling came over him. He wasn't sure what it was, but he felt comfort from it.

"Do you have a preference?" said RomMen.

"If I had my choice, Captain, I'd prefer communications. I seem to have a knack for that." He displayed a sly look.

"It so happens we have a need for someone with skills in communication. If you think you're up to it, give it a try."

"Great," said Pyzor, overjoyed by his answer.

Ronous got up, allowing Pyzor to sit at the communications console. Pyzor looked at the panel, studied it briefly, adjusted the chair, then said, "This'll work just fine, Captain. I presume you have your own coded channels that allow you to communicate with your support craft and sleds."

"We're still communicating on the original codes from the construction station," said Captain RomMen, struck by the idea. "Perhaps you have a point, Pyzor." He thought for a moment, then said," You are correct, we'll change the codes. Contact Lo'Gon, he's probably in the officers lounge. Get him up here."

"Aye, Captain." Soon after Pyzor passed the word, he called.

"Bridge, Lo'Gon here, is there a problem?"

"Lo'Gon, the Captain requests your presence on the bridge."

"I'm in the middle of eating, perhaps when I finish."

RomMen heard the conversation and nodded his approval.

"Enjoy the rest of your meal," said Pyzor.

Lieutenant Zyene came out of the CCC and approached RomMen. "Excuse me Captain, but I'm not sure about some of the functions for the weapons systems, sir." she looked somewhat puzzled. "I think it's something that needs to be addressed."

"Show me at the weapons station," said RomMen.

They went over to the console where she sat down and pointed. "Look at these controls, Captain. What do you think?"

"Wait a minute, hold it right there." He turned his palms up in a pushing movement. "You're out of my area of expertise. Explain your findings, analysis, and give me your recommendations to correct the problem, whatever it is, and we'll go from there."

"That's just it, Captain. I don't know what they are. These functions on this console are definitely related to the weapons system, but I've never seen them before. The configuration is totally new. I'm not even sure what the intended usage is or what the results would be. I have been trying to research this on the computers; but I'm continually being blocked by security codes."

"Lieut. Zyene, I want you to keep this quiet. You and I will have to discuss this with Carter."

"The same system is on the carriers, but not the war cruisers," she said.

"You're a fine officer Lieut. and I appreciate your bringing this to my attention."

"Thank you, Captain," a confident look on her face.

"Captain," said Pyzor, "Captain Carznot reports challenging an unidentified spacecraft near Kaladon. It left without incident."

"Understood," the captain replied.

Lieut. Lo'Gon went through security to the bridge. "And, who is this?" he asked in a hostile tone while looking at Pyzor.

"He's the new communications officer. Lieut. Lo'Gon, this is Lieut. Pyzor," said Carter, easing the tension.

Lo'Gon quickly changed his own demeanor. "Welcome Pyzor, glad to have you aboard."

"Thank you, Lo'Gon, I'm happy to be here."

Lo'Gon quickly shifted his gaze, looked at Captain RomMen, and said, "What is it you want, Captain?"

"Lo'Gon, I want you to change the codes on our interior communications channels and from *Star Wolf* to all our support craft, including the spacesleds."

"Well, I see no need for that, Captain. No one else knows our codes, so what does it matter if we change them or not?"

"I didn't ask your opinion, Lieut. That's the second time you objected to my orders. The next time will produce grave consequences. I want it done as soon as possible, and that's an order. Do I make myself clear?" displaying anger, his voice ending in an ominous growl.

"Perfectly," said Lo'Gon, scowling. "I'll get what I need and be right back."

The fool, Carter thought. *You don't argue with the captain, especially if he's a Tygerian. I've heard that growl before and know what it means.*

Coincidentally, Carter was watching Lo'Gon as he passed where Pyzor was sitting. Without warning, Pyzor jerked his head around as if startled by Lo'Gon's presence. Lo'Gon didn't see it, but KorRak did also. KorRak looked at Carter as if to ask what it meant. He simply raised his eyebrows and shrugged his shoulders, indicating he wasn't sure.

Lo'Gon returned in a few minutes, ready to work. He opened a control panel at the rear of the bridge and it took about an hour for him to change all the codes, except one, which they left unchanged to enable them to communicate with the *Bangar*, Captain Carznot's war cruiser. Pyzor watched intently to all that Lo'Gon achieved. "I'm going to the support craft to change those also," Lo'Gon scoffed sourly as he went by.

"Captain, may I use your conference room for a few minutes?" Carter asked, now showing some concern at tension he neither needed nor understood.

"Of course, be my guest."

"Would you also get Lieut. Pyzor relieved and have him join us?" As Carter headed for the conference room he motioned for KorRak to follow him.

In a few minutes Captain Ronous came to the bridge and relieved their newest recruit.

"Lieut. Pyzor," the captain spoke quietly. "Carter wants to see you in my conference room." He pointed the way.

He entered the room, but hesitated when he saw KorRak and the admiral sitting at a large table waiting for him.

"Well, Pyzor," he said, motioning for him to sit down. "Your natural talent appears to be very useful, doesn't it?"

"Sir, I'd like to know something before we get into the business of lieut. Lo'Gon. What are your intentions with this array of powerful spacecraft you have under your command?"

"Pyzor, this is a rare group you're traveling with. We don't have a country or planet in any solar system we can call home. The *Star Wolf* is as close as we'll get for as long as we survive. After we escaped from the arena at Calverone all of us felt like we needed each other, and figured we'd have to work together to stay alive. After Kaladon, perhaps we can help some of the other solar systems against aggression from races like the Tygerians. So, it appears this is what we'll be doing for a long time."

"It seems as though I'm in a similar situation." Pyzor softened. "If you have room for someone like me, I'd like to join your group."

"We always have room for anyone who wants to join us," Carter said, smiling.

Pyzor's expression changed and said, "He might be a spy." Carter's eyes widened at that statement. KorRak reacted quite similarly.

"Please explain why you have reason to think so." He waited briefly for the translation.

"He didn't change any of your communication codes. You can prove me right by trying to communicate with *Bangar*. Use any channel you wish, if you get through it'll be your proof.

KorRak if you can hear me, nod your head yes, he thought. KorRak looked at Pyzor suspiciously and nodded. *Now, ask Carter if he heard me communicate with you,* he thought again.

KorRak sat staring at Pyzor for moment.

Please, he thought.

Reluctantly KorRak looked at Carter and said, "Did you hear anything Pyzor just said to me?"

"No."

"Yes, KorRak," said Pyzor. "I can read your thoughts as I read Lo'Gon's thoughts when he agreed to change the communication codes. Now you also know my secret."

"Did you know about Pyzor's ability?" he looked at Carter.

"Yes. And I know you'll keep his secret too, right?"

"Not a problem," answered KorRak, shaking hands again.

"I suppose this gesture is one of your customs?" said Pyzor.

"No, it's one of Carter's. We just adopted it because we like its implication of friendship and trust."

"Pyzor," he said, showing concern, "did Lo'Gon say anything about the Tygerians?" "Yes he did," Pyzor replied. "I caught a slight thought about contacting them sometime in the near future. He already sent Lord GorDon the interior communications codes programmed during construction. I guess that's why he didn't want them changed. Who is Lord GorDon? Lo'Gon felt your word would be fear, when he thought of him."

"He's a war lord in the Tygerian Empire," said KorRak.

"I guess we must decide what to do next," Carter said.

"I can change the codes. And there's probably a few more things I can do to help. But I need some items off my vessel on the moon first," said Pyzor.

"Perhaps we can turn this situation to our advantage. Would you mind if one more person knew about your mental abilities?" He asked anxiously. "If you say no I'll respect your decision."

"If you mean Captain RomMen, it's fine with me," said Pyzor.

★   ★   ★

The large rear door came down on the platform after they landed, closing off the room that housed the spacesleds of the *Star Wolf*. They had returned Pyzors' container of life to the small spacecraft on the surface of the moon and retrieved his most cherished possessions. Pyzor had a chance to pay his last respects and was carrying a satchel of some kind.

"Geez, marooned and hopeless. Must've been pretty hard for him, until now," Carter said to KorRak.

He just nodded.

It was hard to believe Pyzor was only a teenager. He was very mature in some things and immature in others. He was also intelligent for his age. Part of growing up, Carter figured. He put his things in a stateroom, then went to the bridge to man the communications station.

Now that they had a large enough crew, they could man three full watch sections. During battle stations they had the best operators at all stations.

A number of volunteers were interested in warrior training. But to have a full complement on every vessel they would need 2,000 warriors. Since they weren't planning on an invasion any time soon, there was no need to have very many on board. KorRak was promoted to captain and he had Lieut. Wydorf, nephew of the late General Wydorf in charge of the warriors. From these he also chose an added security detail.

Lieut. Pyzor changed the codes on *Star Wolf* without Lieut. Lo'Gon's knowledge. He also changed them on the support craft as well, with the exception of *Bangar*.

"Permission to come on the Bridge?" said Captain Mytlaq.

"Granted," replied security. Carter turned toward her and realized she had completed her training when he saw the insignia on her uniform.

"Captain RomMen, am I to understand we have another war cruiser captain on board?" he asked, almost jokingly.

"Carter, she's a fully qualified war cruiser captain," RomMen replied, stopping the joke cold.

"Captain Mytlaq, I have an assignment for you," said Captain RomMen. "I want you to assist *Bangar*. Captain Carznot will brief you on arrival." She smiled at Carter and he followed her off the bridge.

"Congratulations, sweetheart," he said in the lift. "I'm happy for you and I know you'll do just fine."

Her rough official edge fell away in the privacy of the lift. Carter found himself being embraced and kissed. "Thank you, my love. I appreciate your confidence in me." She smiled and left to board her war cruiser. The doors closed and he was left alone with the lingering fragrance of her perfume. Ten minutes later a much more business-like Shanza had her crew together and was headed for Kaladon aboard the *Lynzar*.

★   ★   ★

Regent BryQat found Lord GorDon studying a tactical plan in his war room. "My lord, Admiral ZynTak has arrived with his fleet from the emperor. We also received a message from Admiral MyrAak. He will arrive tomorrow with Res'Itz."

"Well, Regent BryQat, that's excellent." The warlord allowed himself a smile. "Schedule a war conference for late tomorrow, we must start planning our invasion.

"Based on intelligence reports from Kaladon, our little secret is out. The government is setting up new defenses, raising an army and constructing new fighters. This will not help them," said GorDon, grinning.

It was late evening and the war conference began. The group spent days and nights in the war room, going over various plans, counter-plans and more counter-plans. They were thorough, if they were anything. Finally Lord GorDon decided everything was ready. Only one thing remained.

"Regent BryQat, I want you to remain here. I shall go with the fleet to direct the invasion myself," said Lord GorDon. "Have Res'Itz made ready. I will be there shortly."

Res'Itz was somewhat puzzled at the chain of events. He was sitting on a bench in a large round room. Then a Tygerian came in, handed him a sword, and said, "Prepare to defend yourself," as he turned and left the room.

Res'Itz sat there wondering what he meant. Why would he have to defend himself?

Lord GorDon came into the room and Res'Itz saw he had a sword in his hand, too. "I wonder if you learned anything while you were magistrate at Calverone," said Lord GorDon, wearing a big smile.

"What are you going to do with that?" asked Res'Itz, pointing at GorDon's sword.

"I guess you'll have to defend yourself, because I'm going to kill you," said GorDon, smiling again. He would rather it had been Carter, but maybe next time.

"Now wait, Lord GorDon. Why would you want to kill me? I haven't done anything to you. I've cooperated with you all along," said Res'Itz, pleading.

"Please, don't think me the fool," he said, as he swung at Res'Itzs' head. The frightened magistrate ducked just in time and meekly swung his sword at Lord GorDon in a feeble attempt to fight back. They parried back and forth for a few minutes, Res'Itz still asking why, and GorDon not answering.

He never really had a chance during the whole sick farce. Res'Itz made a last valiant swinging move toward Lord GorDon, who sidestepped, partially blocked the swing with his sword, then ran him through. Res'Itz screamed, as he felt Lord GorDon lift up on his sword, cutting his flesh while withdrawing his sword. He looked down at the open wound in his chest, then at the bloody sword in GorDon's hand. His eyes rolled back in his head as he slumped to the floor.

"A fitting end for a magistrate of the arena at Calverone," said Lord GorDon, standing over the body. "Someday, BryQat, I'll have Carter lying at my feet. Nothing would please me more."

"To the fleet. We are off to conquer," yelled the seasoned war lord, now frenzied with the sight of spilled blood, as he held his sword in the air and he walked briskly out of the room.

It was a terrifying spectacle to see so many spacecraft emerge from the canyons and valley floors of MarQ, right through the holoshields heading upward toward open space. Thirty-two vessels of various designs and purposes made the Tygerians grand armada complete. Lord GorDon, his confidence level at its highest in years, was racing toward Kaladon with fire in his eyes. Admiral MyrAak's fleet was leaving at the same time for the Na'Reen solar system with his fifteen spacecraft. What a sight it was, indeed.

$$\star \quad \star \quad \star$$

The *Lynzar*, commanded by Captain Mytlaq, had sentry duty on the opposite side of Kaladon. It was beyond short range sensors and couldn't be detected by Plaxar.

"Captain Mytlaq," said the operations officer, "contact on long-range sensors, it's traveling in hyperspace toward Kaladon."

"Communicator, send message to *Star Wolf*, please advise," said the

Captain. "Set battle stations, energize shields, arm all weapons. Communicator, signal on all channels, stop and be identified." She thought for a moment, *I must be nervous on my first assignment, shields are automatically energized when battle stations are set*, she thought, somewhat embarrassed, but smiling.

All stations rendered compliance to her orders.

The travelers stopped as ordered to get a better look at who blocked their way. "Captain, receiving a signal."

"Visual," ordered the Captain, without giving a reply. The large monitor above the control panels came on.

"We come in peace. Why do you block our way?" he said.

Captain Mytlaq looked at the being in the other vessel as it came into focus and it struck her as rather odd. She thought he looked familiar. "Communicator, send this message: `We are the sentry of Kaladon. Identify yourselves and state your business. We are peaceful as well, but do not provoke us, or you will find we are as capable in battle as we are in peace'.

Since Mytlaq had set battle stations before the smaller craft could scan them, their shields now protected them from any detailed examination by other spacecraft. This also allowed them to disguise their readiness, although any vessel's commander, friend or foe, would have strong suspicions.

"Captain, they're energizing shields and arming weapons," said operations, his voice raised but still calm.

"Fire forward batteries," ordered Captain Mytlaq.

Black space erupted with streaks of fire as the four forward blaster cannons threw a controlled burn speeding toward the vessel nearby. All four shots hit the vessel simultaneously. Apparently his shields were not completely energized, because it exploded with enough force to have destroyed a craft three times its size. "Is the contact still on visual?" said the captain, glancing up to see a blank screen. *Hmm, a bit overkill*, she thought, but still smiling.

"No, captain," he replied, humor in his tone.

"Communicator, send a message to *Star Wolf*: `Contact was hostile, became aggressive, craft destroyed. All is well with *Lynzar*!' News of the skirmish had set off a cheer on *Star Wolf*.

Captain Mytlaq had no way of knowing this was the same craft Captain Carznot had encountered earlier. The Bendoatiis, arrogant as most of them were, didn't have the sense to be tactful or try to get through peacefully.

"Captain," said communications, "*Bangar* requests assistance. Four spacecraft approaching. Present disposition unknown."

"Acknowledge, communicator. We're on our way," she said. "Make 95% normal speed to rendezvous with Bangar."

"Make 95% normal speed, aye captain."

★　　★　　★

"Battle stations," ordered Captain Carznot.

"Weapons armed," came a report.

"Shields energized, battle stations set," came another.

"Now I guess we wait," said the captain. In a few minutes they arrived. "Spacecraft approaching Kaladon, stop and identify yourselves," said Captain Carznot. "Visual." The monitor came on and it was blank, since both monitors must be on for a visual.

"What is it you want?" replied a voice.

"I am the sentry of Kaladon. Identify yourselves and state your reason for being here," said Captain Carznot.

"There is only one of you and four of us, and you would dare issue this challenge," replied a voice.

"I must assume you do not have peaceful intentions or you'd identify yourselves. I must warn you, don't provoke us, as we are here for the protection of Kaladon. Now answer, or be on your way," ordered Carznot.

After a few moments a new voice broke the silence. "If you won't answer him, perhaps you'll answer me," said Captain Mytlaq. This new player in the stand-off startled the leader of the foursome that had been threatening before.

"Very well." As his image appeared on the screen, he said, "I am Captain Skree from Pendari. Three of these vessels are being delivered as ordered by the government of Kaladon. The fourth is for our return voyage."

"I am Captain Mytlaq, and I will be happy to escort you."

"Kaladon, Captain Mytlaq calling."

"Captain, I'm curious; what are you doing out there?" said General Sizdroz. "We thought you were farther out in space."

"Carter thought perhaps we should keep an eye out for any approaching vessels. Tygerians being very sneaky, sir."

"Tell Carter we thank him for the help," said General Sizdroz. "You could also tell him the three spacecraft we ordered from Mylaar arrived ten days ago."

"Yes, sir, general, I'll do that." said Captain Mytlaq. When the craft were close to landing, Captain Mytlaq turned back to rendezvous with Carznot.

★　　★　　★

As soon as Pyzor was relieved at the communications station, he came to Carter and asked if he'd follow him. "Where are we going?" he asked.

"The CCC, I'd like to show you something," he said softly. They walked into the room and Pyzor sat down at the control center for the weapons computer.

You're telling me you've got another area of expertise, he thought. Some of the computers were voice activated, while others were keyboard-dependent.

Yes I am, thought Pyzor. "Take a look at this and tell me what you think."

"We'd better get Lieut. Zyene in here, because I'm not sure just what it is I'm looking at," he said. "Bridge, Carter here."

"Go ahead, Carter," said the Communicator.

"Ask the captain to have Lieut. Zyene come to the CCC."

"The captain acknowledged the request."

In a few minutes she came into the CCC as ordered. She found Pyzor and Carter still looking at the monitor.

She observed without a word. "Oh my word!" she exclaimed, shocked by what she saw. "That's what I've been searching for. I used to think it was still in the design phase and not yet operational."

"Well, they said this was the most advanced vessel ever built, so I guess it belongs here, whatever it is. It all looks Greek to me."

"Huh!, what do you mean, Carter? What is this Greek you're referring to?" asked Lieut. Zyene.

"Never mind. It's just a strange saying we used on earth." "Every weapons station has these odd sequences, except the war cruisers. I haven't been able to pursue this any farther because on every occasion I've been blocked by security codes," she said. "I brought this to Captain RomMen's attention a short while ago."

"I'll try to break some of these codes in my spare time, and perhaps Lieut. Zyene and I can get you some solutions," he said.

"Sounds good to me," Carter said, as he turned and left. He stopped and told captain RomMen about their discussion.

*   *   *

"General Sizdroz," said Empress Dovina, "what's the status on our defense capabilities? Do we really have any possible hope for surviving the invasion from the Tygerians?" This was a standard question with a changing answer.

"Based on the capabilities of our defenses, *Star Wolf* and the support craft they have, the use of the six war cruisers we purchased from Pendari and Mylaar, and our army, I would say it greatly depends on two things." More noncommittal than ever, he continued. "One, the accuracy of the report Lord GorDon received on the amount of damage we sustained from his initial attack. And two, their confidence in the effectiveness of the force they're bringing with them. Your highness, we are dealing with too many unknowns. In all honesty I can only tell you this: we will do the very best we can. Our defense must hold, because we all know our very existence depends on the outcome of this battle."

"I don't mean to take my frustrations out on you, General, but I'm sure you understand how I feel," said Dovina, now very concerned. "If I thought it would help, I'd challenge Lord GorDon to a duel and pick a champion to fight him."

"Your highness, we don't even have a champion on Kaladon to do battle with Lord GorDon. Moreover, I'm not sure a one-on-one confrontation could stop a planet-wide battle."

"I never said my champion was on Kaladon," said Dovina.

★   ★   ★

"Captain, I'm picking up 12 contacts in deep space moving toward Kaladon," said communications.

"Communicator, transmit message to Carznot: `Need assistance. 12 spacecraft approaching from deep space. Unknown origin'," said Captain Mytlaq.

"Message sent, Captain," replied communications.

"Operations, set battle stations," ordered the Captain.

"Weapons armed," came a report.

In a few seconds the operations officer said, "Captain all stations reported set for battle stations, shields energized."

Captain Mytlaq nodded that she heard both. "Prepare to fire all forward batteries, pick a target for each cannon pair, but do not lock."

"Weapons station prepared to fire. Captain, targets located, but not locked."

"Very well," said the captain. "Communications, transmit to the approaching spacecraft. `We are the sentry of Kaladon. Stop and identify yourselves'."

"Message sent Captain," replied the communicator.

This surprised the 12 vessels en route, they thought this bold Captain in front of them had either a lot of courage or was a fool. Since they had no record of its presence, each considered it best to approach with caution. With many new weapons systems on war cruisers, none was exactly sure what he might face, especially from one so bold.

If this is a pre-invasion force, at least Kaladon will be warned, she thought. "On visual," ordered the captain. His image appeared as he spoke.

"My name is Captain Bellost. We are on a mission of great importance. We are from Krynta and Pendari, coming to lend assistance to Kaladon against the Tygerian Empire."

"This is Captain Mytlaq and we welcome you." She quickly assessed codes on the monitor to confirm the speaker's words.

"I will be pleased to escort you to Kaladon, Captain Bellost," said

Captain Carznot.

This transmission had somewhat startled the communications officers on all 12 craft. They weren't even aware this other war cruiser was in the area.

"We will be honored for the escort," replied Captain Bellost. The 12 war cruisers fell into formation behind Carznot.

"Kaladon, this is Captain Carznot."

"Captain Carznot, we receive you. According to our monitors you have 12 guests. Please explain," said Captain Moratz.

"Krynta and Pendari are offering their assistance. Shall I let them pass?" Carznot chuckled at this unexpected fortune. Their code information is verified and visual confirms."

"Yes, yes, of course," replied Captain Moratz, very excited.

In leaving the group and heading back to rendezvous with Captain Mytlaq, he assessed the computer schematics of the new arrivals. One blaster cannon on each battery, with two forward and two aft. The *Bangar* and *Lynzar* each had twice the firepower of the Krinian and Pendarian war cruisers and their cannons were much larger. Still, help was help.

★   ★   ★

"Captain RomMen, I think we're about as ready for the Tygerians as we'll ever be. Again I congratulate you on the successful training of the crew, especially in the limited time afforded us," said Carter. RomMen only nodded in reply. "Make course for Kaladon and signal the *Bangar* to meet us. We should get his communication codes changed before the fireworks start."

"I agree," said RomMen, somewhat puzzled. "Fireworks? What are fireworks?"

"Well, Captain, after spending all that time on Earth, I'd have thought you would know what fireworks are," Carter said, grinning.

CHAPTER 13

INVASION

"Communications, contact Jackson. Have him assemble his crew for sentry duty at Kaladon."

"Yes sir, Captain," said Pyzor.

"Bridge, Capt'n Jackson here."

"Captain, make all preparations for space flight. You're to relieve Carznot on sentry duty. You'll be briefed upon arrival."

"Capt'n Jackson, aye." He was pleased to have an assignment and eager to get started. One could hear the locks disengaged as the *Raven* separated from *Star Wolf* and was on its way.

"Pyzor, have Carter call the bridge."

In a few moments, "Bridge, Carter here."

"Carter," said RomMen. "I wanted to inform you that I have ordered *Raven* to relieve *Bangar* on sentry duty. We need to effect minor repairs and get his codes changed before the Tygerians arrive."

"I concur and thanks for keeping me informed, Carter out."

The clinking sound was much louder from the metal to metal contact as *Bangar* attached to *Star Wolf*. A repair crew came aboard to perform the needed minor repairs. Lieut. Lo'Gon was also available to change the communication codes. An hour after he finished, Pyzor checked the traitor's work. The codes needed to be changed, but his superiors thought it best not to make an arrest at this time. *Foolish,* he thought. After the completion of his work he made his report to Captain RomMen.

"Captain," said Lieut. Wooz, "I'm picking up 32 contacts from the farthest probe launched. They're headed for Kaladon."

"How long before they arrive?" asked the Captain.

"Approximately three hours and maximum alert codes were sent as required. Kaladon knows, sir."

"Very well on all reports," said RomMen.

★   ★   ★

Lord GorDon sat on the Bridge of his command vessel. He was quite comfortable listening to the chatter and activity going on around him. "My Lord," said Captain BenNak, "we'll arrive at Kaladon in three hours, sir. Are there any final instructions before we arrive?"

"Yes, captain, have the admiral meet me in the officers' lounge." As lord GorDon got up to leave, personnel of all rank snapped to attention.

Lord GorDon and Admiral ZynTak exchanged pleasantries, then got down to business. "Admiral, I've been thinking about Kaladon and what concerns me greatly is that Plaxar wasn't damaged during our initial attack. I suppose those witless Bendoatiis have gotten themselves killed attempting to obtain that information." The battle-seasoned veteran showed concern. It was caution that had helped him plan against his foes in ways they could rarely outmaneuver him.

"My lord, with the fleet we have at our disposal I hardly think Kaladon could offer much resistance. If I recall they have no spacecraft, except this mythical one commanded by the Earthling. And according to our intelligence reports, all but a handful of their fighters have been destroyed. Just what, if any, experience does this Earthling have in commanding a spacecraft? I mean, Earth doesn't even have space travel, unless you consider sitting in an antiquated piece of junk while orbiting your planet space travel. And how can Ozlonz build a respectable defense system in just two months?" He quickly added, "however, I do understand My Lord's discretion."

"I heartily agree with what you say, but sometimes we must expect the unexpected, don't you think?" replied Lord GorDon with a slight frown. He sat there in deep thought, while pondering the many times Carter had eluded capture and avoided certain death. "My commanders have dealt with this Earthling before. He's very elusive and I wouldn't take him too lightly. Nothing would please me more than to have him on the other end of my blade." *Perhaps some day soon, fortune will smile upon me*, he thought. "Admiral, we'll proceed in accordance to plan; I want you to instruct the fleet not to damage the palace in any way or they'll answer to me. Is that understood?"

"Yes, sir, my lord. I'll issue that order at once." He got up and hurriedly left the room.

He sat there alone, his mind wandering. *Has Lo'Gon failed me? Perhaps he hasn't had any opportunity to contact me. Or this Earthling has foiled our plan.* He wasn't very concerned about Lo'Gon's safety, the only thing of importance was the spacecraft. And he was obsessed with the idea of acquiring it. *What's that fool Lo'Gon waiting for,* he thought, as his anger swelled from within.

He stopped short of banging his fist on the table while struggling back to reality. *I must control myself,* he thought. *No one must see me losing control.* He quickly went to his quarters.

★ ★ ★

"Kaladon, this is *Star Wolf*," said Pyzor.

"*Star Wolf*, Captain Moratz here, proceed with your message."

"Long-range scanners picked up 32 vessels on a course for Kaladon. Didn't you receive our message?"

"We received your message, but were unable to confirm your findings. Are you sure your scanners are accurate?"

"Captain, is General Sizdroz there?"

"No, he isn't, *Star Wolf*," said Captain Moratz firmly. "And Lieut., we're all on Kaladon, can you be more specific on your next transmission. We're at the palace in Plaxar."

"Understood," replied Pyzor. "Plaxar, would you please find General Sizdroz and have him contact us. We'll be there in an hour. Admiral Carter or Captain RomMen would like to talk with the General as soon as possible."

Pyzor looked to RomMen and said, "That captain could be real trouble for us."

"My thoughts exactly," said KorRak. "We had a little problem with Captain Critz at Ozlonz and now it's Captain Moratz."

"If we don't hear from General Sizdroz soon we'll have Captain Mytlaq land and confront him," Carter said to the small group now gathering on the bridge.

It was a half hour later and they still hadn't heard from Sizdroz. "Pyzor,"

Carter said. "Contact Plaxar again and see if we can talk to Sizdroz."

"Aye, Admiral," said Pyzor, setting up the sequence with his left hand. "Plaxar, *Star Wolf*. Is General Sizdroz available?"

"*Star Wolf*, this is Captain Moratz," came a cool reply. "General Sizdroz is busy and isn't here right now, but I'll tell him you called when we can confirm your report on the Tygerians."

"Enough of this," RomMen said, angrily. "Contact *Lynzar*, if the area is clear, have her land to confer with General Sizdroz."

"*Lynzar, Star Wolf*?"

"*Lynzar* here, go ahead."

"Captain RomMen orders you to scan the immediate area, if it's clear; land and confer." Lieut. Pyzor briefly explained the problem with Captain Moratz. He referred to the Captain's anger and his own concern that the Tygerians were not very far away. "We do not need this problem," he concluded.

"I concur completely," Captain Mytlaq replied. "I always wanted to give that little nibor a piece of my mind."

"Navigator, scan the area. If clear, set us down on the emergency padport near the palace."

General Sizdroz and the empress were standing in the throne room discussing strategy when suddenly they heard a loud and explosive noise. They immediately recognized the sound of landing thrusters igniting. As soon as the craft touched down, Captain Mytlaq ordered, "Keep the main engines on line."

The lower hatch opened in a downward direction. Mytlaq, in full dress uniform, including her sword, didn't wait for it to drop, but jumped the last couple of feet as the ramp descended. Four warriors, also in full dress uniform were right behind her. They approached two security guards at the palace steps.

"I'm sorry for the disturbance," said Mytlaq, "but I have important information for Her Highness and General Sizdroz."

Before the guard could answer, Sizdroz and Dovina were coming down the steps, already hearing Mytlaq's words. "Shanza, are you the captain of this war cruiser?" she asked in a show of surprise.

"Yes, Your Highness, I am," she replied, giving her the customary bow befitting an empress.

"That's wonderful, I envy you." She momentarily recalled the fun times they used to have with the military.

"Please forgive the interruption, Captain, Your Highness, but why did you land just to give us a message?" asked the General. "Perhaps your communications systems have failed?"

"I wish to inform you that our deep space sensors, deployed with your approval, have picked up 32 Tygerian spacecraft. They will arrive about mid-day. We have been trying to relay this information to you for the last hour, General."

"General, we've been unable to confirm this," cut in Captain Moratz, after rushing out from the communications room. "And therefore I saw no reason to bother you."

"Bother me? Bother me?" exclaimed General Sizdroz again, his voice getting louder with every word he spoke. "Just exactly what do you mean by that, Captain?" The general was angry and upset at the same time. "These people," pointing to Shanza, "have the most advanced technology available and you chose not to bother me because our antiquated systems couldn't confirm this."

"General, I—, I—."

Before Moratz could answer. "Captain we are about to engage in the most important battle of our history. Our very existence depends on the outcome. We may well be destroyed or enslaved. And you don't want to bother me?" He paused momentarily. "Captain, you are relieved of your duties; go join the warriors at the military complex in sector three and tell General Engort why I sent you."

Captain Mytlaq struggled with herself not to laugh at his humiliation, but the fool deserved everything he got. "Please contact *Star Wolf* as soon as you can, General."

Dovina smiled and waved goodby, as Captain Mytlaq went back to her vessel. Amid the deafening noise and swirls of dust the *Lynzar* took off for space.

★   ★   ★

"*Star Wolf*, General Sizdroz here, please reply."

"General, this is Carter, glad you called. Have all your war cruisers rendezvous with us as soon as possible. We'll shuttle the captains and you to the *Star Wolf* for a war council."

"Understood, Carter, and thanks. But I'll stay and handle things down here. Just keep me informed."

"Well, Captain, I guess we'd better get ready," Carter said.

"Lieut. Pyzor, recall all support craft."

In a short while all the spacesleds shuttled in all the captains and attached the support craft to *Star Wolf*. They all assembled in the conference room for their council of war. The other captains were in awe of the *Star Wolf's* size and armament. None had ever seen a vessel this large before.

In less then an hour of planning, some of which was heated and loud, they all agreed on a surprise plan for the Tygerians. The Captains were shuttled back to their spacecraft and proceeded to their predetermined positions. While none had reflector devices they would lie in space just beyond short range scanners and surprise the Tygerians when they arrived. Although they were out-numbered, each felt they had a chance, because the element of surprise rested with them.

The defenders figured to use a triangle attack, sending nine war cruisers in from two points, and Carters' group would attack from the third.

The *Star Wolf* would lie in wait, with its reflector device energized, and try to destroy the battle cruisers. As soon as the attack on the surface started, the carriers and *Star Wolf* would launch all available fighters. Captain RomMen coded a message to General Sizdroz, informing him of the plan. He approved the plan immediately, as he thought it truly would give them an edge. This would benefit him on the ground, too.

★   ★   ★

"Captain RomMen," said Pyzor, as he came on the bridge from the CCC, "why don't we launch space mines?"

"What did you say, Lieutenant?"

"I broke another security code on the weapons computer and

accordingly I found out that all spacecraft have space mines in their arsenal, homing space mines, sir. We can launch them into the path of the Tygerian fleet. The effectiveness might be poor, but anything will help, even if it's only antagonistic."

Carter was listening to the conversation and was impressed by the idea. "Captain, how long before the Tygerians arrive?"

"Bout an hour."

"That enough time?" asked Carter.

"It is," he said, nodding his head. "The war cruisers can launch about 20 mines each and get back before the attack starts. Kaladon's between us and the Tygerians, so that should afford them the cover they need. The orbit of Kaladon will send the mines right in their path. We'll use an outer orbit so they won't come back at us or interfere with our scanners."

"Excellent idea, Captain," Carter said.

RomMen turned to Pyzor and said, "Launch the war cruisers."

Pyzor relayed the order and in a few minutes they left for Kaladon. En route they were briefed on exactly what to do. Their weapons officers were checking their computers and tech manuals for proper procedure. Upon arriving at their designated position they launched the mines and headed back.

The *Star Wolf* moved into position to await the arrival of the Tygerians. Their fleet was closing fast. Short-range sensors confirmed their position. "They're about a half hour away, said Pyzor.

"Let's get to battle stations," said RomMen.

Lieut. Wooz positioned the switch on his panel and the alarm sounded. Everybody rushed to their assigned battle stations.

"KorRak, I want three extra security people on the bridge during battle stations," said RomMen.

"Yes, sir," KorRak replied sharply.

Carter heard RomMen's last order and nodded his head in agreement. It was an excellent precaution that would enable them to keep better watch on Lo'Gon.

"Shields energized," reported operations.

"Weapons armed," reported weapons.

"Very well on all reports."

After about five minutes all personnel were at their battle stations and *Star Wolf* was ready. All four support craft reported manned and ready to detach. Forty-two of the two hundred fighters would be useless, as there was still no one to fly them.

"Energize reflector device."

"Reflector device energized, holographics normal Captain," Lieut. Wooz reported a moment later.

"Communicator, have the warriors board the spacesleds, in preparations for landing on Kaladon."

"Lieut. Wydorf acknowledges your last order, Captain," said Lieut. Pyzor.

★   ★   ★

Suddenly, there was an explosion. Lord GorDon looked up at the admiral and noticed he was already getting up to investigate. "Explain, Captain, now."

"One of our war cruisers has been damaged by an explosion." He conferred with his operations officer. "We're not sure what it was. No asteroids in this sector, but we have detected a field of small objects about three meters in diameter, crossing our path," the captain replied, also wondering what they could be.

There were a few more explosions, equally faint along with one large one. "Captain BenNak, contact the fleet, have them go to alert status, set battle stations, and get those shields energized, fast," barked Admiral ZynTak.

"Yes sir, Admiral. At once, sir." A few minutes later, after getting his report, there were a few more faint explosions.

Admiral ZynTak stepped over to Lord GorDon. "My lord, we're on alert status. We've scanned the entire area and have detected what we believe to be space mines, twenty-three to be exact. As you already know some have detonated. Since we are making our final approach I have taken the fleet out of hyperspace. We'll be slowing to sub-light in a moment.

"We sustained damage on seven of our war cruisers and a supply craft was destroyed. Two war cruisers cannot continue and have to be repaired.

One sustained damage to its weapons systems and can only use rear batteries, and yet another has damage to main engine control and won't be able to return to hyperspace. The captain of that war cruiser seems to think it can be fixed in a short time. The other three war cruisers have received minimal damage, because their shields were energized."

"Thank you, Admiral, for the report. I'm very pleased by it, but not the damage we sustained," said Lord GorDon, displaying a satisfied smile. "You have come a long way in your proficiency since we last served together."

"I requested this assignment directly from the emperor to serve under you in this district, my lord."

"Space mines, huh? Destroy them as we pass," replied Lord GorDon softly. "I know of only one place that installs space mines on spacecraft, and that's Ra'Tor. We haven't been able to get them for our vessels. Yet suddenly we're in a field of them." He sat quietly and the bridge quieted with him. Suddenly he stood, smashed his fist into his other hand, and in a loud voice, said, "It's him again. It's that accursed Earthling. Use caution Admiral," he pointed and shook his claw nervously. "Don't ever underestimate this Earthling."

"Understood, my Lord." He was now as concerned as his boss.

"It has to be him. It's that new spacecraft from Ra'Tor. That's where those space mines came from. Curse him, will I ever see him dead?" cried Lord GorDon.

"Excuse me, Admiral, but it's time to split the fleet and get into position to start our attack," the captain interrupted.

"Reduce speed to sublight. Make the split and have transport craft prepare to land warriors on the border of the Esterk province as planned," ordered Admiral ZynTak.

"Yes, sir, Admiral," the captain replied eagerly.

★   ★   ★

"Your highness, we are detecting the Tygerian spacecraft on our short range sensors coming around the horizon," said General Sizdroz. "It's in the hands of our Maker now."

"We'll do fine," said the empress, perhaps attempting to convince herself. "Go get em, Carter," she said softly. "We've been through a lot worse in the arena and survived."

"You care for this male a great deal," he said to her.

"I don't dare think about him, General," she replied. "I can't get emotionally involved with anyone at this time. It might cloud my judgment. Besides, he belongs to someone else. If we survive—." She paused. "We'll see."

★   ★   ★

"Lord GorDon, we aren't picking up any contacts on our sensors," said the captain. "Where can they be, my lord?"

"I wasn't expecting a sky full of spacecraft, but I was expecting some resistance," replied Lord GorDon, a bit puzzled.

"I sense a trap if there ever was one, my Lord," said the admiral anxiously. "Operations, inform the fleet. Prepare to start the attack on my order."

"Aye, My Lord," replied operations.

"He's out there, I know he is. I can feel it," said Lord GorDon. "Why doesn't he do something? What's he waiting for, and why aren't we intercepting their internal communications signals? Perhaps Lo'Gon has failed me after all." Lord GorDon was blurting his thoughts out loud. "Captain, are we picking up transmissions from anyone?"

"Communications are quiet, my lord," the captain replied.

"Something must give him away, even though he's got a reflector device. Perhaps when he fires his first shot we can detect its origin. If only I knew more about that cursed device."

★   ★   ★

"Captain, looks like they're getting into position to start their attack," said Carter.

"Weapons, concentrate on the two bombing cruisers on the right side of your screen, but don't lock on."

Pyzor was getting excited, this being his first battle.

"Carter, you ever get that feeling where everyone's just waiting for someone else to make the first move? I mean, Lord GorDon has to know we're here and watching him," said RomMen.

"What's he waiting for?" said Carter. "Does the thought of our presence here make him more cautious?"

"Maybe it's because he doesn't know our exact position," said RomMen.

"To tell you the truth, Captain, I'm not sure what he's waiting for either," said KorRak.

"Captain, there's a message coming in on a general code," said Lieut. Pyzor.

"On speaker," ordered Captain RomMen.

"Are we playing a little hide and catch game, Carter?" said a deep voice. "I know you're out there, hidden behind your little reflector device. I don't scare you, do I?"

"What the hell's he doing, playing mind games?" he said to RomMen. "Do you know who that is?"

"Yeah, heh, heh," chuckled RomMen. "I know who it is."

"So do I," cut in KorRak. "I'd know that voice anywhere, even though it's been years since I heard it."

"Well, don't leave me in suspense, guys. Who is it?"

"It's Lord GorDon himself," said RomMen.

★   ★   ★

"Attack!" yelled Lord GorDon angrily. Immediately the bombing cruisers started firing their destructive capsules at Plaxar. They were moving into position and firing as they went. Their targets were some of the outer areas of the city, home to at least two military bases. They had no idea two groups of war cruisers were approaching them from space. The Tygerians were so confident of their superiority, they didn't seem to care that they might encounter any significant resistance. Nor did they check beyond short range sensors for any surprises from space.

*   *   *

That's exactly what Captain RomMen had counted on. Tygerian overconfidence would ensure the effectiveness of a surprise counter attack.

"What are you waiting for, Captain?" he said softly while standing near him, not wanting anyone else to hear his question.

"There are at least ten spacecraft tuned to our approximate position, and they're waiting for us to fire our weapons. I don't want to launch our support craft into a hail of cannon fire. We need a diversion, which we'll get as soon as the other spacecraft arrive and start firing. Patience, my friend," he said softly.

"Excellent decision, captain," he replied, a little annoyed with himself for not thinking before he asked.

"Weapons, prepare to fire forward batteries at previously designated targets. Make that at two second intervals," ordered RomMen. "Lieut. Pyzor, immediately following my order to launch, I want our war cruisers to attack the transport vessels landing warriors. The carriers are to launch fighters as soon as they're free of *Star Wolf* and to report to General Engort. The carriers will then engage the war cruisers."

Suddenly one of the Tygerian war cruisers exploded and another one nearby lifted and spun around, gyrating erratically. "The Kaladonian fleet has arrived," said Captain RomMen about the obvious. All watched the Tygerian war cruisers go from their position near *Star Wolf* to engage this new threat.

"De-energize reflector device. Launch," ordered Captain RomMen. As soon as the support craft were clear RomMen focused his attention on the battle. The support group was now on its own. "Lock and fire," barked the captain. Immediately four shots were fired and in two seconds, four more. "Energize reflector device." They moved *Star Wolf* and prepared for another target.

*   *   *

Monitors in the entire Tygerian fleet lit up. "There it is," yelled Lord GorDon excitedly. "Bring us about, quickly!" The Tygerians repositioned six of their war cruisers and fired their forward weapons at *Star Wolf*. There was one explosion. GorDon had missed with the other shots. He was maneuvering for another shot. All on the bridge of the Tygerian war cruiser saw fiery flashes hit two of the three bombing cruisers. On the second hit they exploded into huge fireballs. They looked back only to see *Star Wolf* disappear from view.

The explosions so startled the Tygerian captains near the bombing cruisers that conflict momentarily halted. "Lord GorDon, they had their shields energized," said Admiral ZynTak, a shocked look on his face. "Their weapon blasts went through their shields, like they weren't even there."

"How could Carter have possibly known those two spacecraft were the only two here that still had the older, less effective shields? He will not have that much success against the rest of our fleet," said Lord GorDon.

★   ★   ★

"They've started bombing Plaxar, your highness," said General Sizdroz. Lord Nemarg ordered all fighters launched. Blaster cannon emplacements started firing at the incoming Tygerian war cruisers as soon as they were in range, a little late. One cannon shot hit a war cruiser and immediately the emplacement was attacked and destroyed. A different cannon battery hit the same war cruiser that was hit before and it was enough. The crew of the cannon emplacement cheered, but it was short-lived. Another war cruiser destroyed the cannon emplacement a few seconds later. There were more then 40 cannon emplacements around Plaxar and 20 in Ozlonz, all firing at the Tygerian fleet.

On one side, nine Kaladonian war cruisers, coming out of light speed, were met by six Tygerian war cruisers. The element of surprise was with the Kaladonians, but the experience and seasoning of battle rested with the Tygerians. In a sense they were very evenly matched. The sky burned with the fire-fight. Kaladonian loyalists defeated the Tygerians quickly, but not without irreparable loss. Six war cruisers spun out of orbit to burn in an atmospheric crash that would incinerate any still on board. Two were Kaladonian and four were Tygerians.

On the initial attack the Krynians didn't fare as well. They lost three war cruisers to the Tygerians' two.

Three other Kaladonian war cruisers joined the fight; all began firing at the same Tygerian craft. Their shields simply could not maintain enough energy to overcome such force. As soon as the power to their shields dropped low enough, the vessels exploded. Immediately the three newest additions turned their efforts toward the other Tygerian war cruiser to finish it off. It wisely broke off the engagement and returned to join the rest of its fleet.

A tactic being used by the Kaladonians and Krynians was to attack in a group of three or more. It was Captain RomMen's strategy for attacking a spacecraft.

It appeared the third bombing cruiser was inflicting plenty of unanswered damage on Plaxar, so Lord GorDon gave the command to land. The whole conflict had taken about 30 minutes. "Admiral ZynTak, continue the effort here. Plan on destroying everything in sight," ordered Lord GorDon, burning with the old bloodlust that he so often felt. "I'm going down to the surface near the palace in Ozlonz with the second group of warriors." Between the warrior cargo craft and undamaged war cruisers, better than eight thousand ground troops would land on the first wave, with more waves to follow. In a half-hour the second wave was landing near Plaxar as planned. An hour and a half after the first exchange Lord GorDon was standing on Kaladonian soil.

★   ★   ★

Captain RomMen had stayed fixed on the last bombing cruiser for ten minutes, trying to get in position.

General Engort took over control of the fighters without a word, letting RomMen's expertise go uninterrupted. A lull in the face-off gave RomMen an opportunity to contact General Engort. "General," he said, staying above the noise of battle, "bombing cruisers have to reduce power to their lower shields before they can launch capsules."

Engort hit his com switch and within minutes six fighters from *Raven* fell into formation behind Captain Centarkoh, flying full speed at the bombing cruiser's vulnerable underbelly, while dodging destructive capsules. All began firing simultaneously at the same general location. Shortly after they veered off, the bombing cruiser exploded. Still, they lost three fighters during the attack. It was a painful and difficult way of reducing the Tygerian space superiority.

The remaining six fighters, including Captain Centarkoh's, spotted a damaged Tygerian war cruiser. Captain Centarkoh and his group swarmed in for the kill. In a short time there was a smoke plume emitting from the rear of the vessel. It blew apart and debris was burning as it fell into Kaladon's atmosphere. Just as the pilots eased off, a shot from out of nowhere hit yet another fighter. Lieut. Torroan never knew what hit her.

The Tygerian loss was better than Captain RomMen expected. To his best count, he figured more then 12 war cruisers and all three bombing cruisers were either destroyed or disabled. *The odds are becoming more even,* he thought, with a smile.

Captain Mytlaq had trouble of her own. While diving under all the firing she was below 300 meters of the planet surface. She could feel her war cruiser shaking as the energy from her shields arched to the surface. She realized, almost too late, that she was much too low. Circling around, she gained altitude, and attacked one of the warrior cargo crafts that had already unloaded its cargo of ground troops. With the concentration of firepower from her war cruiser, the vessel was doomed. It arched, then blew, killing the fleeing warriors closest to it.

Maneuvering the *Lynzar* over the palace, Captain Mytlaq could see Tygerian warriors getting closer. If command headquarters were disrupted on the surface, it could cause severe problems. They needed more fighters and warriors to repel this threat. She contacted Captain Centarkoh, who confidently said he would take care of it.

In a few minutes Captain Centarkoh, adrenaline rushing from cheating death earlier, swooped down on the Tygerian warriors with 12 fighters from the *Vandor*. But the Kaladonian loyalists did not have complete superiority. Shortly after the attack began a Tygerian war cruiser came to assist. As the vessel approached, the *Lynzar* intercepted and started firing point blank, so close that shocks from the impacts nearly shook *Lynzar* off course each time she fired. *Lynzar* had twice the firepower of the smaller war cruiser, which quickly veered, breaking off the encounter. Captain Mytlaq stayed with it, and just as it started fading and attempted to go to light speed, the Tygerian vessel exploded.

Another cargo craft had landed to drop off warriors just outside of Plaxar. Captain Carznot came flying in after it with six fighters to assist. It was just clearing the treetops when he hit it with every weapon he had. In a few seconds the slower, unprotected craft broke apart and fell to the ground. Captain Carznot's joy was short-lived when he realized it had already unloaded its cargo.

He saw Captain Mytlaq's craft and followed her up to engage the rest of the Tygerian fleet. Both captains preferred the underneath approach, as both maneuvered for a quick run. There were some definite advantages to the tactic. While their own war cruisers were hit many times, their high-energy power plants produced shield strength that never dropped below 70 percent. Lord GorDon and his admirals had grossly underestimated Kaladon's strength and persistence.

The *Star Wolf* de-energized its reflector device to launch spacesleds, and monitors across the Tygerian fleet lit up to show a new threat. Immediately after the spacesleds took off, *Star Wolf* disappeared again. Carter went with Lieut. Wydorf and the warriors down to Plaxar and then on to the palace in Ozlonz. They were escorted by the *Lynzar* and eight fighters. A pass over the palace showed approaching troops, but no damage. That seemed odd to everyone, considering the chaos all around it.

In the sky there were bigger problems. Captain Carznot on the *Bangar* found himself pursued by three Tygerian war cruisers, pounding him with exceptional force. His shields were weakening and death seemed eminent. *Oh well*, Carznot thought. *One hell of a fight!*

As Carznot braced for an explosion, one of the Tygerian war cruisers suddenly listed left after a hit from four blaster cannons. Then another took a lateral hit. This unexpected offensive rocked both war cruisers and startled their captains. They regrouped when they realized another war cruiser had joined the battle, with eight fighters for support. All veered off in retreat, but only two made the jump to light speed in time.

"Thanks, Captain. That's one I owe you," said Carznot, as smoke emitted and debris fell from his damaged superstructure. He landed safely a few miles from the palace.

The *Star Wolf* had taken a pounding, because two war cruisers finally figured out its location. They suffered some damage, but their shields held. The two war cruisers soon learned the error of their ways as the *Star Wolf* destroyed both of them.

Both carriers returned and positioned themselves on each side of *Star Wolf*. Admiral ZynTak saw this, but didn't quite understand the situation.

During their absence from *Star Wolf*, the *Raven* annihilated three war cruisers and *Vandor* destroyed two. The Tygerians had disabled two more Kaladonian vessels, both of which were still burning internally in space.

When *Star Wolf* de-energized its reflector device directly in front of Admiral ZynTak's war cruiser, he was spellbound by its size and visible armament. Admiral ZynTak wisely realized the battle was lost.

The Tygerians had nine of their 32 spacecraft remaining including GorDon's command craft, Admiral LanDok's, and seven smaller war cruisers, some of which were also damaged. The great Tygerian fleet was almost destroyed. He faced three very powerful vessels, and a war cruiser. On one side were three war cruisers and the other side had two. They were trapped, not that an escape route would've mattered. They'd fight to the end no matter what the results. Never surrender, that was their code.

With Kaladon in charge of the air, warriors were the next concern. Lord Nemarg's fighters along with fighters from the *Star Wolf* and both carriers started pounding the now-panicking Tygerian warriors. They could not understand where their air cover was or what had gone wrong. Kaladonian troops marched to meet them, the first since the battle began. They were fierce in battle and their fighter craft were extremely effective. The Tygerian's suffered exceptional losses.

In now-calm space Captain RomMen slowly walked to the communication console, opened a channel and said, "Commanders of the Tygerian Empire, I give you the opportunity to stop this madness. Surrender or perish."

"Captain RomMen, is that you?"

"Yes, Captain ZynTak." He didn't know ZynTak had been promoted to admiral. They were friends at the academy on Felina.

"No wonder Kaladon had such success against us. The Earthling wasn't responsible for this, it was you," replied Admiral ZynTak. "You knew the status of the bombing cruisers' shields, and where you could inflict the most damage. All the rest of the tactics, our weaknesses, everything. It was you, wasn't it?"

"You're absolutely correct, Captain." He paused a moment. "Lord GorDon will never take another command from me and imprison me in disgrace because of his asinine nephews. Now tell him to give up this madness or we'll destroy the rest of his fleet. You don't have much time. If any transmissions emit from your vessels we will open fire immediately."

"Communications, monitor the last two transmissions."

"Got em, captain," replied Lieut. Pyzor. "Your pals are in the two larger war cruisers. I plotted them both."

"Order all vessels to fire at the remaining Tygerian war cruisers on my order."

"Weapons, prepare to fire."

"Prepare to fire, aye, captain," replied weapons.

"Command sent," replied Lieut. Pyzor. A few seconds later, he said, "Message acknowledged from the carriers and the rest of our fleet, Captain."

Lieut. Lo'Gon sat very quietly at the small table just off to the side. He was waiting for someone to call his name and give him away. He saw Pyzor, *worthless creature,* he thought, had not stopped looking at him since he returned to the bridge. Perhaps it was nothing, but he wasn't sure.

Captain KorRak was standing on the bridge near the weapons console enjoying all that had transpired thus far. He had no love for the Tygerian Empire either.

"Captain, command craft is transmitting," said Pyzor.

"Fire," barked RomMen.

"Fire," ordered Pyzor, transmitting to all spacecraft.

Star Wolf started firing and both sides fired simultaneously as blue-white streaks of cannon flash clouded the monitors. The war cruisers kept firing until the danger of heat threatened to melt the mechanism.

After the firing stopped and everything was calm, Captain RomMen received a report from damage control, that *Star Wolf* had taken many hits, but took them well. They had minor damage on a few decks and the exterior superstructure was scorched in two places, but intact. All fires were out and damage control was on top of everything. *Vandor* had damage to one of its landing tracks, and *Raven* had no damage at all. Of the three remaining war cruisers, so new they weren't even paid for, only one had survived. But it, too, was damaged and had to leave formation for the planet surface. Not so good for her allies. Of the 12 war cruisers from Krynta and Mylaar, ten had been destroyed. The only Tygerian war cruiser remaining was the large command craft of Admiral ZynTak.

CHAPTER 14

A NEW BEGINNING

Lord GorDon put a portable amplifier to his mouth, and yelled, "You, in the palace, this is Lord GorDon, warlord of the Tygerian Empire. Throw down your weapons and surrender. The palace is surrounded and there is no escape." He waited a short while and received no reply. Warlords were rarely in the mood for dispensing surrender mercies, but GorDon was far more intelligent than he was bloodthirsty.

Deciding to wait no longer Lord GorDon walked up the steps, looked around carefully, and went in. He was followed by 20 of his elite warriors. As he walked toward the far end he could see an officer on one side of the throne and three warriors on the other. He continued, unconcerned, toward the bottom of the steps. Then something caught his eye that made him stop. He looked to his left, while motioning for his warriors to form a semi-circle on both sides.

A stunning female in a long flowing gown stepped from behind the curtain and walked toward the throne. She stopped, faced the intruders, and said, "Lord GorDon, warmonger of the Tygerian Empire?" There was laughter from his troops at her words. Determined to go on with a plan she wasn't sure would work, Dovina went right for his ego. "I challenge you in a duel to the death for your intrusion. And I shall pick my champion."

"And just who is your champion?" spat Lord GorDon. He had taken the bait. "Or perhaps I should ask first, who are you to demand such a challenge?"

"I am Empress Dovina Zordek, ruler of Kaladon," she replied firmly, as she sat down. "And I address a murderer."

"Not anymore you're not," said Lord GorDon, arrogantly ignoring her accusation. He went up the steps about half-way, stopped and glared up at the person before him.

"Don't I deserve the respect of a customary bow when approaching an empress?" she said, trying not to act concerned.

He stood staring at her. He did not acknowledge second thoughts readily. But this time, he was entertaining the idea and showing them in his expressions. Recovering, he said, "I only bow to my emperor and royalty that have earned my respect. What you say is meaningless. You should be groveling at my feet for leniency. I have destroyed your fleet and demand your surrender. Kaladon is mine." He stood poised like a boxer and his voice grew louder as he spoke.

"You don't have to beg for anything, your Highness," Carter said, walking briskly to her side from the curtain's edge. "In fact, Lord GorDon, you are very much mistaken. Your magnificent armada has been destroyed and Empress Dovina Zordek, ruler of Kaladon," he waved his arm toward her, "demands your immediate surrender," he smiled as he finished his speech.

Lord GorDon stood there, staring at him with a look of contempt, waiting for the near instant translation. *Could this be the Earthling?* he thought.

"Oh, how rude of me, your highness," Carter said. "Where are my manners? I apologize for the interruption."

The empress stood. "Lord GorDon, my champion," she motioned with her outstretched arm, still smiling. "His name is Carter. He's an Earthling. Perhaps you've heard of him."

"Lord GorDon, what a pleasant surprise. We finally meet face to face, and you're not just a voice on a communications channel from a spacecraft which we destroyed."

Lord GorDon gave a long low, nearly inaudible growl. He was ready to pounce as he stared up at Carter. He had never been in contact with the creatures from Earth, and he was having a hard time keeping his composure in the face of one who did not cower in his presence.

Finally, he spoke in a quiet controlled voice. "I'm happy to make your acquaintance at last. You've been in my thoughts many times of late. You'll never know how glad I am to finally meet you in person. Perhaps fate has brought us together and your luck has finally run out." GorDon's expression seemed to change in mid-sentence, getting louder as he spoke. He slowly removed his cape and stood like a coiled spring ready to unwind, his hand on the hilt of his sword, his eyes locked onto his mortal enemy, ready to do battle.

So preoccupied was GorDon that he never noticed Kaladonian warriors slip up behind his to disarm them.

So menacing he was that Carter could see why his frightening reputation was deserved. He appeared to have regained complete control of himself.

"Wait," interrupted Dovina, in a loud crisp voice. "There will be no bloodshed here. No weapons are allowed to be drawn in the palace. Continue this outside." Everyone, including Lord GorDon, did as she ordered without question.

The forecast was to be clear with occasional clouds, but at present the sun was not shining. The air was tainted with the odors from war. Death and destruction were visible everywhere. The mood was nearly as dark as the cloud cover when Lord GorDon walked down the steps.

Captain Mytlaqs' war cruiser landed near the palace. The sound was deafening even at that distance from the palace. Word had spread of GorDon's whereabouts. Twenty fighters performed a fly-by as armored vehicles and hundreds of warriors ringed the palace entrance.

The access ramp lowered beneath the war cruiser as Captain RomMen, KorRak, Mytlaq and Jackson emerged. They were followed by Lieutenant Pyzor and Lo'Gon, Admiral ZynTak, Dr. Zark, and six members of the security force from *Star Wolf*. All were well armed. Admiral ZynTak was the only one in chains.

As they approached, the growing crowd of onlookers around Lord GorDon and Carter grew quieter. When they drew closer the crowd went silent. RomMen stepped out in front saying, "Well, if it isn't the infamous Lord GorDon himself. Don't tell me you've come all this way just to congratulate us on our victory? Or do you have some other reason for jeopardizing your safety?" Captain RomMen broke into a broad grin as he spoke. He made an abrupt about-face, grabbing someone behind him. "Here, I believe this belongs to you." Holding Lo'Gon by the front of his garment, he threw him toward Lord GorDon. "We don't like spies in our midst. Perhaps you do. The only reason he's still alive is because we never gave him the opportunity to betray us."

Lo'Gon stumbled a few times trying to regain his balance but he finally fell at Lord GorDon's feet. Two security guards, one on each side, picked him up and put him in chains.

Lo'Gon was never so shocked in all of his life when Captain RomMen grabbed him. *How could they have possibly known about me?* he thought. *None of this ragtag band could have known what a code 31 was. Nor about the communication codes. How? How was this possible?* He was physically drained and mentally sickened at getting caught. *I wonder if they know about Ri'Zar's daughter in the engineering spaces. She helped design the damned weapons systems, and I'm being blamed for denying any knowledge of them,* he thought. He was looking over at Pyzor and noticed he was staring back. *Hideous creature,* he thought.

Pyzor looked at Lo'Gon and displayed a slight grin.

Reality finally set in as GorDon looked around. Warriors defeated, armada destroyed. This was a situation he had never known, although several enemies had made his empire pay dearly for his incursions. This time he knew he was definitely not in control. None of his warriors had any weapons. They, too, were being put in chains. He didn't care what happened to Lo'Gon, but he did care about his warriors. All his careful planning had gone wrong. *How could this have happened?* he thought, barely able to keep from speaking aloud. *Somehow I lost control and things just got out of hand. I will kill this cursed Earthling.*

While holding that thought, he looked over at RomMen and it suddenly became very clear. His eyes got bigger as the truth finally dawned on him for the first time. Walking up to him, he said, "It was you." he growled loudly, pointing a claw at him.

"It's Captain RomMen to you, and don't you ever forget it."

"BryQat told me it was a mistake demoting you and sending you to the arenas. I guess perhaps he was right." He was nodding his head toward RomMen, indicating he was correct on this issue. "This was my only mistake in this whole campaign. I acknowledge your skills, Captain." He clicked his heels and nodded his head again, an honoring gesture in Tygerian society.

GorDon finally succumbed to the realization that he was defeated. *My great fleet destroyed,* he thought. *My victory snatched from me by these idiots. No wonder the enemy knew my weaknesses. The enemy was not only this accursed Earthling, but one of my best captains, as well.* Pondering this he thought, *Perhaps an honorable defeat was still possible.*

Lord GorDon turned to Empress Zordek. "Are you going to deny me my challenge?" he asked, as he bowed before her in the custom befitting an empress. She was shocked by his sudden display of respect, as was the crowd.

Before she could respond he quickly stood, drew his sword, and came at Carter, swinging. He waited until the last, split second, then side-stepped, moved just enough for GorDon to miss him with his sword, and bumped him on his shoulder as he went by. Lord GorDon went sprawling face first onto the hard surface next to the padport, falling so hard he even lost his grip on the sword. It made a screeching, rattling sound as it slid across the hard surface a few feet from him.

GorDon rolled over and sat up blood dribbling from small cuts and scratches on his face. He looked at Carter with a hatred such as Carter had never seen. Slowly he got up, never taking his eyes off Carter, picked up his sword and walked cautiously back toward him. Many in the crowd were amused at the great Lord GorDon lying face down on the hard surface, but they stifled their laughter. The embarrassment only infuriated him more.

Carter drew his sword, only it didn't glisten this time as it came out of the sheath. Instantly, he thought the sword had lost its power and his confidence wavered. Pyzor sensed this. He noticed the sword was different from any he had ever seen. Reading his thoughts he said, without speaking. *"It is always the bearer of the weapon, not the weapon itself, who wins the fight."*

"Thank you," thought Carter.

GorDon swung his sword and he blocked the blow. *He's strong, but not any more than KorRak,* he thought. His confidence was returning, thanks to Pyzor. They parried back and forth for a short time, and he realized he had a real fight on his hands. GorDon was constantly pressing and he knew he had to slow him down. Getting in a few nicks here and there were enough for him to realize that were it not for his speed he might have lost by now.

Soon GorDon started to get the edge, both mentally and physically. In addition to his strength, he was the best swordsman Carter had ever fought. His sword wasn't doing anything, so all his fighting drew simply from the skills he possessed. Nobody noticed that the clouds were breaking up until the sun shown through.

GorDon backed off a moment, to catch his breath. Carter was glad of that. Suddenly GorDon lunged in for another round of fierce sparring. Carter blocked his thrust, elbowed him in the chest and gave him a hip roll, which threw him on his back in the dirt. Carter swung his sword down at him, but GorDon rolled away just in time. This only increased his rage. Carter was getting in a few licks, but he didn't move fast enough for GorDon's last move. He felt the sting from a cut on his left leg. He could feel the wetness from a bleeding wound. This also forced him to limp and gave his opponent cause to smile. GorDon could tell he was now gaining momentum. "You're very good," said GorDon, confidently. "Much better than Res'Itz."

The sun shown brighter, and his sword started to reflect its splendor. The weapon started to glow slightly, and with each movement it became lighter in his hand. Inexplicably, he felt strength flowing from it. The pain in his leg eased, and he became more aggressive.

Pyzor, watching intently, noticed the change in the sword. He grew more intrigued as the transformation was taking place, both in the device and in the one carrying it. Pyzor didn't believe in magic, but he did understand that the universe held many strange mysteries. Certain metals reacting with direct sunlight must be one of them. Sparks flying from clashing swords broke Pyzor from his trance and GorDon from his cockiness. GorDon also noticed a nick in his blade and this concerned him very much, as it had never happened before.

They fought their way onto an ornamental wooden deck near a fountain on the side of the palace. Without thinking Carter shifted his weight to his left leg to use it as a pivot point. He lost his balance trying to run his sword into GorDon's side. When Lord GorDon blocked the move, Carter almost fell. He saw this and while parrying, maneuvered around and bumped him toward his left leg again. It threw Carter off balance again, but this time he went sprawling. He landed on his right shoulder and winced in pain. The momentum rolled Carter onto his back, with his right arm pinned beneath him. During the fall he lost his grip on the sword. He groped for it, almost panicking. It lay a few inches from his right shoulder. They were both gasping for breath.

Nobody noticed Pyzor step out in front of the crowd a few feet. As small as he was everybody just looked over him. He was watching intently, ready. He was holding something in his hand in front of him. It was metallic in color and barely visible.

Carter couldn't really move. Lord GorDon had him wedged between his legs, standing over him, the point of his sword pressing in his chest. "Now, Carter, I shall avenge my defeat on you. Much more than I did Res'Itz. So, the champion loses after all!" He raised his sword above his head for the kill. In a desperate move, Carter reached across with his left hand and grabbed his sword. He swung it across as Lord GorDon's sword came down toward his head. Just before their swords made contact he moved as far as he could to his right. When their blades hit, sparks flew, and this time it cut Lord GorDon's sword in half. The severed half kept coming and thudded into the wooden deck an inch from Carter's head.

This shocked Lord GorDon and put him off guard. He froze, momentarily, staring at his sword. Carter swung back through in the opposite direction and cut him right across the lower part of his chest. The deep unexpected wound stopped him cold. He staggered backward a few feet and sank to his knees, his forearm pressed tightly across his chest. Carter immediately got up, a little bloody and still limping, to face him again if necessary. GorDon looked down and gasped in horror as he saw blue blood oozing rapidly out of the wound. He then looked up at Carter, in utter disbelief. The hilt of his severed sword suddenly became very heavy and it slipped from his grasp. He fell over, face down onto the hard surface, gasping out a final breath. With no speeches and no melodramatic pause, GorDon simply died.

The crowd remained silent for a moment, then gave a sigh of relief. Some cheered, while others stood quietly in shock at the abrupt ending of the great Lord GorDon. He was a legend, feared throughout the galaxy. Now he was a cadaver on the wooden deck. Carter got up, very shaky on his feet and soaked with sweat. His wounds were slowly oozing blood as

Pyzor grabbed him and helped him to the wooden bench so he could sit down. Dr. Zark pushed through the crowd to reach him.

Criminal, he thought, *if the champion dies too, because the doctor can't get to him.* Shanza was right behind him.

As she approached Carter, she saw Pyzor standing next to him. "I'm sure he'll be just fine, Shanza."

"Oh! Pyzor, I was so terribly worried he might be killed," She put her arms around Carter and gave him a hug.

"No, Shanza," he whispered. "He certainly had a tough battle, but he was never in danger of being killed."

She backed up a little and stood looking at Pyzor, somewhat mystified by what he said. Answers would come later. Right now Carter needed medical attention and a little tender loving care.

Empress Zordek would confer with Generals Sizdroz and Engort about the fates of these prisoners, including Lo'Gon. It was decided they would be forced to help clean up the destruction they had caused.

Depending on their behavior, many could be put to death. It would send a message to the Tygerian government that its armed aggression would not be tolerated in the Tarn solar system. In the interim, Kaladon needed time to recover from an invasion that failed in its aim, yet succeeded in its destruction. Millions had died and many thousands were homeless as the aura of destruction loomed everywhere.

★ ★ ★

A special session of the government convened to recognize some of the many who contributed greatly toward victory. The timing was perfect because weeks of funerals and removing rubble had sent morale plummeting.

The ceremony wasn't a lengthy process and at the end the empress proceeded to present the awards for heroism to all who deserved them, and there were many, including Captain RomMen. After all the awards were presented, Empress Dovina stood and raised her arms and said, "My fellow citizens of Kaladon, I have ordered changes in our governmental structure.

The old senate is hereby abolished and I remove all of its power. In its place I will allow a group of lords to help govern Kaladon. They will be elected by the people of their province and will be known as the Lords of Kaladon."

"And finally, I shall have one more lord in my government. This person shall be Lord of the Skies. This will be the eyes and ears of Kaladon, the sentry, whose presence allows those below to sleep without fear and to work without worry. This lord will be in charge of the powerful space armada we shall build to protect our world and the Tarn solar system against any foe. We realized almost too late the advantages of having a powerful space fleet. Our neighbors have agreed to form an alliance with us and contribute toward the common goal of lasting peace in the Tarn solar system."

Geez, she's pretty good at this speech stuff, Carter thought.

"I appoint Franklin Carter to this position. And henceforth, he will bear the title `Lord Carter'. He will answer to me and this government for as long as it shall exist. May we all have many years of peace." The whole assembly stood and cheered.

Huh? he thought. *She's got to be kidding.* His eyes got wider as he stood there listening. He couldn't believe what she just said. He basked in praise he had never dreamed was possible. His appearance certainly didn't match his new title. His left leg was bandaged, his right arm lay useless in a sling and he had some difficulty walking. But it didn't matter. He just couldn't believe she did this. The honor she had bestowed on him. *A lord in the government, whew,* he thought, *this was too much.*

Shanza assisted him as he limped past Captains RomMen and KorRak, who surprisingly bowed as he went by. The two congratulated him and shook his left hand. Glancing to the side he saw Captains Jackson, Carznot, and Lieut. Pyzor giving him a thumbs up. *Must've been Jackson's idea,* he thought. He smiled, nodded, and returned the gesture with his left hand. Then he turned and continued toward the empress. He went up the steps about halfway and stopped.

She raised her arms once again to quiet the crowd. He bowed as best he could and then stood straight. He saw something in her eyes he'd never seen before, and it wasn't just friendship. "I pledge my honor and my life to serve you, and to defend Kaladon against any and all aggression." Pausing a moment, he added, "May you live a long and happy life, and govern your people well." The crowd began to cheer even louder. He turned and limped back down the steps to where Shanza was standing. She took his left arm and offered herself as a crutch. They crossed the large room, went through the open doorway and out of the palace. At the top of the steps, they looked out along the horizon and up at the sky toward space, his new domain. The planet Krynta was visible off in the distance and it was a beautiful sight. He pondered over and over in his mind. *Who would have ever thought I would find happiness in a world so very far from Earth. Earth ... somehow it didn't seem as important as it once was*, he thought.

THE END